ALL I WANT FOR
CHRISTMAS

ALL I WANT FOR
CHRISTMAS

Sherrilyn Kenyon

Lori Foster

Dee Holmes

Eileen Wilks

St. Martin's Paperbacks

NOTE: If you purchased this book without a cover you should be aware that this book is stolen property. It was reported as "unsold and destroyed" to the publisher, and neither the author nor the publisher has received any payment for this "stripped book."

This is a work of fiction. All of the characters, organizations, and events portrayed in this novel are either products of the author's imagination or are used fictitiously.

ALL I WANT FOR CHRISTMAS

"Christmas Bonus" copyright © 2000 by Lori Foster.
"A Night with Emily" copyright © 2000 by Dee Holmes.
"Santa Wears Spurs" copyright © 2000 by Sherrilyn Kenyon.
"The Proper Lover" copyright © 2000 by Eileen Wilks.

All rights reserved.

For information address St. Martin's Press, 175 Fifth Avenue, New York, NY 10010.

ISBN: 978-0-312-97680-4

Printed in the United States of America

St. Martin's Paperbacks edition / November 2000

St. Martin's Paperbacks are published by St. Martin's Press, 175 Fifth Avenue, New York, NY 10010.

10 9 8 7 6 5 4

CONTENTS

The Proper Lover

Eileen Wilks

ONE

Emily Eleanor Smythe was bent on ruin.

She lay quietly in the darkness beneath the cozy mound of covers and listened to her cousin Letty snoring softly beside her, and counted: *three thousand eighty-five, three-thousand eighty-six* . . .

Normally Emily slept in her own little room, but Christmas was only a week away and the house was packed to the eaves with Baggots and Baggot spouses and children. She'd been moved into her cousin Letty's room for the duration so that a great-aunt could have her bed.

Uncle Rupert liked gathering his family around him for the holidays. He had promised the young people a sleigh ride, weather permitting; there would be excursions to gather holly; a trip or two to the village; carol singing and present-making; and, of course, Christmas Eve services at the church. Neither mistletoe nor a Yule log would be part of the merrymaking, however. Mistletoe and Yule logs were not sufficiently respectable for a Baggot.

After tonight, Emily wouldn't be sufficiently respectable, either. That was an unfortunate but necessary part of her Plan.

Three-thousand ninety-nine . . . four thousand.

She drew a shuddering breath. It was time. She had heard the last footsteps in the hall four thousand seconds ago; everyone must be asleep now.

Her heart pounded as she eased back the covers and slid her legs off the bed. It was a high bed, and Emily was short. She landed with a soft thump, but Letty's snores didn't falter.

Emily bent and retrieved a large bundle from beneath the bed. Even if Letty woke, she told herself, she would only think Emily was pulling out the chamber pot. That is, she might think that if she didn't see Emily sliding in her stockinged feet, one slow step at a time, toward the door, the shawl-wrapped bundle of clothing an incriminating bulk beneath her arm.

The floor was cold. The air was cold. It was close to midnight, and the fire that had been kindled earlier in their fireplace was little more than coals now, giving off little heat and less light. Emily's arms had popped out in goose bumps by the time she reached the bedroom door. She reached for the handle.

Out in the hall, something creaked.

Her hand went to her throat, where her pulse hammered so hard it seemed her heart was trying to escape her flesh.

It was just the house, she told herself when the noise didn't come again. Houses made noises all by themselves, especially on cold winter nights—proof enough to Emily that houses weren't entirely insentient. *This* house didn't like her. She was convinced of that. It was a solid, respectable house, just like the family who lived in it. All of the Baggots were forthright, conventional people who knew their places and understood their worth.

Emily wasn't a Baggot. Her mother had been, but

her mother had run away with dashing Edward Smythe twenty-two years ago. Somehow Emily had ended up all Smythe, with very little respectable Baggot blood in her veins.

It would be just like this house to creak loudly while she was making her escape. And Aunt Dorothea was a light sleeper. If she woke up and saw Emily sneaking out . . .

Emily's imagination grabbed hold of the idea and quickly built an image of the scene. Her oldest cousin, George, had a loud, boisterous manner at the best of times. When he was angry, he got even louder. Letty would be crying; she liked the drama of tears. Abigail would be shrill and self-righteous. And her uncle would yell and yell, his face growing red and blotchy. Then Marcus would start yelling at the others to shut up and leave her alone.

But the worst—the very worst—would happen after the yelling ended. Then her aunt would speak to her. As much as Emily dreaded the loud-voiced arguments her uncle and cousins enjoyed, she feared her aunt's shriveling tongue more.

Aunt Dorothea was very much a lady. She wouldn't raise her voice. She would be cool and civil and withering, and Emily would shrink into a tiny, miserable spot that grew smaller and smaller with every word. Sometimes Emily thought she might disappear entirely if she had to listen to one more quiet lecture on her inadequacies.

When her aunt found out what she'd done tonight . . . She shuddered. She mustn't think about that, or she'd lose what little store of courage she possessed.

She gripped the handle of the door, but it was suddenly hard to turn it. To take that next step. Though Emily was often in trouble, she had never done anything truly *bad* before. Misguided, foolish, impulsive—oh, yes. She freely owned those faults. But she never set out to do the wrong thing. It simply worked out that way.

This time, though, she knew what she was doing was wrong.

Yet staying here would be worse. Being ruined would not be pleasant, but in the long run it was bound to be better than being married to Sir Edgar or to Ralph Aldyce. Emily thought of her Plan and turned the handle.

Emily and Letty were sharing the bedroom nearest the stairs, and there was a small window on the landing. Moonlight snuck up the stairwell, giving Emily enough light to avoid tripping on the worn spot in the runner in the hall. She reached the stairs and started down, moving as carefully as a soldier maneuvering behind enemy lines.

At the foot of the stairs she breathed a little easier. She untied her shawl and took out the contents—her warmest woolen dress, which was loose enough to wear without a corset and was buttoned up the front, making it easy to dress herself in the darkened hall. She pulled it on over her nightgown, did up the buttons all the way to her neck, then sat on the bottom step to tug on her half boots.

Oh, drat. She'd forgotten a hat. Well, she had the shawl. Emily hadn't dared sneak her pelisse out of the wardrobe and hide it under the bed, but the ratty old shawl wouldn't be missed. She'd just have to wear it over her head like an old countrywoman. The warmth would be necessary. Her destination was a mile and a half away.

She pulled on her mittens and was seized with a sudden urgency, a need to be out of this house. Opening the front door didn't frighten her the way opening her bedroom door had. She had never been outside alone at night, but Emily's fears centered around what she knew, not on the unknown. The unknown was a world she was seldom allowed to explore, a fascinating realm aglitter with possibilities as well as perils.

She turned the key quickly and stepped outside.

Earlier that day it had snowed lightly, frosting the ground, grass, eaves, and everything with white. Emily watched her breath turn white, too, and laughed aloud—white air, white ground, and big white moon smiling down on her through tatters of clouds. Happiness hit as suddenly as a storm, and she skipped down the steps, then did a spinning dance, arms raised.

Free. She was out of that house, out here on her own, with the moon and her own crisp white breath for company, and she was free. For now, only for now, but even this small bite of freedom was enough to make her giddy.

She started walking along the drive, angling toward the woods that lay east of the house. The moon was full, giving ample light, but clouds hid half the sky. One ragged cloud streamer drifted across the face of the moon like the trailing end of a scarf or shawl,

reminding her to pull her shawl up over her head as
she hurried on. She left the smoothness of the drive
for the crunch of brittle, snow-topped grass. The
woods loomed just ahead, looking dark and mysteri-
ous enough to serve as the setting for any number of
fairy tales. But Emily knew them well, and she knew
herself, too. The path she needed was wide and well
trodden, and she had an excellent sense of direction.
She wouldn't get lost.

Not on her way there, at least. No, the dangerous
part of her journey waited at the end of her trek. At
Debenham Hall. In the last bedroom on the ground
floor of the west wing, if Betsy, the upstairs maid,
was correct.

As she entered the woods, the top of her head
brushed against the outflung branch of a fir, which
promptly dumped snow on her head. Drats. She'd forgotten to keep a grip on the shawl, and it had slid to
her shoulders. Emily brushed the snow off her hair,
gathered the shawl up over her head once more, and
shivered.

Betsy had to be right. She didn't want to be ruined
by the wrong man.

James Edward Charles Drake, Baron Redding, second
son of the Earl of Mere, was bosky. On-the-go, half
flown, slightly castaway. Not yet three sheets to the
wind, he judged, for his hand was steady enough
when he reached for the decanter he'd brought back
to his room.

In the circles in which James moved, gentlemen
were expected to be able to hold their liquor, a social

skill James found amusingly ill-named. It wasn't the capacity of a man's bladder that was applauded, but his acting ability. As long as a gentleman was able to act sober, he could be as drunk as he pleased. As drunk as a lord, in fact.

James toasted himself for possessing this necessary skill and downed another swallow of his host's brandy.

Debenham did keep a good cellar, he conceded. A good cellar and an obliging wife, two amenities that he had expected to make this house party agreeable. Lady Debenham was a lovely creature with lovely breasts—great, large breasts with great, large nipples that had stood out like bull's-eyes when she'd bared them to him an hour ago. While her husband stood nearby, watching and smiling.

And the other guests, too. Watching and smiling. And snickering, a couple of them.

Damn it, James was not a prude. No one could call him a prude. Just because he didn't care to boff the man's wife while he watched did not make him a prude.

Even half drunk, however, James was pretty sure what this situation did make him. A fool. He should never have accepted Debenham's invitation. James didn't object to the man being a rake; how could he, when he was one himself? He'd attended any number of house parties where the guests played musical beds, as well as out-and-out debaucheries involving members of the muslin company.

But this house party was something quite out of the ordinary.

"Bad ton." He nodded emphatically. This caused
the room to spin, but only a trifle, confirming his opinion that he wasn't—quite—drunk. "Perfectly accept-
able for a man with a frisky wife to turn a blind eye.
Bad ton to turn both eyes on her while she frisks. *Very*
bad ton to ask a guest to top her under such circumstances."

Having settled the matter to his satisfaction, he
leaned back, crossing his feet at the ankles. The unsteady light from the fireplace sent shadows prancing
over an untidy room. The fire provided most of the
light, since the one candle that still burned in the candelabrum was well-nigh guttered. No servant had
drawn the drapes or tidied the room; a tailored jacket,
several cravats, a greatcoat, and sundry toilette articles
were dispersed casually about the room.

James's person was as untidy as his bedchamber.
He lounged on the bed, his unfastened cravat dangling
around his neck, his shirt hanging loose. He'd pulled
his boots off himself, no doubt smudging the glossy
finish and incurring Dobbs's future wrath.

He sighed. He wished his groom-cum-valet was
here, and that he himself wasn't. He should have suspected something was wrong when Debenham had
said he couldn't house his guests' servants. But it was
common knowledge that Debenham was pretty well
blown off his legs. James had assumed the man
couldn't afford to feed a lot of valets and grooms in
addition to his guests. It hadn't occurred to him that
Debenham wanted to restrict the number of witnesses
to an orgy.

The fact was, James admitted gloomily as he

swirled the liquor around and around in his glass, Debenham and his lovely wife had shocked him. Embarrassment had caused him to reject the man's notion of hospitality rather bluntly and retire to his room while the party went on without him.

At some point, James expected to see the humor in this situation. Here he was, one of the ton's best-known rakes, hiding in his room like an offended maiden. Yes, that would undoubtedly tickle his sense of humor . . . eventually.

"I should have known," he muttered, scowling at the brandy. His father had cut Debenham in public last month. That should have warned him. The Earl of Mere might be a womanizer, an indifferent landlord, and a worse father, but he was always good ton.

Still, the house party had served its purpose. The earl had been furious when he found out James planned to attend. No doubt he would have disinherited James on the spot if he hadn't already enjoyed that pleasure. Not that the earl cared what his second son did, except for cursing his disobedience. Now that James's older brother had amply secured the succession with his own heir and a spare, James's existence was entirely superfluous.

"Su-per-flu-ous," he said aloud, rolling the word off his tongue in careful syllables. If he could still string together a word like that, he wasn't drunk enough. Yet. But when he tipped the decanter in the general direction of his glass, nothing came out.

Blasted thing was empty.

Only thing to do, he decided, was to get some more. No point in ringing for it. If the servants hadn't actually been invited to join the party—and James didn't put even that past his host and hostess—they were abed by now. He would fetch it himself.

His decision made, James rolled off the bed and onto his feet. The floor showed a tendency to roll as if he were aboard a ship, however, so he gave it a moment to settle.

Tap-tap. Tap-tap-tap.

The floor had steadied, but now he was hearing things. He frowned.

Tap-tap-tap.

He really *was* hearing something. A tapping, at the window. He turned his head.

By God, there was a woman there. Or a witch? A witch, floating at his window with a great black cloak pulled over her head . . . No, no. No need for her to float. He was housed on the ground floor, owing to a dearth of inhabitable rooms in Debenham's neglected family seat. And as he moved closer he realized the black cloak was really an enormous shawl. Beneath that shawl her face was a pale oval, the features blurred by darkness. She looked young, though.

Not a witch, then. A Cyprian.

He smiled. Debenham must have recovered from his pique and sent James one of the women he'd imported for those of his guests who didn't have a wife handy to pass around. His brandy-fumed brain found an explanation for the ugly shawl: It was cold outside.

Poor thing. He'd better let her in and warm her up.

It was a casement window, fortunately, low to the ground and easy to unlatch. He swung it open and, mindful of the the courtesies, managed a bow without toppling over. "Do come in, my dear."

TWO

Emily was glad the window was set low to the ground, since her ravisher was too busy bowing to offer any assistance. She climbed over the sill without any great loss of dignity.

Soon she would lose more than her dignity. She glanced nervously at the bed that sat squarely in the center of the room, the covers all a-tumble. In spite of being country-bred, Emily had only a dim idea of what would happen to her tonight, save that it would involve an embarrassing degree of intimacy. And that bed.

She looked at the man standing in front of her. In the dim light, she couldn't see him clearly—but she saw enough to know she had found the right room. This was definitely the man she had encountered in the woods yesterday, the rake whose kiss had changed her life.

He had the look of a fallen angel, with his dark, untidy hair and his dark eyes set deeply beneath straight black brows. Compelling eyes, she had thought yesterday. Tonight they looked hazy, but that might be the poor light. His mouth was beautiful, as perfectly carved as any Greek statue's.

As for the rest of him . . . oh, my. With his shirt undone and his cravat loose, she saw a good deal more male flesh than she was used to seeing, and the shape of him was . . . firm. Delightfully firm. Something fluttered deep in her belly.

She clasped her mittened hands together. "You must be wondering why I'm here."

"Much too cold to stay out there." He moved closer—alarmingly close—and touched her cheek. "Your face is chilled."

Not as chilled as her hands and feet were. Strangely, though, when he stroked her cheek, she began to feel warmer. "This is very irregular, I know, but I do feel we should introduce ourselves. I'm Emily Smythe."

"Emily." His eyes were dreamy now, and his fingers trailed down her throat, stopping where they met the high neck of her gown. "What a lot of buttons you have, Emily. I am James Drake, Baron Redding— a courtesy title only, borrowed from my father and signifying nothing."

She nodded. "Yes, I know. I mean, I know your name. I asked someone after—after what happened." After he had flirted with her and kissed her, and her sneaksby cousin, who had followed her into the woods, saw it, and carried the tale home ahead of her.

He pushed the shawl off her head, and off her shoulders, too. The sudden intimacy of having her clothing removed here, in a bedroom, by this man, made her hands clutch at the material in a sudden flare of panic.

His eyebrows went up. "I don't think you're going to need this." He tugged.

Of course not. She made herself let go, and the

shawl fell to the floor. She shivered. "Don't you think you should close the window?"

"Of course. I'm not quite myself. Or perhaps too much myself. What do you think, my dear—do we find *in vino veritas,* or *in vino dementia*?"

"I think it is rude to toss Latin around unless one knows that the person one is speaking with is acquainted with it." She would have liked very much to learn Latin, but Uncle Rupert thought such knowledge unseemly in a female.

He chuckled. "Very true." He lifted one of her hands as if he were going to kiss it, then stopped, surprised. "Mittens?"

"It *is* cold outside. And rather chilly in here, too, with the window open."

"I keep forgetting." He shook his head, then grimaced. "We're not on a ship, are we?"

"Ah—no."

"Didn't think so. Remind me not to move my head so quickly." At last he turned to the window, his brow furrowed as if he were thinking. Unfortunately, he didn't seem to be thinking about closing the window, because he just stood there. "I could have sworn Debenham wasn't happy with me, after what happened."

"Lord Debenham?" She knew who that was, of course, having seen him in the village several times. The last time, he had looked at her in a perfectly horrid way. But she'd never spoken to the man. No one in the neighborhood did, due to what her aunt called his excesses, though Emily had never been able to discover precisely what excesses he practiced. "What do you mean?"

"You weren't there?" He turned around—and wobbled slightly. "No, you weren't. I would have noticed." He gave her a singularly sweet smile. "You look just like her."

"Her? Who?"

"The wood nymph."

But *she* was the one he had called a wood nymph when he was flirting with her, just before he stole a kiss. Emily frowned. Did he call every young woman a wood nymph? And why was he leaning so far out the window? "My lord, are you feeling well?"

"Call me James," he said cheerfully, and brought himself back into the room, closing the window at the same time. "I don't like being 'my lord'-ed in bed."

Emily's face heated. She shouldn't be bothered by his assumption that she was here to visit his bed, since he was quite right.

"Don't frown so, pretty nymph. I'm slightly on the go, but not in-ca-pac-i-tat-ed." He rolled the word out one syllable at a time.

"Oh, you're castaway!" That was a relief. She'd begun to fear that her chosen ravisher was a few bricks shy of a load.

It had been many years since Emily had listened in on the impromptu parties her father and his fellow officers had sometimes held. Emily hadn't actually seen those convivial gatherings, of course, but the quarters an officer without private means could afford for his family had invariably been small enough to make eavesdropping easy. She remembered how silly they had gotten after tipping the bottle too freely.

She also remembered finding her cousin Ralph

once, after he'd been into her uncle's port. He'd been casting up his accounts in the bushes. "You aren't going to be ill, are you?"

"Not a bit." He slipped an arm around her waist and drew her close. "I'm well able to take care of you, pretty one."

He hadn't held her yesterday, when he'd kissed her. No one had held Emily this closely for years. James's long, firm body felt distractingly . . . different. He smelled different, too. Like brandy and sandalwood and something else, something warm and strange and desperately interesting. She wanted to put her face in the crook of his neck and sniff him.

How embarrassing. "You, uh, obviously know why I'm here."

"I may be half sprung, but I'm not stupid." He smiled slowly. "And I may be a fool at times, but not foolish enough as to refuse such a lovely gift. A lovely going-away present." He nuzzled her cheek. "I'm sailing for America in two days, pretty nymph. Bought my fare after I had a run of luck at cards. You can give me some last memories of England to take with me."

"America?" For a second she forgot what he was doing and why she was there, as other longings rushed in. "How exciting!"

"Very exciting." His voice was low and thick, and he put his hand on her breast—right over it, squeezing lightly. "Especially when you look so much like her."

She swallowed. "*Her.* You said that before."

"Not too drunk to perform," he murmured ruefully, "but too far gone for tact." And then he went and

sniffed her neck, just as she'd thought of doing to him
... no, he was nibbling on it, tickling her skin with
the tip of his tongue. How odd! How—wonderful. "I
spoke of a pretty wood nymph I once stole a kiss
from. Or perhaps she was a dream. But no dream
could be as delightful as the way you taste ... here."

She felt the scrape of teeth—lightly, oh, so
lightly—but it startled her so much she jumped, and
his hand slipped away from her breast. Did *people* do
that? She'd seen her uncle's dogs once when the bitch
came in season, and the male dog had put his teeth
on the bitch's neck.

Surely the rest of it wouldn't be like what she'd
seen the dogs do. Would it?

He kissed the place he'd nipped. Sensations slid
through her, rich and layered—the tiny sting where
he'd nipped, the soothing press of his mouth ... no,
not so soothing, for it made her want to move. To tip
her head so he would go on doing that ... and that.

He was sucking at her skin now. Dogs certainly
didn't do *that*.

Her hands had found their way to his shoulders.
His shirt was thin, the linen a barely noticed barrier
between her fingers and his skin. He felt so *interesting*. Her fingers had begun a tentative exploration of
bone and muscle and skin, one hand slipping up to
explore the nape of his neck, when he muttered something about his pretty nymph.

What was it with him and nymphs?

Nurse had been right. Men obviously were capable
of lusting after persons who were total strangers to

them. James had no idea whose neck he was nuzzling so delightfully.

Why this would bother her when indiscriminate male lust was necessary to her Plan, she didn't know. But it did. Emily's lips tightened. "Let's get on with it, shall we?"

He lifted his head, smiling, which made his eyes crinkle up at the corners in a way she found quite charming. And annoying. He was amused, drat him. "Far be it from me to keep a lady waiting. Aside from Lady Debenham, that is, who can wait indefinitely as far as I'm concerned. Although it may be her husband I've disappointed, in which case I don't think we should count that, do you?"

"You're not making any sense."

"No? Then let us, as you say, get on with it." And he bent and scooped her up into his arms.

Emily squeaked and threw her arms around his neck. He took three quick steps—and dropped her. Right onto his bed. Then he came down on top of her.

Her eyes went wide and her body stiff. *Remember the Plan,* she told herself as he kissed her, full and hard on the mouth, which made her eyes close and her heart drum a mixture of panic and pleasure. She told herself to cooperate, to put her own arms around him, but he slid his hand up her bare calf to her knee.

And he didn't stop there.

Oh, my.

THREE

Lust and brandy made an intoxicating brew, especially when stirred with a dash of amusement and a whiff of temper.

So she wanted to get on with it, did she? James was more than ready.

He landed on top of her more heavily than he'd intended, due to the brandy. Fortunately, the liquor component of the brew hadn't affected the lust component at all. He couldn't remember the last time he'd gotten this hot, this hard, this fast. He bent to catch her mouth with his.

She tasted even better than she had yesterday in the woods . . . no, no, that had been a different woman. A young, gently born innocent with more curiosity than was good for her. He'd seen that curiosity shining in her big eyes as clearly as he'd seen her innocence, and it had had a surprisingly erotic effect on him. So he had stolen a kiss, giving her a taste of the answers she unknowingly sought.

And giving himself a memory that clung with unreasonable persistence.

Not that he'd kissed her then the way he was kissing her now—no, the way he was kissing the strumpet in his bed. It was important to keep the two women straight. One was an innocent, off bounds. The other was a pretty bit of muslin, her breasts delightfully unbound by anything as annoying as a corset. A pretty strumpet, ready and willing to please him in whichever ways he chose to be pleased.

There was no reason to prefer the innocent over the strumpet. And he didn't. Of course not. But maybe it wasn't too great a sin if thoughts of her tangled up in his mind with the feel of this woman's soft skin as he ran his hand up her leg, pushing her skirts up as he went, enjoying her mouth the way he would have liked to enjoy the wood nymph's mouth.

For a woman eager to get on with things, she was oddly passive. She wasn't moving, wasn't gasping or grasping at him. She wasn't even kissing him back. But that thought was dim next to the bright heat of lust, dim and slippery. It slid down the hasty slope of heat and sensation and vanished.

He stroked the curls at the top of her legs. She made a funny sound. A squeaky sound. His mind hazed by brandy and lust, James paid little attention to that.

But he did notice her legs. They were clamped tightly together.

Even brandy-bemused, he knew her legs weren't supposed to be closed to him at this point. He lifted his head, cupping her mound reassuringly with one hand. Her eyes were tightly closed. Her hair . . . for the first time he noticed her hair. It was in a braid.

Had he ever bedded a strumpet with braided hair? It seemed wrong, somehow. "Ah—sweetheart? Is there a problem?"

"Oh, no. But are you—" She swallowed. "Are you *sure* this is what you're supposed to do?"

Was he *sure* . . . Oh, God.

Thoughts crowded in then, darting around too quickly to grasp—but he tried. He tried. James held himself completely still, afraid that any movement would send him sliding off in some unpredictable direction. "Emily," he said as steadily as he could, his hand still resting on her intimately. "Emily, where do you live?"

Even in the poor light, he could see the rush of color to her face—and that her eyes stayed closed. "I told you. At Rosehill Manor."

She had told him . . . yesterday, in the woods. He had asked a pretty maid where wood nymphs stayed when they weren't wandering about, enticing strangers with their beauty. She had given him back a merry chuckle and said she couldn't speak for nymphs in general, but she herself lived at the western end of the woods. At Rosehill Manor.

"Oh, God." He hurled himself away so violently he nearly rolled off the bed. "What—" His chest heaved and he tried, he tried very hard, not to shout. "What in the name of heaven *are you doing here*?"

"Getting ruined," she said in a small voice. "Is that all there is to it? Somehow I thought there would be more."

James began to curse.

Emily lay flat on her back on the big bed, confused, aching, and embarrassed. She was damp in a place she didn't even have a name for. He had touched her there, and it had felt good. Beyond good. Amazing, really. Not to mention scary. She had never dreamed feelings like that existed.

He didn't seem embarrassed or confused. No, he was angry. Emily regretted that without understanding it. She must have done something wrong, which wasn't surprising when she didn't know anything about being bedded save that a bed was involved.

His anger didn't upset her, though, the way her relatives' anger did. Perhaps because he wasn't yelling. Cursing didn't bother her, not when he did it in a low voice that reminded her of the way Ned, the groom, spoke to the horses sometimes. Quietly, so they wouldn't be alarmed. He even used some of the same words Ned did.

Ned always refused to tell her what those words meant. Emily's curiosity, never far from the surface, rescued her from the pain of embarrassment as she straightened her skirts. "What does 'shagging' mean?"

"Never mind." He was certainly a man of sudden movements. This time he threw himself all the way off the bed and onto his feet. "Get up."

Obediently she sat up. "Am I ruined now?"

"Not if I can help it, by God." He grabbed her hand and dragged her harum-scarum off the bed and onto her feet, then grabbed her shawl and threw it at her.

She caught it, frowning unhappily. "I guess this means you'd like me to go."

"Preferably before your father arrives." He sat on the chair and picked up one of his boots.

She was beginning to get a bit angry herself. "My father is dead, and I don't see why you are being so uncivil."

"Your brother, then, or your uncle." He was struggling with the boot, which didn't seem to want to admit his foot properly. "Whichever male relative is slated for the role of outraged guardian."

"I don't have a brother, and my uncle wouldn't come to this house even if he knew I was here, which he doesn't. He doesn't approve of Lord Debenham and his wife. Or of you," she added pointedly.

"Good for him." He grunted and the boot slid into place. "We're still leaving before whoever is supposed to catch you here shows up."

"Catch me? I know you're foxed, but I'm not. I'm not crazy, either!"

"You're female. Amounts to the same thing." The other boot went on with one fierce tug and he stood, stamping his feet to settle them properly, then reached for his waistcoat.

Faintly, from another part of the house, came the shrill sound of a woman's laughter. "Are Lord Debenham's other guests still awake, then? I saw lights at the front of the house before I found your window, and I was worried you might not be in your room and I would have to wait." She tilted her head. "Why *were* you here if everyone else is still at the party?"

"You ask too many questions. Put your mittens on." He grimaced. "Good God, mittens. That should have tipped me off, even if I was too drunk to notice what you are wearing."

She bristled. "What's wrong with how I am dressed?"

Unexpectedly, he grinned. "It isn't exactly the sort of thing a Cyprian wears when she calls on a gentleman. But I was too busy noticing what you weren't wearing to pay attention to the style of your gown."

"What do you mean?"

"No corset."

Her skin heated. "You are certainly blunt."

"You object to my mentioning what you are or aren't wearing under your gown, but not to what I was doing beneath it?" He shook his head.

Her cheeks got even hotter. "You wanted me to remind you not to move your head quickly that way."

"I'm sobering up fast." His jacket was so tightly fitted that it was almost as much of an effort to don as his boots had been. "Nearly stepping into some conniving female's marriage trap can have that effect on a man."

"Marriage—oh, is that why you're upset?" Relief made her smile at him reassuringly. "I am not trying to trap you into marrying me! Good heavens, that's the whole *point.* Uncle Rupert thought you should marry me when he heard about you kissing me—"

"And just how did he hear about it?"

"My cousin Francis," she explained patiently. "He's eleven, and he's a dreadful little snitch. You would think that he would have better things to do than sneak after me into the woods, just hoping to see something he could tattle about, wouldn't you? Anyway, he saw you kiss me and told Aunt Dorothea, and of course she told Uncle Rupert, who thought you should marry me, but Aunt Dorothea told him not to be a fool. She has noble connections, you see, so she hears a great deal of ton gossip, and she said you were neither honorable enough nor green enough to be caught that way, and that very likely you wouldn't offer for me if we had been caught *in flagrante delicto,* which I think is Latin for being ruined."

"My compliments to your aunt on her astuteness. I am certainly not going to offer for you."

"There, now." She was pleased to have her surmises confirmed. "I didn't think you would."

"But neither do I care to be part of the sort of scene your uncle or whomever has it in mind to stage when he finds you here, so you might as well go ahead and wrap up in that hideous shawl. You're going out the window with or without it."

"You don't believe me!" She was as surprised as she was insulted. "You still think I am trying to trap you into marriage. I suppose I should make allowances, since you don't really know me, but I *never* lie."

"Never?" His eyebrow cocked up in a skeptical way.

"I'm no good at it, you see. That's one of the reasons Aunt Dorothea despairs of making me into a proper young lady."

"I can see why she might be concerned," he said dryly, handing her mittens to her. "A disinclination to lie is something of a social disability, but I would say it was the least of your aunt's worries."

"It isn't that she wants me to *lie,* exactly." She pulled the mittens on. "But there are a great many subjects one is not supposed to mention in polite conversation, and I can never get it right. It all seems to involve a great deal of pretending, which is rather like lying, isn't it? And it is very difficult to never ask any questions, even when one really *wants* to know the answer. Aunt Dorothea says that if I possessed a proper elegance of mind such questions wouldn't occur to me, but I sometimes think that a truly elegant mind is much like an empty one. Look at the Trowbridge twins. They are considered terribly well behaved, and in a week's time they seldom have a complete thought to share between them."

A smile touched his lips. It made him look more like the charming young man she had met yesterday, and less like the hardened rakehell he was supposed to be. "It sounds as if your aunt has her hands full with you."

She sighed. "That's what everyone says."

"So if your goal isn't marriage, why are you here? And don't tell me it's because I kissed you yesterday."

"But that *is* why I'm here."

His smile hardened. "I may be good, sweetheart, but I'm not that good. Not enough to tempt a young lady to cast virtue aside with, ah, such wholehearted abandon on the basis of a single chaste kiss."

"I wouldn't call it chaste. It wasn't like the way you were kissing me just now, but I don't think it was chaste, either."

He shook his head and turned to grab the huge greatcoat adorned with four capes from where it had been tossed across a chair. "You're still leaving."

"All right, but I need to know if I am completely ruined now."

"You're not ruined as long as no one knows what happened tonight." He thrust the window open once more. "And I'm damned well going to see to it that no one does."

"They will when I tell them." She spoke absently, her mind on other things as she wrapped the shawl around herself and followed him to the window.

It did sound as if there were more to the type of intimacy that resulted in ruination for a single woman, or children for a married one, than what they had already done. She couldn't help wondering what that might be. Considering everything they *had* done . . . of course, he hadn't stripped. She was almost sure he had to remove at least some of his clothing for It to happen. Whatever It was.

"And why would you be totty-headed enough to do that?"

It took her a moment to recall what she'd said. "Oh. Well, there is really no point in all this if I don't tell them."

His lips tightened. "It will be your word against mine." He stepped over the sill.

"I suppose that means you don't have a problem with lying."

"Not at all. I have been well trained to take my place in polite society." He stepped over the sill and turned, holding out one hand. "Come on, quickly, now."

He certainly was eager to speed her on her way, wasn't he? It was probably for the best, but Emily suspected that, even if they hadn't done *everything,* they had done enough to keep her from ever marrying. Which was her goal, of course, but being half ruined was apt to prove frustrating. She doubted she would ever find out what else was involved.

"You don't have to go with me."

"Don't be a ninny."

"You sound less like a rake and more like Cousin George all the time." It was very disappointing. Reluctantly, she took his hand, and he assisted her over the sill as gracefully as if she had been climbing down from a carriage.

His words were less courteous. "I suppose you consider your crack-brained behavior tonight perfectly reasonable."

"Under the circumstance, yes. I—Oh, dear." She looked up. "The clouds have moved in. It's dark as pitch out here."

"Damn and blast. I don't suppose you were intelligent enough to supply yourself with a lantern."

"There was plenty of light when I came here. The moon is full." Of course, she could find her way back in the dark if she had to. Emily never got lost, and, indeed, she had trouble understanding how other people could.

But perhaps she would keep that information to herself for now.

"The moon isn't doing us much good now. Did it not occur to you that you would have to return, too? And that the weather just might change?"

"I hadn't planned on being evicted before morning. I think it most unchivalrous of you, sir."

"On the contrary. It's probably the only chivalrous

thing I've ever done. Which is no doubt why I'm
making such a muck of it—lack of practice." He
sighed. "Back inside with you. We can't go anywhere
until I find a lantern."

FOUR

James was not a happy man. He didn't like feeling a fool. He hadn't even noticed that it was as black as the back side of hell out here—and that was the least of his folly tonight. Sexual frustration clawed at him, making his skin tight, his cock hard, and his blood churn with lust, guilt, and less identifiable emotions.

Nobility was vastly overrated, in his opinion. "Get back inside," he snapped.

Unexpectedly she giggled. "I just noticed. You put your waistcoat on inside out."

Her giggle was light and girlish. It tugged at something inside him that he didn't want touched. It also increased the prickling of guilt without doing a thing to ease his arousal. "How old are you?" he asked suddenly.

"Nineteen. You know, I quite thought that was one of those questions one wasn't supposed to ask."

Nineteen. It could have been worse. "I think our acquaintance has been unconventional enough that we needn't worry about the dictates of polite conversation."

She nodded seriously. "Good. I am a poor hand at that, anyway. How old are you?"

"Twenty-six."

"Really? I thought you must be at least thirty."

That paid him off nicely for his temper, especially

since she was totally unaware of having delivered a set-down. "No doubt the marks of dissipation on my face misled you."

"No, I don't think so. I haven't noticed any marks of dissipation—that is, assuming you mean the wrinkles and red squiggly lines around the nose and eyes that Lord Debenham has. I just expected you to be older. I didn't know one could become a hardened rake so young."

"I started young. That, too, is something for which I have been well trained." He held out his hand. "And now, perhaps, do you think we could go back inside?"

She sighed and climbed back through the window without allowing him to assist her.

He followed quickly, unbuttoning his greatcoat. "Close the window, would you? I'll be back as soon as I can. God knows where I'll find a lantern."

"I'll help," she offered, folding her deplorable shawl and laying it neatly on the chair. "I know the house fairly well."

His eyebrows lifted. "I thought the local gentry didn't recognize Debenham."

"Oh, they don't. Not the current one. The old lord was respectable, however, and his housekeeper used to give us plum cakes—my cousins and me, that is. We weren't supposed to pester her, but she was a very motherly woman and seemed to enjoy our visits. So I do know where the kitchen is, and that is probably where you'll find a lantern."

"Nonetheless, you are not going with me." He tossed his greatcoat on the floor, since her shawl now occupied the only chair.

She frowned. "You'll find it more quickly if I am with you."

"I don't want you seen wandering around the house with me. In fact, I want your word that you'll stay here while I go looking for a lantern."

Even in the poor light, there was no mistaking the stubborn set of that pointy little chin. "You have no authority over me."

"If you don't promise to stay in this room while I'm gone, I will lock you in."

She sniffed and turned to tug off her mittens and slap them, one at a time, on the dresser next to the candelabrum. "I dislike high-handed persons who order others around and won't listen to perfectly reasonable suggestions."

He didn't think she would recognize reason if it reared up and bit her on that delightful bottom. "Oh? You liked me well enough earlier, when you were trying to seduce me."

"Nonsense. I wouldn't know a thing about seducing anyone. I was counting on you to handle things." She used the smoldering candle stub to relight the others, and the room brightened.

How had he thought her anyone but who she was? Even drunk, even with the dim light, he should have recognized her. She had a piquant face, heart-shaped, with a straight-and-narrow nose and a too-wide mouth that looked made for smiling. Or kissing. And God, but he wanted to kiss her again. And again.

He needed to get out of here. "I was enjoying handling things, too. Until I realized who you were."

A pair of very fine blue eyes fringed by lashes several shades darker than her taffy-colored hair regarded him reproachfully. "And then you stopped."

"Shockingly inconsiderate of me."

"Well, yes, it was. Though I expect I'm still mostly ruined, aren't I? I do hope it will be enough."

"Enough for what? Other than trapping me into marriage, that is, which is not such a good idea as you might think."

"You keep harping on that idea. I came here to *avoid* marriage, not to trap anyone into it. In fact, I *promise* not to marry you."

"How remarkable. Aside from an adventurous widow or two, I cannot call to mind any ladies of my acquaintance who are opposed to marriage."

"I don't object to marriage. Just to marrying Sir Edgar or Ralph Aldyce."

He was beginning to believe her. In spite of logic and past experience, he was beginning to believe that she really hadn't come here in a crack-brained attempt to force an offer from him. "Can't say I recognize the names. Local lads, I suppose?"

"Yes. At least, they are both neighbors, but I don't think anyone would call Sir Edgar a lad." Her nose wrinkled. "He's over forty."

"Ancient indeed." James tried, he really did, but he couldn't keep from laughing. This was one of life's better jokes. "Let me see if I understand. You came here to be ruined so you wouldn't have to marry one of your suitors?"

"I can see you think that's amusing, but it isn't funny to me."

"You have no idea." He shook his head, grinning.

"You see, I came here to avoid a marriage my relatives sought for me, too."

Her eyes widened. "You? But—but you're a man! No one can make you get married! Besides, you're going to America."

"When I accepted Debenham's invitation, I hadn't yet won the stake I needed for the fare. And I wanted to make something clear to my father." He shrugged. "Stupid of me. The earl isn't sufficiently aware of me to understand the point I was trying to make."

"But why would your father force you to marry? And what point were you making? And—"

"Never mind about me." She was a curious little thing, wasn't she? "Emily, you have to go home and tell no one where you've been. When the time comes, refuse your suitors if you don't fancy them."

She shook her head. "No, my aunt and uncle are determined that I marry one of them. Of course, they have been wanting that for some time, especially since I wasted my chances during my Season, but they weren't absolutely set on it until they heard about you kissing me."

"Do you know, I was expecting that this would somehow be all my fault."

"Don't be tiresome. I'm not blaming you—though I must say, it seems odd for you to go around kissing strange females. I daresay that is the sort of thing rakes do, however," she added, "and I don't mean to take you to task for your habits."

His lip twitched. "Thank you."

"The real fault is mine. I am well aware of it. I should have stopped you, or fainted, or at least slapped you. I shouldn't have spoken to you in the first place," she added with less conviction, more in the manner of one conscientiously repeating a maxim. "Especially since it was obvious you were part of Lord Debenham's party."

"No doubt your aunt told you so."

"Yes, among other things." She shuddered. "It was horrible. I have a horror of being yelled at, and told how ungrateful I am, and that I am driving my loved ones to an early grave, and—and a number of unpleasant things."

Gently he said, "I am sorry my kiss caused you so much trouble. Yet I don't think that your adventure tonight will help you avoid, er, being yelled at."

"No, it will be quite horrid when they find out. But it will prevent me from marrying Sir Edgar. Or Ralph."

"Emily, I do understand how unpleasant it can be when your family is hounding you. But they can't make you marry where you don't wish to."

"Yes, they can. And it's no use telling me to have resolution. Marcus always tells me that. He's my favorite cousin, and he means well, but it doesn't do any good to tell me to have resolution, because I *don't*. Sooner or later, I would have given in and done what they wanted. I always do. So I had to make it impossible for me to give in."

"That makes about as much sense as lopping off your foot to avoid twisting an ankle."

Her shoulders drooped. "I thought you might understand, since you're in a similar situation yourself."

That unfamiliar tugging was back. He didn't like

it. It made him want to touch her cheek, to offer comfort—oh, now, there was a ludicrous thought. The only kind of comfort he knew how to give a woman was the sort that came from a long, sweaty bout between the sheets.

He turned and grabbed the empty brandy decanter. It had occurred to him that his earlier mission would serve to explain his wandering around the house, if he was seen. "Our situations are not the same. When word got out about my attendance at this party, a few more hostesses crossed me off their lists. But you would be completely ostracized. Do you have any idea what that would be like?"

She nodded gloomily. "I'll be sent to live with my great-aunt in Yorkshire. I've been threatened with it often enough, so I know that's what will happen. Great-Aunt Regina is the only one on my father's side of the family who acknowledges me. She's a Methodist, and she doesn't approve of visiting the sins of the fathers on the children. She also disapproves of dancing and wearing colors. And men. She won't have a footman or a butler because she thinks men are limbs of Satan. It will be awful there—but better than marrying Ralph or Sir Edgar."

Ralph and Sir Edgar must be remarkably inept suitors, if they couldn't make themselves appear to better advantage than Great-Aunt Regina. James looked at her small, sad face and decided he'd better leave now, before he did something else foolish. "Are you going to promise to stay here while I'm gone, or do I have to lock you in?"

"I don't see a key in the door."

Damn and blast. She was right. "Emily, you really do have to stay here. If anyone should see you—"

"It wouldn't matter. I have promised not to wring a proposal from you."

"Strange as it seems, I'm worried for your sake, not my own."

She smiled. "That is nice of you, but it isn't necessary."

Nice? He hadn't been called "nice" since before he left the nursery. James ran a hand over his hair. "Look, aside from the danger of you being seen— which I realize you don't consider a problem—I don't want to risk you seeing Debenham and his guests, either. They, ah . . . you shouldn't see the sort of things they're up to, that's all."

She nodded wisely. "Debauchery."

"Not that you have the faintest idea what is meant by the term, but yes. And not ordinary debauchery, either, though that would be bad enough. Debenham . . ." How to discourage her without saying too much? "Why do you think I was alone in my room when you came?"

"I did ask you that. You told me not to ask so many questions."

"Did I?" He grinned crookedly. "Well, I was here because the party became too bawdy for me. And, as you keep pointing out, I am a rake."

"Goodness." Her eyes were wide. "I wonder what—"

"Never mind 'what.' Will you take my word for it that it would be wrong, even dangerous, for you to leave this room?"

"I suppose so. Though I am *very* curious about what behavior is too licentious for a rake." She looked at him hopefully.

He laughed. "No, I am not going to tell you. Do I have your promise to stay here while I find a lantern?"

She nodded reluctantly.

He turned, but her hand on his arm stopped him. It was a small hand, the palm wide, the fingers short and blunt. A practical-looking hand, at odds with her disposition.

He wanted to nibble on those short, practical fingers.

"You'd better let me give you directions if you want to avoid the other guests. The kitchen is on the west side of the house."

What he had better do was get out of there before lust drowned out what shreds of conscience he still possessed. "The others are in the Long Drawing Room, or were. I'll go through the main hall at the front of the house and blunder around until I find the kitchen."

"But the Great Hall is right in front of the Long Drawing Room. If you don't want to be seen . . ." She bit her lower lip thoughtfully. He wanted to do that for her. "You know where this wing joins the main house? Turn left at the first door past the half flight of stairs. That's the portrait gallery. The door at the far end opens into the library. There are two—no, three doors leading from it. You want the west one. There's a bust of Julius Caesar next to it. His nose is chipped. That door leads to the little dining room, and if you go straight through it to the door on the opposite wall, you'll be in the hall that leads to the kitchen."

His eyebrows went up. "You do know the house well."

"The old lord used to let me use the library sometimes. He gave me a tour once, too, before he became an invalid."

Once? Debenham's father had died three or four years ago. That was a long time to retain such a detailed mental map of a rambling old house. Either her directions were as imaginative as her plan for avoiding marriage, or she wasn't the widgeon she seemed. "Bookish, are you?"

"Oh, no. My cousin George's wife, Mildred, is something of a bluestocking, which Uncle Rupert doesn't like, but my aunt considers her unexceptional otherwise. Mildred is very high-minded," Emily assured him. "During the Season she holds literary salons. She invited me to one and I thought it a crashing bore, so obviously I am not bookish."

He smiled. "Yet you liked visiting the library here."

"It has a number of books about other places, you see. India and China and the Sandwich Islands and— oh, all sorts of fascinating places." She smiled shyly. "America, too. I am *extremely* curious about other places and peoples, and books are the next best thing to seeing them in person, aren't they?"

That's when James forgot. He was thinking about her big, wistful eyes, and that she would never see the distant lands that fascinated her. He was thinking about *her,* and forgot to be on guard against himself.

So he kissed her.

FIVE

Emily didn't close her eyes. James was going to kiss her again. And this time she wanted to see everything.

He was smiling when their lips met. His mouth was warm, but the skin on his cheek was cold from their brief venture outside. She discovered this intriguing contrast when her hand flew to his face as he nibbled at her lips. Her fingers slid from cheek to jaw, exploring smooth, cool flesh so unlike her own, for a hint of roughness underlaid it.

His eyes were nearly closed, the lids heavy, as if he were so focused on the pleasure of her mouth that he had no attention left to give to sight. Emily didn't mind. She liked being free to look at him. He was beautiful.

When his tongue teased at the corner of her mouth, she sighed in pleasure—and when her lips parted, his tongue slipped inside, shocking her into stillness. Fascinating her. He tasted of brandy and darker flavors, a blend so rich and intriguing she had to explore it. She touched her tongue to his.

He groaned and pulled her up against him, and it felt wonderful—her breasts pressed against the hard wall of his chest, her body molded to his.

Time hung suspended as their breaths and mouths mated. How odd, she thought dimly. She felt closer to him now, with her clothes still in place, than she had when he had touched her everywhere a gentleman shouldn't touch a lady.

It grew harder to keep her eyes open. There was so much to feel, so many sensory clues to investigate. She began to pulse in the place he had touched earlier, and a restless ache built and bubbled inside her. She had to move. So she rubbed herself against him.

He made a strangled noise, gripped her arm with his free hand, and moved away from her. His eyes were hot and dark and blank.

Her gaze slid to his throat, where his pulse throbbed. "Does this mean you've changed your mind about me leaving?"

"*No!*" He dropped her arm as if she'd burned him, then turned quickly and left, slamming the door behind him.

Emily didn't move. Feelings squirmed around inside her, disturbing her body, her breath, and her mind. These feelings were both like and unlike what she'd experienced before. They were stronger, yes . . . but that wasn't the only difference. And it was important that she understand what had changed. She wasn't sure why, but she knew it was important.

Restlessly she tidied James's things while she tried to make sense of desire. She did know that was what she was feeling, but naming it didn't help. Never had Emily been as curious about anything as she was about these feelings. For once, though, her curiosity worried her. She was afraid that if she kept kissing James, she would grow to crave the taste and feel of him.

She was afraid she already had.

Oh . . . *that* was it. That was what was different. This time, she had kissed him back, knowing it was James she was kissing. Wanting *him*, not just those delicious feelings.

She wanted James. It made all the difference.

She wanted to learn everything about him—the textures of his skin, and whether he liked gooseberry tarts as much as she did. The name of his horse. His birth date. Who his friends were, and if he liked fishing and dancing. What questions rose to trouble him in the middle of the night, when the world was dark and lonely.

Oh, my.

She stopped moving, his jacket in her hands. Maybe he was right. Maybe she should hurry home, before she learned more than she could afford to know about him. But never again would she have a chance to explore the way he made her feel. She couldn't imagine letting someone else touch her that way.

Should she try to persuade him to let her stay the night—to finish what he had started? Or was that horribly wicked, more sinful even than her original plan? She hadn't the excuse of necessity now, only—what was that?

The noise came again, a faint thump out in the hall. There hadn't been enough time for James to reach the kitchen and return, but maybe he had found a lantern somewhere closer. She started for the door.

And heard a woman's voice, muttering a most unladylike curse.

Emily's eyes widened in horror as the handle of the door slowly turned.

*   *   *

James found a lantern and the brandy without en-
countering any of the servants—some of whom, from
the sound of things, had been invited to participate in
the revels. He grimaced as he padded quietly through
the darkened dining room. On the other side of the
wall one woman squealed, another giggled, and two
men sang the chorus to an obscene ditty, accompanied
by the rhythmic slapping of flesh against flesh.

His lip curled in distaste. At least Emily was tucked
up safely in his room. As safe as she could be in this
house, that is. Which wasn't safe at all. Especially
when her only protector wanted badly to finish what
he'd started.

He could have her. And not just because of her
crack-brained plan to ruin herself, either. She had
liked what he had done to her. Even when he'd been
treating her like a lightskirt, she had enjoyed his
touch. Her body might be untried, but it was naturally,
beautifully responsive. Pretty Emily Smythe was as
hot and sweet as a man could wish . . . and defenseless
against one unscrupulous enough to use her innate
sensuality to get what he wanted.

She was also infatuated with him.

James knew women too well to have missed seeing
that. He could have kissed her right out of that ugly
dress, right into his bed and onto her back. He could
have gone on to answer every question she had about
how men and women fit together, and plenty she had
never thought to ask.

Oh, yes, he could have her. Partly because she
wanted to be ruined. Partly because he knew how to

overwhelm her senses with a passion she was too in-experienced to handle. And partly because she wanted him.

She wanted *him*.

And that made all the difference.

The knowledge acted as a sweet kick that went straight to his groin—and what remained of his conscience. He had seen trust shining in her eyes as clearly as he'd seen the infatuation, and knew he would damn himself completely if he violated either one.

But James knew himself better than Emily did, and trusted himself far less. If he didn't get her out of here quickly, he was very much afraid he would end up taking more than she could afford to lose.

Because he wanted her, too. Not just her sweet woman's body. *Her*.

James didn't notice the door to his room was ajar until he reached for the handle. When he did, he froze. He was sure he had pulled it closed when he left. Hell, he'd slammed it. And she had promised to stay put. He'd thought he could trust a widgeon who never lied—but then, he had only her word for it that she didn't lie. Which probably meant that he was the idiot.

Oh, God, if she was wandering around this house . . . He shoved the door open with his foot.

Someone was in his room, all right, but it was the wrong woman. Lady Amelia Debenham lay on his bed. He glanced around the room. No badly dressed nymph lurked in the corners. Either she had left, or—

Debenham's wife uncoiled from her supine position, giving him glimpses of long white limbs as she swung her legs off the bed and stood. That offered him a different view, this time of full, mostly bare breasts. She pouted. "You don't look happy to see me, James."

"You surprised me." Now, there was an understatement if ever he'd made one.

She shrugged. The gown's bodice slipped from scandalous to indecent. "I don't hold a grudge. Not everyone enjoys a public performance, so I came for a more private one."

"I *do* hold a grudge, however. I didn't like being surprised that way."

She swayed toward him. No, she was weaving. The lady was drunk. "Are you going to be mean to me? How ungennnul—ungeneral—how rude." She twined her arms around his neck. "Be nice to me, James. As nice as I plan on being to you."

"Sorry. I'm not interested." And it was true. For the first time since Emily climbed in his window, his body was definitely not interested.

She didn't move except to stretch high enough to lick his neck. Her breath reeked of spirits and less pleasant things. "Don't you like me? You liked me in London. You thought I was pretty, I know you did."

No, he didn't like her. He didn't much like himself, either. But he could use her. "Let me put these things down, sweetheart," he said. "I can see I'm going to need my hands free."

It was very dusty under the bed. No doubt that was why Emily's eyes were watering.

That Woman giggled and said something about too

much brandy. James said something, too, but his voice was low and Emily didn't catch the words. Not over the rubbing, rustling sounds.

Her eyes watered some more.

More sounds. A long, slow kiss. Cloth rubbed against cloth. Emily wondered miserably if James was gong to bring That Woman *here,* to this bed, and do everything to her he'd done to Emily earlier. And more.

"Oh, honey," That Woman said. She sounded reproachful. "You're not trying."

"I'm doin' my best. Had a lot of brandy before you showed up, you know. Wasn't expectin' you. Not my fault."

Why were his words all slurred? He sounded like he had earlier, when he was foxed.

"Well, you're not trying hard enough." She giggled. "That's a joke, isn't it? Not hard enough."

"Are you laughing at me?" He sounded angry.

That Woman tried to reassure him. She tried several things. Emily couldn't tell exactly what she was doing, but she understood enough to make her want to crawl out of her hiding place and pull That Woman's hair—and James's hair, too. And then hit him.

But after a few endless, cloth-rustling minutes, That Woman told him pettishly to "sleep it off" and Emily heard the door close. She thought That Woman was gone, but she didn't know if James had left with her. It was very quiet. . . .

"You may as well come out from under the bed."

His voice was crisp and normal again. She scowled

and shoved back the bedclothes and stuck her head out. "You mean you knew I was here? All the time you and she were kissing and everything, you knew where I was?"

"Where else could you be? You promised not to leave the room. And you don't lie, do you?" His face was hard, like his voice, and his eyes glittered as if he were angry.

"I would have left when she showed up if there had been time. As it was, I barely managed to duck under here before she came barging in. She didn't even knock."

"She assumed she would be welcome."

Yes, she had, hadn't she? Emily drew on her memory and came out with a phrase she'd heard Ned use when the mare took a nip out of his shoulder.

His eyes widened. "*What* did you say?"

"You heard me."

The ghost of a grin touched his mouth. "Don't know what it means, do you?"

There was a certain lack of dignity to holding this conversation while she was on the floor. There wasn't much dignity in scrambling out from under the bed, either, so she just did it and got it over with. She stood and tried to brush some of the dust from her gown. Her nose itched. "I don't think the maids ever clean under there. It's terribly dusty. I was afraid I would sneeze and interrupt you two."

"Perhaps I should mention that to Lady Debenham when I take my leave, so she can speak to her house-keeper about it."

She gave him a reproachful look. Then sneezed.

That angry glitter was gone now, replaced by amusement. Drat him. "If that's the best you can do, you needn't have worried. Kittens sneeze louder than that."

She sniffed. "Do you have a handkerchief? I didn't bring one."

"There should be some in my satchel. Help yourself."

It seemed intimate to rummage through his belongings. But then, he didn't object to intimacy with a woman, did he? With *any* woman. She took out a neat square of linen, used it as it was meant to be used, then crumpled it in her fist. "Why did you pretend you were drunk?"

He shrugged. "I had to get rid of her. I do draw the line at some things, and tumbling the very experienced Lady Debenham while a virgin hid under the bed would be a little much, even for me."

"But why did pretending you were drunk get rid of her? She was drunk, too, so I don't think she had any moral objections to it."

"You ask too many questions. Put your shawl on. I'm getting you out of here before anyone else comes calling."

But Emily's curiosity had her in its grip now. There was something wrong with the way he was acting. Something that didn't fit. Acting . . . that was it! He was *acting*. But why? "She seemed to think that you couldn't—well, you know—because of the brandy."

He strode over to the chair and grabbed her shawl. "Brandy has an unfortunate effect on a man's virility sometimes. And now that I've ruined my reputation as a rake for your sake, do you think you could put this on and hustle your charming bottom back out the window?" He thrust the shawl at her.

Absently she accepted it. "But it didn't have that effect on you earlier." Emily might not be entirely clear on what happened when a man bedded a woman, but she knew more than she used to. A great deal more, now that she'd felt James's body on top of hers. "When she said something about 'not being hard enough,' did she mean—oh, dear. I don't know the word for—"

"And I am not going to enlighten you." He grabbed her arm and dragged her to the dresser. "Light the candle in the lantern, will you? I need to get my coat on."

She lifted the lantern's hood obediently, but her mind wasn't on what her hands did. The puzzle she was working on was too important. "That poor lady."

"You feel sorry for Lady Debenham because she didn't get what she came for?"

She turned around. He looked impossibly good, she thought wistfully, with his dark hair all rumpled and the capes of the coat widening his already broad shoulders. Even scowling at her that way, he was gorgeous. "Don't be dense. I feel sorry for her because she's so sad and lost. Is that what happens to a woman who becomes debauched?"

He spoke more gently. "Yes. That's just what happens."

"Oh." Slowly she tugged on her mittens. "I suppose that's why my aunt and uncle are determined to save me from ruin, then. At any cost."

"I'm sure it is." He buttoned his coat.

"And why you want me to leave." Maybe even why he'd kissed That Woman. He had known she was there, listening. He'd wanted to show her how bad he was, how lost she might become if she went ahead with her Plan. That meant he cared, didn't it?

"I want you to leave so that I can play with women who are more my type. Experienced women."

"Just because I don't lie doesn't mean I can't tell when someone is lying to me." She smiled. "You're not entirely honest, James, but you are kind."

"I'm an idiot," he muttered, and thrust open the window. Then he stood there and cursed.

When she moved up beside him, she saw why. It was snowing. Hard.

SIX

"Oh, this is beautiful!" Emily's eyes glowed as brightly as the lantern James held. "It's like walking in sparkles."

No, James thought. The way the lantern's light reflected off the falling snow was pretty. But *she* was beautiful. Crazy, but beautiful. "The snow may be lovely, but it's dangerous. We can't see more than a couple feet ahead of us." They walked in a shifting bubble of white lit by the single candle in the lantern, with darkness all around.

At first they had been able to follow the house, but the back lawn was taken up by an overgrown formal garden that had forced them away from the wall. They walked now between two snow-topped hedges. James was almost sure this path would lead them to the gazebo—but from the gazebo to the woods there would be no convenient yew borders to steer by.

Emily looked more guilty than alarmed. "Maybe we should turn back."

He took her arm. "Don't worry. I'm not going to drag you off into the woods unless I'm sure I won't get us lost. We'll turn back if we have to."

"I'm not worried. Not about that, anyway."

At least there was no wind. The air was almost uncannily still, and somewhat warmer than it had been earlier. But the snow was falling thickly. The lantern's light didn't reach far, busy as it was reflecting off the dancing flakes.

He glanced at her, and smiled in spite of himself. "If I didn't know better, I'd say you were enjoying this."

She laughed and tilted her face up. Snowflakes caught on her eyelashes and glistened. Her cheeks were rosy from the cold. "Why not? I've never been outside at night before when it was snowing. Uncle Rupert doesn't trust the night air even in the summer."

"One more new experience for you tonight." If this snow didn't let up, they would have to turn back. And she might well have another "first" to add to the list.

"Yes, and it's quite as magical as the rest."

"Damn it, Emily." He took her arm and turned her to face him. He wanted to shake her. Or kiss her. Or both. "Being ruined is not a solution to your problems."

"Why not? You said you came here to avoid marriage, too. And *don't* tell me 'That's different.' "

"I also said that I was stupid to do it. Emily, the scene you overheard with Lady Debenham—"

"You didn't want her, and not because of the brandy. You wanted to give me a disgust of—of kissing. Or maybe of you."

He sighed. She understood too much. And too little. "The point is that I've played out a lot of scenes much like that one. Too many. You call me a rake, but you haven't faced what that means. If this house party had gone the way I thought it would, I would have bedded my host's wife, and I would have enjoyed it. And forgotten all about it, and her, in a few days."

She didn't like that. He could see that much, but he couldn't tell exactly what feelings she struggled with. Disgust, probably. And the pain of losing whatever infatuation she'd felt for him.

She started walking again. "Have I told you about Sir Edgar and Ralph?" she asked.

James kept pace with her easily enough physically. Mentally, he had no idea where she had hared off to. "What, are they rakes, too?"

"No. At least, I think Ralph might like to be one if he weren't so busy trying to make everyone think him a pattern-card of all the virtues. He just thinks slimy thoughts."

"The same kind of thoughts I have about you, you mean?"

"It's different when Ralph does it. He doesn't even like me."

"An odd sort of suitor."

"Oh, he pretends to like me, but I have known Ralph Aldyce ever since I came to live with my aunt and uncle, and he can't fool me. I have never liked him. Never. He stole my kitten when I was thirteen because I wouldn't let him kiss me." She brooded over that a moment. "I pushed him in the pond. Of course, I got in trouble when he tattled, since no one believed dear little Ralph would have tried to kiss me, but it was worth it."

"You don't think he might have changed since then?"

"No. He has clammy hands and a weak chin and

he pinches the maids, and I'll bet he tries to kiss them, too, for all that he pretends to be so proper." Her mouth pursed in distaste. "And he wears a green waistcoat with yellow stripes. It makes me bilious."

He couldn't help smiling. "A truly ugly waistcoat, I take it."

"Oh, yes. Aunt Dorothea agrees with me about his waistcoat, but she says, 'Beggars can't be choosers,' and that if I won't take Sir Edgar, I have to take Ralph. And I *can't*. When he thinks no one will notice, he looks at me like a drunkard gazing at a bottle of wine. It is all lust," she finished darkly. "Lord Debenham looked at me that way the time I encountered him in the village."

Alarmed, he spoke quickly. "Stay away from Debenham, Emily. His actions are every bit as slimy as his thoughts."

"I know that! But Ralph wouldn't have to keep his sliminess to himself if I married him, would he? And I don't think I could stand that. I'm not real to him, not a person, just a—a way of having those kinds of thoughts."

He didn't think he could stand her wedding—and bedding—the disgusting Ralph, either. "And Sir Edgar? Does he look at you like he is having slimy thoughts, too?"

"I told you, he is over forty."

"Even men over forty have those kinds of thoughts."

"Do they?" Her nose wrinkled. "I hadn't realized. I expect he is too much of a gentleman to let a lady know what he is thinking, then. Sir Edgar *is* a worthy

man—at least, my uncle thinks so, and he ought to
know, being exceptionally worthy himself. But he has
a loud voice, and he doesn't listen. He yells at his
dogs."

"Is he cruel to animals?" A man who abused animals shouldn't have any smaller, weaker creature put
in his care. James's jaw clenched at the thought of
Emily's delicate beauty being entrusted to a brute.

"N-no. Not exactly, though he is a firm believer in
discipline. He is very fond his dogs, actually. But
he *yells* at them."

They had reached a crossing with another hedge-
lined path. He thought the gazebo lay straight ahead,
but he couldn't be sure . . . then he remembered how
well she had directed him through a house she hadn't
been inside in years. "Do you know how to reach the
gazebo?"

"Oh, I—I'm not at all sure."

She was right; she was a deplorable liar. "You have
a complete mental map of these gardens, don't you?"

"Well—not a *complete* map." She looked very
guilty now. "I just tend to remember things like that."

"Which way is the gazebo?"

"Left?" She smiled hopefully.

"Emily."

She sighed. "All right. We go straight another fifteen feet, then the path curves at an arc of about thirty
degrees. It straightens out at the gazebo."

He smiled slowly. "You've studied geometry."

She clapped her hand over her mouth. "I am not
supposed to tell *anyone* about that. It is unbecoming
in a female to flaunt that sort of knowledge."

"Did you share your cousins' lessons?"

"Oh, no, Uncle Rupert would never have allowed that, but I did so want to know. I have always been curious about maps, you see, and finding one's way around, from having traveled with my father and mother when I was little. Then, after I read about Sir James Cook's travels, I wanted to know how he knew where he was. I couldn't find any books about navigation, but the vicar was kind enough to lend me a book on geometry."

"And you understood it, without any sort of instructions?"

"It was a basic sort of text, I imagine. And geometry is so tidy, the way the theorems build on each other. I liked it." She sighed. "I'm afraid I got the vicar in trouble. Uncle Rupert's face was ever so red when he found out."

She wasn't an empty-headed widgeon. She just might be a mathematical prodigy. James shook his head, took her hand, and started down the path that he had no doubt would, after another fifteen feet, curve at an arc of thirty degrees to take them to the gazebo. "Tell me more about Sir Edgar and his dogs."

"You don't understand why that bothers me, do you?"

"Keep talking, and maybe I will."

She gave a little gurgle of amusement. "No one ever says that to me—'Keep talking.' You are very easy to talk to, you know. I wonder if we would have been friends if we had met in London, when I had my Season."

"I doubt they would have let you anywhere near

me, my dear." The aunt and uncle had apparently
done their duty by her, giving her a London Season.
James wouldn't be abandoning her to any real mis-
treatment by returning her to them. The thought
should have reassured him. Instead, he felt . . . disappointed? How foolish. Had he thought, for even a second, that he could be her white knight and charge in
to save her from the dragon?

Hell, he was the dragon she needed to be rescued
from.

The gazebo loomed up suddenly in front of them,
a dim white bulk intruding itself on the tiny world
trapped by their lantern. "I think we had better wait
here and see if the snow lets up," he said, mounting
the steps beside her.

The candle in the lantern had burned down, so he
set it on the floor and knelt to replace it with one of
the spares he had brought along in his pocket. Emily
drifted restlessly around the small, half-walled struc-
ture. "Perhaps it is just as well we didn't meet until
now. I probably would have given you a disgust of
me if you had met me at a party. I was *very* stupid
in company."

"I'm sure you are wrong. In fact, now that I cast
my mind back, I believe I saw you at some respectable party I accidentally attended. You were *la belle
jeune fille*, surrounded by so many admirers that a
man had to fight three duels to get close enough to
see your face, much less claim a dance."

She laughed. "You are confusing me with one of
your flirts. I didn't take at all. I told you, I was stupid."

He lit the new candle from the old, seated it, and replaced the glass-paned hood. "Nonsense. Your mind may wander down unpredictable paths, but they are charming paths. And as pretty as you are, I can't believe you lacked admirers."

Her face lit up. "You think I am pretty? And charming?"

Also dangerous. To both of them. He straightened, leaving the lantern on the floor. "I'm sure you were considered an Original."

"No, I was considered a ninny. Aunt Dorothea had warned me so often about everything I mustn't say and not humiliating her that I got all stopped up. Like when you have the grippe and can't breathe right? Only this was conversational grippe. I couldn't talk right. Either I didn't say anything at all, or I sort of sneezed words all over the place. I did have one offer," she said with a hint of pride, stopping in front of him. "But he was a younger son with no prospects other than his lieutenant's pay, so Uncle Rupert wouldn't let me receive it."

He looked at her upturned face. Long strands of hair had worked their way free from her braid, and there was a dirt smudge on her nose. And what he felt for this dusty innocent was stronger than a tugging. Too strong to shut out, to ignore, to push away.

It hurt. Like the sharp sting of frostbitten flesh warmed by returning blood, it hurt.

"Did you want him?" he asked abruptly. "Your younger son with no prospects."

"I expect I should have. Why is it that a young man of twenty is still a boy, when an unmarried female of that age is practically on the shelf? Anyway, I couldn't feel a tendre for him. He was nice, but very silly. He wrote a poem to my left eyebrow." She giggled.

"It *is* a lovely eyebrow." He reached up to trace it, and discovered that her skin was icy. "And I am an idiot. Why didn't you tell me you were cold? That shawl isn't enough." He began unfastening his greatcoat.

"I'm not cold."

"You look enchanting with blue lips, but I'm a conventional man. I prefer them rosy."

"Put your coat back on. It would be miles too big for me, and you'll freeze without it."

"A little cold won't hurt me." He dropped it over her shoulders.

"My goodness, it's heavy. But very warm." She snuggled her cheek against the material and smiled. "It smells like you. All right, I will borrow it for now, but you have to take turns with me."

"If you like."

She looked at him suspiciously. "Do you promise?"

"You were going to tell me about Sir Edgar and his dogs."

"You haven't promised."

Stubborn as well as curious, wasn't she? His smile flickered. "Very well, I promise to take turns with the coat. Tell me about Sir Edgar." He would feel better if he knew that one of her suitors was worthy of her. "What are his waistcoats like?"

She grinned. "They aren't a bilious green, but they are snuff-stained. I did try to like him, but he doesn't *talk* to me. Or listen to me, either. Mostly he talks to my aunt or uncle, though every now and then he'll tell me I'm a pretty chit or a good girl—much the way he might toss one of his dogs a treat."

Hardly a courtship designed to appeal to a young lady. "He may be shy."

"Sir Edgar? Oh, no. My aunt and uncle encourage him to think I am shy, though. The less he talks to me the better, so he won't discover I am not what he thinks."

"And what is that?"

She sighed. "A quiet, well-behaved miss."

His lips twitched. "It does sound as if he hasn't been paying attention."

"Aunt Dorothea says he is fond of me." She said this dolefully, as if she were announcing the man's intention to beat her thrice a day after they wed.

He touched her cheek. It was still chilled. "Is that so terrible?"

"Yes. Oh, yes, it is. He is very like my uncle, you see, who is also fond of me. Sir Edgar would want what was best for me, but he wouldn't listen to what *I* want, and he would yell at me when I did something he didn't approve of, and grow disappointed in me. It is quite deadly to always be disappointing those who care for you, isn't it?"

He thought of his father. "Or those who are supposed to care about you. And don't."

She nodded. "Like my aunt—although I shouldn't say that, for perhaps she is fond of me and unable to show it. But I *would* do things Sir Edgar didn't approve of. If eight years in my uncle's household hasn't taught me a proper elegance of mind, how will marrying Sir Edgar change that?"

"Sometimes when an older man marries a much younger lady, he enjoys indulging her. Especially when there is a degree of, ah, fondness." Especially when the randy old fart was enjoying all that lovely young freshness in his bed. James had to consciously relax his hands to keep them from making fists.

"You are forgetting his dogs. He is fond of them, too, but that doesn't keep him from yelling at them. No, if I married Sir Edgar he would squeeze me out of myself, a little at a time, until I simply wasn't there anymore. Unless I did something really dreadful," she added, "like run off and starve in a ditch."

He couldn't help smiling at her notion of what her alternatives were. Yet an overbearing, self-righteous man could be deadly to a merry spirit like hers. But wouldn't it be just as deadly for her to be ostracized, condemned by family, friends, and neighbors, packed off to live with her dour great-aunt—if she wasn't put out on the streets to survive as best she could?

He wanted to make everything right for her. And couldn't. "I know you don't want to be told to have resolution—"

"Because it doesn't do any good."

"But it's the only thing you can do, sweetheart." He reached up to tuck one of the errant strands of hair behind her ear, and wanted to go on touching her— her cheek, her lips, her breasts. "If you refuse your suitors firmly enough, they will have to stop paying you court."

"Aunt Dorothea says she will have my decision to-morrow. She will make me promise to accept him—whichever 'him' I choose—before she lets him declare himself formally, so I won't have a chance to refuse anyone."

"Then you must refuse to give her your promise."

"But I have never been able to stand up to her. I try, but trying isn't enough." She touched his wrist. "I know I am a great coward, but she makes me feel so small. When she talks and talks at me, I feel as if I would do anything to make her stop. She tells me I am too much like my father and mother—as if that were a *bad* thing." Her voice shook.

He didn't decide to put his arms around her. It happened without him being a conscious part of the act at all. One moment they were talking, and the next he was drawing her to him. He rested his cheek on the top of her head and wished her aunt was a man, so he could throttle the coldhearted bastard. He wished someone would throttle him and put a stop to the heat that raced through his body, warming him better than his greatcoat had, demanding that he pull her closer and closer still, so he could rub his aching groin against her.

He kept his body still. Barely. "A coward wouldn't leave her home in the dead of night to be ruined by a stranger. Mind you, I'm not saying that was a bright thing to do—but it wasn't the act of a coward."

"You don't seem like a stranger," she said shyly.

It was the most natural thing in the world for his head to dip lower, for his lips to draw near hers. A breath away from the kiss, he stopped. His heart

pounded. Was it heat or panic making it race? He had
to draw back.

He didn't move. "The snow isn't falling as hard.
We should leave now."

One mittened hand crept up to touch his cheek. "Do
we have to?"

SEVEN

Emily's heart pounded. Deep inside she quivered with hope and fear, balanced on a keen and dreadful edge between one moment and the next. They knew, they both knew, what she offered with those few words . . . and this time her offer had little to do with her Plan.

And everything to do with him.

The light from the lantern's single candle came from below, making his face more shadow than seen, hiding his eyes while it played lovingly over his lips. She longed to go up on tiptoe and kiss those lips, persuade him to let her stay. Tonight, all night. With him. But it had taken all her courage just to touch his cheek.

His hand rose and captured hers—and pulled it away from his face. Something inside her tore at the rejection.

But he didn't release her hand. His thumb began to trace circles on the damp yarn that covered her palm. "It's a good thing we are here, not in my room," he said softly, "for I've little experience resisting temptation, and I have never been so tempted in my life. But I won't marry you, Emily. I can't."

She swallowed hurt and hope and pride in one hard lump. "Why? Not 'Why *won't* you marry me?'— there's no reason you should. But you make it sound as if you *can't* marry."

The twist of his mouth was sad and bitter. "Money. Both cure and cause of so many evils, isn't it?"

"I . . . I heard that your father had disinherited you."

"Your aunt does keep up on the on-dits, doesn't she?" He dropped her hand. "He did. In an effort to bring me to heel, he continues to withhold the income from another inheritance for which he was, unfortunately, named trustee. My future is uncertain, to say the least. And you deserve better." He moved away to pick up the lantern. "The snow has almost stopped. It's time we left."

She looked out at the night and saw only a few flakes drifting groundward, barely visible at the edges of the area limned by the lantern's light. Drat it all. "I loathe it when people make decisions about what is best for me."

"I know. But I am still taking you home intact, if not untouched."

She slid his heavy greatcoat off his shoulders. "It's your turn."

"Not yet. I'll let you know when I'm chilled."

She held it out. "Maybe I can't keep you from being horridly noble about some things, but you can't have everything your way. If you don't take this, I will leave it here on the floor."

He smiled and took the coat, slipping his arms in the sleeves. "You will allow me to indulge my nobility midway through the woods, I trust?"

She shrugged and started down the snowy, slippery steps. This was it. Her last chance. Her heart thudded hard in her chest. "Oh!" she cried. And fell off the step.

Emily hadn't fallen on purpose since she was small. It was harder to do than she had expected, and she landed awkwardly. "Oof!"

"Emily?" James was at her side in a second. "Are you all right?"

She couldn't look him in the eye, so she stared at his shoulder. "I twisted my ankle."

"I'd better have a look." He pushed her dress up farther than was necessary and took her foot in his hands.

"Ow!"

"I haven't touched your ankle yet."

"It was the angle. You were holding it at a painful angle."

"Hmm." He rotated her foot, and she grimaced and bit her lip and tried to look brave in the face of pain. "I suppose it hurts too much for you to put any weight on it."

She nodded.

"There's no help for it, then. We'll have to steal a horse." When her mouth dropped open, he laughed. "A word of advice, sweetheart—never try to earn your living on the stage."

Emily lay on her back in the snow, growing damp and chilled—except for the fiery tide of humiliation sweeping over her. She had made herself painfully obvious. And he had laughed.

He stood and held out his hand.

No, she wasn't going to touch him. Or look at him. Or speak to him, ever again. She scrambled to her feet by herself, her face still fiery. And he put his hands on her shoulders, pulled her to him, and kissed her.

The world tilted. Her stomach went dizzy, as if she were falling again—but this time she just kept falling. There was no solid ground, only his shoulders to cling to, his body firm against hers. His mouth, warm and hungry, on hers. The smell of damp wool was suddenly delicious, intoxicating. The taste of him, brandy and heat, sent her spiraling into a dark, private place where there was nothing but her. And him.

His lips left hers to press kisses along her cheeks. His hands cupped her face, tilting her head so his mouth could follow the line of her neck from her ear to her collar, and back again.

"Emily," he said then, leaning his forehead against hers. "You have no idea what you do to me, do you? And very little idea what you are inviting me to do to you, I think. So you don't really understand what I'm asking, but still I have to ask. Are you sure? Be very sure, because once I get you back to my room, I won't give you another chance. I won't take your virginity—but I will take everything else."

What did he mean—everything but her virginity? She pulled her head back so she could look at him. His face was hard, unsmiling, his eyes hidden from her in the darkness.

She touched his cheek. "I won't lose myself, you know. I can see how it could happen—these feelings are so *strong*. But I think people only get lost when they look for these feelings in the wrong places."

He gave a hard, short laugh. "And you think I am

the right man, and this is the right place? Oh, Emily. I should explain to you how very wrong you are, but I'm out of reasons. Out of reason entirely, I think."

But Emily understood. More than he would believe, she understood what she risked—and what she had found, with him. She didn't try to tell him, but tucked her hand in his. "I will have to show you, I think."

If he thought it strange that a virgin would offer to show a rake anything about lovemaking, he was courteous enough not to say so. He pressed one last kiss to her lips—a gentle kiss, this time. As if there were something he needed to tell her, too, that wouldn't fit neatly into words. Then he let go of her hand long enough to take his coat off and drape it over her shoulders once more. "Allow me this much."

She nodded. They turned together to go back to his room.

Emily didn't speak. The world itself was quiet, with the peculiar hush that snowfall brings to the country, so that even her thoughts seemed loud and singular, and her heart beat hard and fast. In the soft privacy of that silence they walked back to his room, her hand in his, his coat warm and large and awkward on her small frame.

It would be so easy to trip, Emily thought. She took care to keep the coat bunched up in her free hand, away from her feet, as they moved together toward the moment when she would find answers to some of her questions. *Everything but your virginity,* he had said. What did that mean? Doubtless it involved kisses, and oh, she loved his kisses.

Which was not surprising. She loved him.

Emily wasn't worried about losing herself. The most important thing she had to lose was already his. That was all right. There was so much waiting to be found, in his arms. So she walked on, careful of the dragging length of his coat. And just as careful of her thoughts.

It wouldn't do to think about tomorrow, and all the tomorrows to come. When he would be gone.

He wouldn't enter her. That much James was sure of. Emily would still be a virgin when she left him. He would do everything else—strip her, touch her, kiss her, waken her to pleasure she'd never dreamed existed. And then send her plunging into climax—oh, yes, he wanted that, all of it. Desperately. But he wouldn't breach her maidenhead.

James knew Emily would never pretend to a virginity she couldn't honestly claim, and he knew the men of his class. They wouldn't accept a bride who admitted she lacked that small, significant scrap of flesh. And despite what she thought, marriage was her only chance for a decent life. So he would make sure she would still be able to marry one of her suitors . . . and he would leave Sussex quickly, before he killed the bastard.

But that was all he was sure of.

Amazingly, his hands shook as he pushed the window open and helped her inside. They had left the candles burning, as well as the fire, so the room was cheery and warm after their walk through the snowy night.

She took the greatcoat off and draped it neatly on the back of the chair, then turned to face him. Her gaze was steady, her smile shy.

"How peculiar," he murmured as he crossed to her. He laid his hands on her shoulders, running them down her arms and taking her shawl with them. It fell to the floor, a dark puddle. "You look serene, and I am nervous enough to jump out of my skin." As if he were attempting something he had never done before.

"You don't look nervous. And I don't feel serene."

He reached behind her and slipped the first button loose, bending to nuzzle her neck. "What do you feel, then?"

"As if . . . as if I were running very fast, making my head light and my stomach dizzy. Dreamy, yet wide awake, so awake I can feel my fingertips and I . . . Oh, my. You are awfully good with buttons."

"I'm afraid so." He slipped the last button free and gently pushed her gown from her shoulders. It followed her shawl to the floor. "Emily?"

"Yes?"

"That's the oddest-looking chemise I've ever seen."

"I would think a man who is so good with a woman's buttons knows the difference between a nightgown and a chemise."

He touched the flowers embroidered in white thread on white flannel, and his heart turned over. His women had always come to him experienced, knowing, wearing silks and lace . . . or nothing at all. None had come to him dressed in flannel and innocence.

If he were a better man, he would stop now. If he had needed her less, he might have been able to. But he could, at least, be gentle with her innocence.

He ran his hands along her sides in a caress that was more than chaste, but far less than what his heated blood urged him to do. "Will you let down your hair for me? I want to see it loose on your shoulders and breasts. I want to fist it in my hands when I kiss you."

Her breath caught. "I hadn't known there was so much talking involved."

"In lovemaking, you mean?" He smiled and moved his hands a little higher. His thumbs rested just beneath the curve of her breasts now. "Does it bother you?"

Emily's brain had turned light. Sunshine pooled, thick and happy, in her middle, making her hands unsteady when she pulled her braid in front of her. "I like it," she said softly, meaning his voice, his words that acted as richly on her system as his touch.

"Let me," he said when she had the braid undone, and combed his fingers through the newly separated strands. His knuckles brushed her breast, sending a quick jolt through her.

He did it again. And again. The finger-combing soothed while his hands thrilled as his knuckles, then the backs of his hands, and then his fingertips grazed her breast. His eyes stayed on hers while he lightly stroked her breast.

She wanted badly for him to kiss her again. For once, though, her too-quick tongue found no words.

So she told him with her hands, slipping them behind his head.

The nape of his neck was warm. His hair was cool and slightly damp from their walk in the snow. The feel of him, silky hair and warm flesh, distracted her, and she traced her fingers over his face, studying the planes and hollows with her eyes and the pads of her fingertips.

His breath caught. "Sweet Emily," he said, "I am trying to go slowly, but I've less willpower than I had thought. Boots next."

"Boots?"

"It is the most awkward part of a seduction, love—the footwear. Sit," he said, and led her to the chair where his greatcoat was draped. He knelt at her feet and unfastened her half boots and pulled them off, leaving her in her nightgown and stockinged feet. He ran his hand up her foot to her ankle, to her calf, then rolled down garter and stocking together. "You have such pretty, dainty ankles."

He had seen a great deal more than her ankles. "You didn't remove my half boots before."

"I was drunk and foolish. I'm still foolish, but at least I am sober now. Or as sober as a man in the grip of passion can be." He lifted her foot and shocked her by pressing a kiss to the arch. Then he moved away to sit on the bed and tug at one of his boots.

There was something very domestic about watching him struggle with his boots. If they were married . . . No. No, she couldn't let herself think about that.

"What's wrong?" He stood in front of her in his

shirtsleeves, his jacket and waistcoat having gone the way of his boots.

"Nothing. Do you always throw your clothes on the floor?"

His half smile was quizzical. "I wouldn't have done so if I had known it would make you so sad." He held out his hand. "Miss Smythe, may I have the honor of this dance?" Without waiting for an answer, he pulled her to her feet, put one hand at her waist, and held the other out in the approved way—then spun her into a mad semblance of a waltz, holding her much too close as he danced her around and around. He danced her into laughter, and right up to his bed. Where he stopped.

She stopped laughing. Her heart was pounding and he was smiling when he pulled on the tie that fastened her nightgown. When it, too, lay on the floor, he eased her onto the bed.

He gave her little chance for embarrassment, strewing her neck and shoulders with kisses and shivers. His hands—oh, his hands were everywhere, petting and stroking, making her body restless and achy. The feel of them on her breasts was a wonder to her.

"You . . ." Words and breath were hard to find. "You still have some clothes on."

"Best if I keep them on. We can't entirely trust me, love."

He kissed her again, and she almost forgot—but when she ran her hands over his back, cloth shifted beneath her touch. "But I want to see you." To touch him, skin to skin. "I will never have another chance, and I want to *know*."

He lifted his head. His lips, damp from hers, turned up in a smile, but his jaw was taut. "Curiosity again? You'll learn a man's body fully one day. In your marriage bed."

No, she wouldn't, for she would never marry. But she wasn't going to argue with him now. "I want to know *your* body."

He went very still. Then he shuddered. "I am certainly a fool," he said, but he sat up and pulled off his shirt.

He wanted to leave his breeches on, but this was her only chance to know what was beneath those breeches. She fumbled for the buttons and learned how different a man's body really was. He made a funny, low noise in his throat and pushed her hands away—but only so he could take over.

He didn't look anything like the statue of an unclothed Apollo she had seen once in London. "Oh," she said, her eyes huge. "Maybe it's just as well you aren't going to . . ." He was so *big.* Without thinking, she reached out to touch him.

He caught her hand. His smile was strained. "I have my limits, and that would definitely be beyond them. Keep your hands above my waist, sweetheart, or you'll make me forswear myself."

Skin to skin was better. It was incredibly better, for when he kissed her now, she felt him all along her body, warm and slightly sweaty. It was even more intimate than when he'd touched her *there,* for they were together now in what they did. "I feel so strange . . . as if I should move. I need to *do* something, but I don't know what."

"It's a hasty feeling, isn't it?" He nuzzled her neck, and down to her breast, where he captured the tip in his mouth. She forgot everything in the delicious new sensation. "I understand. God, I do understand. But there's no need for you to rush to the end."

"Is there an end?" She ran her hands over his back. She wanted to go on swimming forever in this rich, intolerant heat, the need that rose like steam, replacing thought and blood alike.

"There is . . . how should I put it?" He circled her nipple with his tongue. "There is a climactic moment, love, which is generally the end for a man, not necessarily for a woman. You'll know when you reach it." He turned his head to lavish the same attention on her other breast.

"I don't—Oh! James." Her hands tightened, clutching at him, for he was touching her where he had touched her once before. The sensation was overwhelming. "James!"

He suckled her breasts and kissed her and touched her. Her legs moved restlessly, and he pushed them wider, and there were sounds—soft gasps from her, a throaty groan from him, a funny, wet sound from where he touched her. She was reaching for something, her body moving now at his command while he murmured words of encouragement and praise. "Like that—yes, love, beautiful Emily, let go, let go. I'm here, you're safe. Let go."

She did. Her body jerked. Everything went white and blank in a flash of purest pleasure—and then she was back inside herself, limp, with little shocks running through her, throbbing where his hand had been.

He had moved, coming fully over her to touch her *there* lightly.

Something replaced his hand. Something blunt and hard and warm.

Her eyes had drifted closed, but they flew open at this strange new feeling. He was so big—he was stretching her, stretching—"Ow!" The hurt was sharp and stinging.

He thrust again, hard. And was fully inside.

His eyes went wide, too. He stared down at her, startled. As if this were as unexpected for him as it was for her. She shifted, uncomfortable, and he groaned. "Emily," he said, and his hips began to move. "Emily." He bent and kissed her.

The hurt faded, and his movement began to feel good, but lingering discomfort combined with the sheer novelty distracted her. The wet sounds were louder. The faint, rhythmic creaking of the bed ropes blended with the sensations that began to build once more.

There was such need on his face, such desire. She stroked him and petted him as he had done her. The flex of muscle in his hips and buttocks fascinated her. She needed to move, to meet him . . . her hips found his rhythm, then lost it again when he speeded up.

Just when things were getting really interesting, he gave a loud groan, went rigid—and collapsed on top of her. His chest heaved, and his eyes were closed. Emily cherished the weight of him, holding him and smiling and smiling.

When he rolled to his side she made a small sound of protest, but he cuddled her close, stroking her hair, and that was almost as nice as the other.

"James?"

"Hmm?" He continued to play with her hair.

"I think you did what you said you weren't going to do."

"I know. I'm sorry."

She tilted her head back so she could see his face. He didn't look sorry. He was smiling. It made tiny crinkles at the corners of his eyes. He had gorgeous eyelashes, thick and curly. "I'm glad you changed your mind."

"My mind had little to do with it. In truth, as stupid as it sounds, I forgot. I knew I should have kept my breeches on." He gave her hair a playful tug, but his eyes were troubled. "There's something about you, Emily, some magic . . . I don't understand what you do to me."

Emily's breath caught at what she saw on his face. She waited, her heart beating painfully hard, for him to go on. If he felt something for her—something more than lust—surely he would speak now.

But he didn't. He kissed her again, and the kiss was sweet, a blend of tenderness and sensual delight that hazed her brain as it woke her body. When he touched her, his hands were careful and knowing and perfect. But he didn't speak of feelings or the future.

And she couldn't. Though her heart cried out for her to tell him she loved him, she couldn't. She had promised not to trap him. So when they made love a second time, Emily was silent.

So was he.

EIGHT

The air was still and cold. The only sound came from the crunch of their boots on the snow. In the east, the sky had faded to a dingy gray. The moon was gone, so they'd needed the lantern to find their way through the woods. But they'd almost reached the end of the path now.

He was holding her hand. They had hardly spoken since leaving his room, but he had held her hand the whole time. Maybe he didn't want to let go, Emily thought. Maybe he didn't want the night to end any more than she did. Even if he didn't say so.

He squeezed her hand. "We're almost there. How had you planned to get back inside?"

"I left the front door unlocked." She looked at the bare, snowy expanse of lawn and field that led to the dark bulk of her uncle's house. And stopped dead. "I see lights."

"Some of the servants must be up." He didn't stop, drat him, but tugged her with him out into the openness.

"No, there are too many lights. The servants would be in the kitchen, not at the front of the house. James, you have to go back now before someone sees you."

The smile he gave her came cursedly near to being lighthearted. "Did you really think I would leave you to face them alone?"

"You have to!" She pulled hard at her hand, but he just kept moving them both forward.

"I'll stand by you, Emily." He hesitated. "If there should be a child—"

"A child?" Her stomach pitched in sudden panic. "Is that possible? I thought—when one of the female dogs goes into season, it takes several days, a week—"

"It's possible." There was a grim note in his voice.

Dear heavens. She'd based her assumptions about mating on her uncle's dogs, but people weren't dogs. She might be with child. James's child. Now, this very minute. The thought made her light-headed—but fear was only part of her giddiness.

"James," she said, her voice shaking. "Some of those lights are moving. They're coming this way."

He nodded. "They have lanterns, too. Or torches. I'm afraid someone noticed you were gone, love. They're looking for you."

"You have to get away!" She pulled frantically at his hand. "At least put out the lantern so they can't see you."

But he only put his arm around her shoulder and brushed her cheek with his lips. "Courage, sweetheart." And kept moving them both forward.

But she didn't have courage. It was too much like resolution, and she was pathetically lacking at that. Emily felt herself shrinking inside as they neared the other lights. She heard voices—her uncle's voice, loud and angry.

Then a gunshot. "Oh, God, Uncle Rupert has a gun!"

"He fired in the air," James said calmly, so far from heeding her words that he tightened his arm, hugging her close. "A signal, I suspect. There must be other searchers out."

"But he might shoot you!"

"That would be stupid of him, wouldn't it? Can't wring a proposal from a dead man."

"But—"

But it was too late. Marcus was the first one to reach them, his young legs having outstripped the others.' "Emily!" he cried. "I've been so scared! Letty woke Mother up and said you were gone, and Mother woke Father up, and of course Aunt Mildred heard them when Father started yelling, so I—"

"Wanton! Harlot!" Her uncle was winded from his run when he reached them, but not so winded his voice didn't thunder out like the wrath of Jehovah. "Sneaking out of the house to shame yourself and your family with this misbegotten bastard—"

"That's enough!" James's voice cut through the tirade like an icy knife. "You may abuse me all you wish, but you will not speak to Emily that way."

"I'll speak to my niece however I wish, and I'll make you wish you were never born!" Uncle Rupert lunged forward, grabbing for Emily's arm. "Come here!"

Her uncle's fingers dug into her arm cruelly, and he yanked at her. She thought she would be torn in two, because James didn't release her. Then Marcus flung himself at his father, prying his fingers off Emily's arm—and earning a cuff for his trouble.

James moved swiftly, putting himself between Emily and her uncle. "Leave her be," he said in a low, deadly voice.

For a moment there was silence.

It didn't last.

Cousin George and Ned from the stable reached them next, followed quickly by the husband of another cousin. Cousin Timothy. Frances, the snitch. Two second cousins from Bath. One of the footmen. Great-Uncle Max. Letty, who was crying, and Abigail, who was shrill.

Loud, outraged voices rose around them like an angry tide. There were questions and threats—the questions shouted at her, the threats at James. He stood beside her, his arm around her shoulders the only thing that kept her from drowning in the clamor. Perhaps he realized that one had to let Baggots yell themselves hoarse before they would listen, for he didn't say anything. Not that anyone gave either of them a chance. They were too busy arguing over what should be done with her, to her, to James.

Just as the sun came peeping over the horizon, her aunt arrived.

Aunt Dorothea was dressed with as much neatness and propriety as always in a dark puce gown and her ermine-lined pelisse. Every strand of hair was smoothed into place. Her hands were folded primly in front of her when she came to a stop in front of James and Emily. Her lips were folded even more tightly together. She didn't look at Emily at all, but spoke to James. "Your name, sir."

He didn't bow. "James Edward Charles Drake, Baron Redding, at your service, madam."

"Hah!" her uncle cried. "That dastard who was kissing you in the woods, missy? Is this how little you appreciate all we've done for you, taking you in, caring for you?" He shook his fist in James's face. "Name your seconds, sir!"

"The Earl of Mere's son," Aunt Dorothea said in her cool, measured voice. Still she didn't look at Emily, making Emily wonder if she had finally vanished. "Your reputation, and the manner in which you lured my niece to you, indicate that you have no honorable intentions. Mr. Baggot, I believe a horsewhip would be more suitable."

"He didn't lure me." Emily's voice was small and shaky. "It was all my own idea. I am very sorry, Aunt. I simply couldn't marry as you wished me to."

"You are wrong, madam." James's voice was every bit as cool as her aunt's. "I intend to offer for her."

"James!" Emily cried as the earth turned unsteady beneath her feet. But her voice was only one of many as the babel broke out again. She searched his face, trying to see something other than the whimsically late arrival of his sense of honor. "James, you don't want this, you know you don't."

Maybe he didn't hear her in all the shouting. He patted her hand and smiled. It was a beautiful smile, meant to reassure her. It failed. If he had wanted to marry her, he would have said something earlier. He offered now to save her from ruin. Or maybe from her relatives.

Eventually her uncle outshouted the rest. "And what do you offer her, sir? Not an honorable name, if half of what I hear is true."

"Nor a roof over her head," Aunt Dorothea said. "If you were hoping to fund your raking with her fortune, my lord, you should know she doesn't have one."

"Neither do I," James said steadily. "As you are obviously aware. But I do have an inheritance from my mother that will come to me in four years."

"Four years?" Uncle Rupert shouted. "Four years, you say? Do you think you can batten yourself on me that long? Or did you intend to drag the poor chit with you to your gaming hells and orgies?"

Emily noticed that she had gone from being a harlot and a wanton to a poor chit. It was typical of Uncle Rupert's rages. They blew hard and hot while they lasted, but they did blow themselves out.

Unlike her aunt's temper, which was cold and deadly. "If you still want her after debauching her, you may have her. But you take her now, as she is. No dowry, no trousseau, not even a hairpin more than what she has on her this moment."

This time James bowed. "Thank you, madam. I accept."

"No." Emily's voice squeaked so badly she wasn't sure anyone heard. "No," she said again, and forced herself to move away from James. "I am very sorry, Aunt, but I will not marry him. I promised not to."

"Emily—" James reached for her.

But her uncle was closer to her now. He grabbed her and and called her a shameless hussy. He told her to be a good girl and do as she was told. She could only shake her head no.

For a dreadful moment she thought he would cry.

If she had thought things were bad before, they got worse. Louder, more confused. And James was no longer by her side. Her oldest cousins were squared off against him, ready to beat him into agreement. Emily could only keep saying, over and over, that it would do no good. She wouldn't marry him. Her uncle yelled, but she didn't give in. Then her aunt started in on her.

Aunt Eleanor spoke in clear, withering sentences. She told Emily everything that was wrong with her—everything she had done wrong in the last eight years. Emily had done so much wrong. She was wrong. Wrong, wrong, wrong, and she shrank with every word.

But still she said no.

At long last, Emily had found her resolution. She wouldn't trap James, wouldn't force him to surrender his dreams. He would go to America, if she could not.

There was a flurry of motion behind her, the sound of a blow struck. She spun around in time to see Cousin George fall to the ground. James pushed past another cousin to reach her. "Enough," he said, and his face was stern. "I'll not have her browbeaten. If you'll let me speak with her in private a moment—"

But they wouldn't. Her uncle boomed out that Emily would by damn accept the suit of the man she'd lain with. Her aunt said that if she didn't, her things would be thrown out of the house, along with her. Which started her aunt and uncle arguing, because her uncle would never countenance such a thing. Marcus screamed that he would go with her if she was turned out, so George started yelling at Marcus. Abigail shrieked that Emily had ruined them all, as if shame were catching, like the measles. And Letty cried.

James had to raise his voice to be heard over the others. "In that case, I withdraw my offer."

The world tilted again.

Someone gasped. Uncle Rupert turned purple, turned away, and dragged Emily off toward the house. James called out her name. She looked over her shoulder and saw him surrounded by Baggots. She caught only a glimpse of his face, heard only a few words of what he said—something about waiting, something about his back, or coming back, and his groom.

Then her uncle jerked her forward, and she saw and heard no more of the man who had been her lover, and would remain her love.

Emily spent the next five days locked in her own small bedroom on the third floor. The servants brought food and took care of the other necessities; Marcus, who was becoming an accomplished sneak, stole the key three times and visited. He smuggled her some books and her needlework. They helped her pass the time until she could be sent to her great-aunt.

The days were the worst.

Emily didn't mind the isolation as much as she had feared she might. There were some advantages to being unfit to mingle with the respectable Baggots, who went right on celebrating the season without her. She might miss the sleigh rides and carol singing, but no one was yelling at her. Her aunt wasn't speaking to her. But the days were still bad, because, in spite of the sternest lectures Emily could give herself, every morning she woke up *hoping*.

The hope lasted all day, wiggling inside her when she heard steps on the stairs or a carriage pull up outside. She couldn't see the yard from her window, only the roof of the second floor of the family wing, so the foolish hope squirmed and churned inside her for half an hour after hearing a carriage.

James had said something about his back . . . or about coming back.

Every night when the maid brought Emily her supper tray, that day's unwanted allotment of hope curled up in a cold lump that sank into her stomach, making her too ill with disappointment to eat.

Belief and hope, it seemed, were not the same thing, for Emily didn't really believe he would come for her. He *had* cared about her. He would remember her. That much she believed. But she was only one memory of many for him, and even if he had truly wanted to marry her, he couldn't afford to. He had made that clear.

But she couldn't seem to stop hoping.

Nights were better. Once she had put the day's hope and the evening's disappointment behind her, she could perform a hasty wash in the chilly air, tug on her nightgown, and blow out her candle. Cheered by a darkness relieved by the familiar warmth of a fire, she could climb into bed and wrap herself up in memories and dreams as warm as the covers she snuggled under.

At night she relived every minute of her time with James. She pictured him on the boat to America.

Sometimes she imagined receiving a letter from him a few years from now, telling her all the strange and wonderful things he had seen and done in the New World.

She didn't dream of anything more personal in the imaginary letter. Not because she possessed the strength of mind to banish such longings, but because they hurt too much. There was comfort in thinking of him prospering in America, and in her somehow learning of it. There was no comfort in imagining what could never be.

But on the fifth night of her banishment, Emily couldn't summon contentment from the darkness. It was Christmas Eve, and she felt painfully alone. She tossed and turned, and found neither sleep nor fantasies to distract her. So when the tapping came at her window very late that night, Emily was wide awake.

She sat bolt upright in bed, her eyes huge. Surely she was losing her mind. She hadn't heard what she thought she'd heard. There was no way—

Tap, tap. Tap-tap-tap.

Emily threw back the covers and raced to the window. She threw back the drapes, releasing the cold air trapped between glass and cloth, and shivered with cold and excitement.

There was a man on the roof outside her window. His shape was no more than a huge, caped silhouette against the star-strewn sky, his face invisible in the darkness—but she knew. Oh, she knew.

Her fingers were thick and clumsy unlatching the window, but finally she had it open. And the man she couldn't see reached in, grasped her face in gloved hands, and leaned in and kissed her.

His lips were cold, the inside of his mouth was warm, and his taste was utterly, wonderfully familiar. "Emily," James said, his voice thick. "I tried to get word to you, but no one from this house would speak to my groom—except for Marcus, and I gather he got in trouble for it, though he did manage to get me word of which room was yours."

"Your groom—that was what you said, that your groom would stay in the village?" And that he would come back. He *had* said he would come back, and here he was. At her window. She laughed from sheer happiness. "Where have you been? Why aren't you on your boat? And how did you get up here?"

"A ladder," he said, "and I'll answer the rest of your questions inside. If you want me to come in."

Of course she wanted him to come in. Her window was smaller than the one at the hall had been, so he had to take off his greatcoat and toss it in first, and she hurried to light a candle with the flint by her bed. When she turned, he was there—there in her tiny, shabby room. Sudden uncertainty made her hug herself instead of throwing her arms around him. "Have you come to say good-bye, then? Before you sail?"

"God, I hope not." He crossed to her and took her in his arms and made everything right in her world once more, if a trifle dizzy. After a long kiss, he pulled his head back. "We've much to do and little time, and I'm thinking too much of that bed beside you, sweetheart. I'm afraid you'll have to make do with what you can pack quickly, plus what we can buy before the ship sails. If . . ." He looked suddenly uncertain. "If you want to come with me, that is."

"Of course I do. But I have to know if . . . that is, you withdrew your offer, so I'm not perfectly sure what you want, but if you are here because of your honor, or mine—"

For some reason, that made him kiss her again. Then he laid his cheek against her head. "I'm an idiot. Emily, I want to marry you, if you'll have me, not for any honorable reason, but because I am madly, absurdly in love with you, and—"

Of course, she had to kiss him.

A long time—a very long time—later, he was doing up the buttons on her second-best wool dress, a process that seemed to take much longer than unbuttoning did. Her nightgown lay on the floor on top of his jacket and greatcoat. His cravat was draped over the bedpost. And her body was still tingling.

The climactic moment he had told her about was even better when it happened while he was buried inside her.

"Better get your things together, love," he said, pressing a kiss to her neck as he finished the last button. "We need to be in Portsmouth in time to use the special license in my pocket before our ship sails."

Our ship. It sounded wonderful. But questions pressed against the happiness, making her heart ache a little. Emily brushed her hair and did it up again quickly, then spread her old black shawl out on the bed to serve as portmanteau. She didn't look at him when she started on the first of her questions. "I don't understand why you didn't say something about your feelings before. And—and why you withdrew your offer."

"Because I could see you were going to hold stubbornly to your promise not to trap me into marriage, and I couldn't stand the way they were treating you. And I didn't want you forced into marriage." He finished tying his cravat. "Does this look as bad as I think it does?"

She giggled. "As bad as my hair, I suspect. James?"

"Yes?" He had his waistcoat on and was struggling into his jacket.

"Why didn't you tell me how you felt?" That still hurt.

He came to her and kissed her lightly. "I'm sorry. I wanted so badly to do right by you, and I've had little experience at that. I didn't know what was right. With any other young miss, the answer would have been obvious. Marriage." He smiled. "But you're not like anyone else. It wasn't until your relatives surrounded us that I realized I did have something to give you."

"Was that when you realized I loved you?" she asked shyly. "When I finally found my resolution and stood up to my aunt?"

He traced a finger down her cheek. "No, sweetheart, though that moved me greatly, I had a pretty good notion of your feelings already. You fairly shimmered with love when you gave yourself to me—which was what made me forget everything except making you mine. But I didn't know what I could give you in return until I saw how your family smothered everything bright and special in you. Then I

knew I could give you one thing others wouldn't—
the freedom to be who you are. It just took me a few
days to arrange things."

She turned and reached for her jewelry box. "You
had to get your money back from the ship's captain
you were to have sailed with, I suppose, and arrange
passage for the two of us. It must have been expensive." She held out her one piece of good jewelry, her
mother's pearls. "These should help."

He folded her fingers around the pearls. "You
needn't worry about money, Emily. Are you ready to
go?"

"James," she said, exasperated, "I know you don't
have any money. I don't, either, but I do have the
pearls and a small dowry. I don't think my uncle will
withhold it once we're married. He blusters and yells,
but he does care about me."

"But you truly don't have to worry about money.
I've, ah, persuaded my father to release my inheritance. It took a spot of blackmail—"

"What? How?"

"The Earl of Mere has been the cause of too many
scandals himself to be concerned with the world's
opinion of him—normally. But it is one thing to be
known as a wicked rake. Quite another to appear ridiculous." He grinned. "I paid a visit to the parents
of the bride my father had been trying to foist on me.
I assured them they needn't worry about their daughter's safety if we wed, since I hadn't suffered one of
my spells in months, and besides, my father never
turned violent when he was suffering from our little
family problem. Why, the last time it happened, I told

them, the earl did nothing more alarming than borrow my aunt's court dress and feathers."

She choked on a laugh. "You didn't! Oh, heavens. You did."

"They didn't entirely believe me, but they were delighted to have an interesting bit of gossip to pass on. My next interview was with my father. I made it clear that unless he released my inheritance, my only goal in life would be to convince the ton that our family was subject to the most foolish sort of madness. Once the gossip started to spread—aided by the way I behaved at Lady Jersey's rout party—he was willing to do whatever it took to get me out of the country."

She was laughing helplessly now. "What did you do at Lady Jersey's party?"

"Suffice it say," he said, handing her shawl bundle to her, "that your neighbors won't be gossiping about you running off with a rake. Instead they'll shake their heads over 'poor Emily,' whose husband barks at the moon." He smiled that tender, devastating smile. "I am as ruined now as you are, you see. No one else will have me if you don't."

So she kissed him again.

The sun was creeping over the horizon on Christmas morning when they finally climbed out her window. There was a ladder to be navigated to reach the ground—another new experience for her, she told him.

"So," she said happily when they both stood on the icy ground. "Am I marrying you to save your reputation, or is it the other way around?"

"Maybe we'll save each other." He took her hand.

"I'll need you in America. I don't want to get lost."
He smiled. "Ready to leave the Old World for the
New?"

She looked at the house, at eight years' worth of
the familiar—and joy bubbled up in her, sweet and
heady. There was so much to learn—about ships and
America and, most of all, about the man smiling at
her on this shiny Christmas morning. The right man.
The one who had taken her virginity and her heart—
and had given her himself, and the chance to find her
resolution. And herself. "Oh, yes. Yes, please."

SANTA WEARS SPURS

Sherrilyn Kenyon

PROLOGUE

Danger. O'Connell felt it on the back of his neck and deep in his bones as he raced his pinto across the dead winter Texas plains toward a town he'd never known existed.

After all this time, he ought to be used to danger. He had lived his life under its constant stalking shadow, and kept it as his faithful companion. Danger was his ally and his enemy.

It defined everything about him. There had only been one time in his life when he had felt safe. But that was a long time ago.

It was biting cold out, not that he felt it much. His thrumming blood kept him warm as he rode through the night.

"You should have been there, Kid. It was like taking candy from a baby," Pete had laughed. "Hah, now that I think about it, I *did* take candy from a baby. I just wish I could see their faces when they wake up and find their money gone."

Then as now, O'Connell hadn't found the words amusing. He knew Pete could be as cold-blooded as they came—the bullet wound in his arm was testimony to that. But not even *he* had thought Pete would steal from an orphanage just two days before Christmas.

The man had no soul.

There was a time when O'Connell had been just the same. When hatred had strangled his heart and left him unable to feel for anyone save himself.

And then he'd met *her*.

His heart lurched, just as it always did when he thought of her. She had shown him another way, another life, and had changed everything about him in the process. She'd given him hope, a future. A reason to live. And life without her had been nothing more than a bitter hell.

In all honesty, he didn't know how he managed to make it through the endless, miserable days that had turned into years.

Somehow, he just survived. Cold. Empty.

Alone.

God, how he missed her. How he ached for some way to go back and relive just one second of the time he'd shared with her. Just to see her face one more time, feel her breath on his skin.

For a moment, O'Connell let his thoughts drift to the past. And like they always did when he was unguarded, they went to a remembered dream of long dark brown hair and eyes as clear and warm as a summer's day. Of a woman who had told him she loved him without making a single sound.

Closing his eyes, he saw her bright smile and heard the music of her laughter as she lay naked beneath him while he claimed her for his own. He clenched his teeth at the white-hot desire that coiled through his belly. And for a moment he swore he could still feel her hands against his back as she held him tight and cried out in ecstasy.

Not even five years could dull the memories. Or his craving for her touch. He could taste the salty sweetness of her body, feel her hot and tight around him, and smell the sunshine that had always seemed to be in her hair.

Catherine had touched him in ways no one had before or since.

"I remember you," he breathed. But most of all he remembered the promise he had made to her. The promise he had broken. And in that moment, he wished Pete's bullet had gone straight through his useless heart.

Lord above, if there was one last wish he could have, it would be to set things right. He'd sell whatever was left of his blackened soul for a way to go back and change what he'd done to her.

But it wasn't to be.

He knew that.

There was nothing left for him to do except see the money back to the orphans Pete had stolen it from.

After that, he didn't know where he'd go. He'd have to find another place where the law and Pete couldn't find him. *If* such a place existed.

Briefly, he considered trying to find *her.* After all, she had been his safe harbor. His greatest strength.

But then, she had also been his greatest weakness.

No, it wouldn't do to seek her out. Too much depended on him staying away from her. Because one thing his brother Pete, had taught him years ago—there was no such thing as a second chance.

ONE

"All I want for Christmas is a man as handsome as the Devil himself. One with a charming smile, at least some semblance of intelligence, and a great, *big,* bulging—"

"Rebecca Baker!" Catherine O'Callahan gasped, shocked at her friend's words.

"Bank account," Rebecca said as she dropped her hands down from the graphic illustration she had been providing. She picked up the frying pan near Catherine, then placed it on top of the black iron stove. "I was only going to say *bank account.*"

Trying not to smile lest she encourage her friend's libidinous conversation, Catherine looked askance at Rebecca as she continued washing dishes.

Rebecca's olive cheeks colored ever so slightly as she walked back to the sink. "Well, maybe I wasn't. *But* as a married woman yourself, you know what I mean. How long am I supposed to go around mourning Clancy anyway? Good grief, it's been almost four years since he died. And I barely knew him before we married."

As was her habit, Rebecca gestured dramatically with her hands to illustrate her next words. "My father practically dragged me to the altar to marry a man almost twice my age. I tell you, snuggling up to a man whose hands and feet are colder than icicles in January isn't my idea of wedded bliss."

Catherine could well agree with that point.

Rebecca sighed dreamily as she idly put the plates on the shelf above her head. "What I'd like to have is a gorgeous, *warm* man I could be cow-tied to forever. A man who could enter the room and make me all hot, and cold, and all jittery." She looked at Catherine and smiled. "Know what I mean?"

Blushing, Catherine grew quiet as she rinsed a large black pot. She knew *exactly* what Rebecca meant. She'd lain awake many a night as memories washed over her of a pewter-eyed demon who had promised her everything, including the moon above.

A man who had made her body so hot there had been times when she was certain she'd perish in flames.

But unlike her friend, she wasn't a widow. For all she knew, her husband could come waltzing up to the front door at any time and knock on it.

As if *that* would ever happen, Catherine chided herself.

When would she give up her useless, unwavering hope of seeing him again? Why couldn't she just put him out her mind?

What was it about him that made her yearn for him after all this time?

Of course, she knew the answer to that question— everything about him. He'd been so wonderful and kind, considerate and giving. Up until the day he left her without so much as a by-your-leave.

She must be insane to still yearn for him.

And after five years, he *might* be dead. Heaven knew, a lot had happened to her since he'd run off.

She'd moved to a new town, started her own restaurant and boardinghouse, and created a respectable life for her and her four-year-old daughter, Diana.

Last summer, after the yellow fever epidemic, she and Rebecca had taken in five of the town of Redwood's orphans.

A *lot* had happened.

Rebecca sidled up to her and took the pot from her hands to dry it. "So, tell me, if not a gorgeous St. Nick to come knocking on the door, what *do* you want for Christmas?"

"Oh, I don't know," Catherine said as she reached to wash a pan. "I guess if I had my druthers, I'd like for our money to be returned. It bothers me that someone would steal from the children right before Christmas."

Rebecca agreed. "I know how much you wanted to spend it on them. It's such a shame. I can't imagine what kind of monster could so something so terrible."

Neither did she.

They didn't speak for a few minutes. Only the sound of sloshing water and clanging dishes broke the silence as they worked.

All of a sudden, the hair on the back of Catherine's neck stood up. Turning her head, she saw Rebecca staring at her.

"What?" she asked.

"Is that really all you want for Christmas?"

Catherine handed her another pan to dry. "Why, yes. I'm quite happy with everything else."

Rebecca arched a questioning brow.

"I am," Catherine insisted.

"Methinks the lady doth protest too much," Rebecca said, putting the pan away. "Can you truly tell me that you haven't once given thought to having a handsome man come sweep you off your feet?"

Catherine laughed halfheartedly. "I already had that happen, and I must say I found the experience less than desirable."

Rebecca shook her head. "You know, I came to work here almost four years ago and never in that time have I heard you speak of your husband. That is who you're talking about, isn't it?"

Catherine nodded, refusing to meet Rebecca's inquisitive brown-eyed stare as she moved to pump more water into the sink. "There isn't much to tell."

Rebecca nudged her away from the pump and took up the motion. "Come on, Catherine. All the children are in bed for the night. Why not open up a little?"

Catherine buried her hands back in the suds and sighed. "What do you want me to tell you? Plain preacher's daughter fell in love with the gorgeous stranger who came to work for her father's ranch? He married her a month after they first met, took her off to Nevada, and left her the first chance he got."

"That's it?"

"That's it."

Rebecca paused. Her brown eyes darkened in anger. "I'll never understand a man who could do something so cold-blooded or mean."

"Me either," she whispered under her breath.

"I don't see how you stand it."

Catherine shrugged. "I got used to it. Five years gave me time to lay aside my hatred. Besides, I have Diana to think about. I'm the only parent she has and I decided on the day she was born that I would never mention his name or dwell on what he did to us."

"Well, I respect you for that. Me, I wouldn't have rested until I found the polecat and skinned him alive."

Catherine relished the image of her husband's tawny skin being flayed from him as he screamed for mercy. Now that Rebecca mentioned it, she did rather enjoy the thought of him being skinned. It would certainly serve him right. "You know, I do want something after all."

"And that is?"

Catherine scrubbed her pot with renewed vigor, wishing it were her husband's head she held beneath the water. "I wish I could lay eyes on him one last time to tell him what a no-good, lousy, rabid dog he was for leaving me."

"That's my girl." Rebecca laughed as she patted Catherine on the back. Then, she leaned forward and said in a low tone, "But the real question is, was he any good where and when it counted?"

"Rebecca!" Catherine gasped, trying her best not to think about just how good he had been *there*.

Though why Rebecca's words continued to shock her after all these years of knowing her, she couldn't imagine. Rebecca had never had an ounce of shame in her.

But then, it was her outspokenness Catherine liked most of all. She always knew where she stood with Rebecca. Her friend never held *anything* back. And after having lived with her husband and his secrets, she found Rebecca's candor a true blessing.

Suddenly a knock sounded on the door.

Catherine wrung the suds off her hands, then wiped her hands dry on her apron. "Why don't you go on to bed?" she said, rolling her sleeves back down her forearms and buttoning them against her wrists. "I'll get the door. I'm sure it's just someone needing a room."

"Poor soul to be out on Christmas Eve without a bed," Rebecca said. She inclined her head to the sink. "You sure you don't want me to finish up the dishes?"

Catherine shook her head. "There are only a handful left, and we already have all the gifts under the tree. Why don't you just go and enjoy what's left of Christmas Eve?"

"All right, then. I'll look in on the kids and then retire. Let me know if you need me."

"I will."

Rebecca headed to the back stairs while Catherine took the lantern off the kitchen table and walked down the narrow hallway to the front door.

Through the lace curtains, she could see the outline of a tall man with broad shoulders.

A smile twitched at the corners of her mouth. Perhaps Rebecca would get her wish after all.

Rolling her eyes at the very indecent thought that flicked across her mind, Catherine opened the door.

She took one glance at the handsome stranger, who had his head turned to look at his horse, and dropped the lantern straight to the floor.

* * *

O'Connell cursed as the lantern's fire exploded on the pine boards of the porch. Reacting without thought, he dropped his black Stetson and saddlebags, and stamped at the flames, his spurs jingling loudly as he stomped. Then, to his chagrin, the flames spread to his boots and set fire to the toes of his left foot.

He hissed in pain as he whipped his black duster off and put out the fire on his smoking boot. Then he quickly used the duster to extinguish the rest of the fire.

Luckily, the fire didn't do much in the way of permanent damage, but the porch and door would need a good washing come morning.

"Good Lord, woman," he snapped as he surveyed the damage. "You ought to be more . . ." his words trailed off as he looked up and met wide, startled brown eyes.

His jaw went slack. Those were the same eyes he'd been dreaming of not more than a few minutes before.

"Catherine?" he whispered in disbelief.

Catherine couldn't move as she stared into the handsome, devilish face that had coaxed her away from everything she had ever known.

Ask and ye shall receive, her father's favorite phrase echoed in her head.

Stunned by his sudden appearance, she took his form in all at once. He was still as handsome as sin. His dark brown hair was short in back with long bangs that draped becomingly into eyes so silvery gray they appeared almost colorless.

Captivating and searing, his eyes could haunt a woman night and day. And she ought to know, since they'd done nothing but torment her since the moment she had first seen them.

That same air of danger still clung to him, seducing her, wooing her. Oh, but he was a man to make any woman's heart pound.

His face had grown thinner over the years, adding sharp, angular planes to it. But they in no way detracted from the perfection of his patrician features. Dark brows contrasted sharply with his silver-gray eyes, and his broad nose still had the tiny bump in the center where she'd broken it.

Glory, but he was scrumptious. Completely and utterly scrumptious, like a rare treat of succulent chocolate after a long abstinence.

He'd always possessed a powerful, compelling, masculine aura that was downright salacious in nature. An aura that reached out and captured the attention of anything female within its mighty grasp.

And heaven only knew, she was far from immune to it.

But the Devil would move his home to Antarctica before she *ever* let him know that.

"What on earth are you doing here?" Catherine asked as she finally found her voice.

"Needing a doctor," he said sardonically, shaking his left foot.

Catherine looked down to see the charred black leather in the bright winter moonlight. A rush of embarrassment filled her.

"Why is it," he asked, "every time we meet, I end up needing a doctor?"

She lifted her chin at his playful tone. Her days of

finding him amusing were long past. "Are you trying to charm me?"

Not even the dark could mask the wickedly warm look in his eyes. "And if I were?"

I'd probably end up surrendering to it.

But she had no intention of letting him know that, either. *Fool me once, shame on you. Fool me twice, shame on me.* She couldn't afford to let him break her heart again. The first time had been painful enough. And in truth, she wasn't sure if she could survive losing him again.

Instead, she sought to protect herself by putting an end to whatever thoughts might be playing through his mind.

"I'm not a girl anymore, Mr. O'Callahan. I no longer dance to your tune."

O'Connell took a deep breath as he sized her up. He'd almost forgotten his old alias. But the cold tone of her voice chilled him more than the winter wind at his back.

Still, it did nothing to daunt the fire in his gut that her presence stirred. She looked even better than he remembered. Gone was the willow-thin frame of her youth and in its place were the luscious curves of a woman full grown.

She wore her hair in that tight bun he'd always despised. Catherine had such beautiful hair—long, thick, and wavy. He, the man who was wanted in six states, had spent hours brushing her hair at night. Running his hands through it.

And he wondered if it still smelled like springtime.

In that instant, he remembered the way he had left

her. Without a word, without a note. He had simply gone off to work and had never returned.

Shame filled him. He should have at least sent a letter. Although, honestly, he had tried to write one a thousand times. But he'd never completed it. What did a man say to a woman he'd been forced to give up against his will?

Especially when he didn't want her to know the real reason he'd left?

Picking his hat up from the porch, he cast a sweeping, hungry look over her body, and wished for the millionth time, that things had been different between them. That he could have had a long life spent by her side, being the husband she deserved to have. "It's good to see you again."

Her look froze him as she untied her apron, then stooped to pick up the broken glass and place it in the cloth. "I wish I could say it's good to be seen by you, but in this case I think you'll understand if I'm a bit cool toward you?"

"Cool" was a mild term for her demeanor. In truth, he suspected icebergs at the North Pole might be a shade or two warmer.

He'd expected more anger from her. The Catherine he remembered would have been cursing him like a slow-walking dog for leaving her.

This Catherine was different. She was composed and serious, not laughing and playful.

Passionate, he realized with a start. That was what was missing. She'd lost the verve that used to have her laughing one minute, sobbing the next, and then kissing him blind two seconds after that.

And without a doubt he knew he was to blame for it. Being abandoned had a way of affecting a person adversely. His gut drew tight. He had a lot to answer for in his life. He just wished she wasn't one of those things he'd messed up.

"Where's your anger?" he asked as he leaned over to help her pick up the mess.

Catherine considered her answer. She should be enraged at him, but oddly enough, once the initial shock of the encounter wore off she found herself completely numb to him.

Well, not completely numb.

In fact, "numb" described his effect on her like "handsome" described Abe Lincoln.

A woman would have to be dead not to feel a vigorous stirring for a man so incredibly handsome as her wandering polecat. Especially a man possessed of such raw, primal appeal.

Everything about him promised sheer, sexual delights. And all too well she remembered the way he had felt in her arms, the strength of his long, lean body caressing hers in playful abandon as he sent her spiraling off into blissful ecstasy.

And right then, with his head just inches from her own, she could smell the raw, earthy scent of him. That leather and musk that had always titillated her. That warm, wonderful smell was a part of him like the innate power and authority that bled from every pore of his body.

And those lips . . .

Full and sensuous, those lips of his had kissed her until she lost all reason, until her entire body buzzed with lust and desire. And those wonderful, sensual lips had teased and tormented her body to the ultimate pinnacle of human pleasure.

Good heavens, how she ached for him. Even after the way he had hurt her!

What are you thinking?

Catherine mentally shook herself. No, she didn't hate him for leaving her the way he had—five years had given her time to lay her hatred aside.

She wouldn't get mad at this point.

She would get even.

He deserved to feel the sting of rejection. Then he would understand exactly what he had done to her. How it felt to be denied and forgotten.

"I got over my anger for you, Mr. O'Callahan," she said tartly, rising to her feet carefully lest she cut herself on the glass in her apron.

She raked a look from the top of his head down to his still-smoking boot, took a step back into the house and spoke, "And then I got over you."

With one last stoic look at him, Catherine closed the door on his stunned face.

TWO

Catherine's words rang in O'Connell's ears as he stared in disbelief at the closed door.

Well, what did you expect? he asked himself as he retrieved his charred duster from the porch.

Her hatred, in all honesty. That he had been prepared for. But her apathy toward him . . .

Well . . .

It was . . . insufferable!

Anger over her rejection blistered his gut. How dare she dismiss him so! What did she think he was, some lost little puppy come to lick scraps off the floor?

Well, he wasn't a lost puppy. He was a man. A man sought by every woman who had ever laid her eyes upon him. Not that he was vain about it. Not overly so, anyway. It was merely a fact he'd long grown accustomed to. A fact everyone who knew him just plainly accepted.

Women had always been partial to him.

In Hollow Gulch where O'Connell had been working the last few months, the women had singled him out the moment he rode into town—baked him fresh pies, batted their lashes at him. Hell, one gutsy blonde had even snuck into his room and hidden herself naked in his bed while he'd been out drinking.

Not that he had been interested in the blonde or any of the others. Unlike any normal, *sane* man, he'd sent her home as soon as he tossed some clothes on her body. And all the while she'd whispered to him the torrid, lusty things she'd do to give him pleasure.

Her salacious comments had set fire to his loins, but even so, she hadn't appealed to him in the slightest. His heart belonged to Catherine. It always had.

And he refused to sully Catherine's memory by bedding down with any other woman. That was the one vow he'd never break.

Hell, he'd given up everything he valued to see Catherine safe.

And she had banished him from her thoughts?

He saw red.

In the last five years there hadn't been an instant when he hadn't been consumed by thoughts of her. Not a minute he hadn't wondered what she was doing. *How* she was doing.

And she felt nothing toward him.

Nothing.

He didn't even warrant her hatred.

"Fine," O'Connell muttered at the closed door as he shrugged his duster on, then settled his Stetson on his head. He grimaced at the front of the brim that had been partially burned away by the fire. "I don't need you to feel anything for me, woman. I don't need you at all. In fact, I can put you right out of my mind, too."

Spinning on his heel, he took a step for his horse. Pain exploded across his foot and he cursed out loud as he limped away.

The woman had damned near maimed him! And all the while she felt nothing toward him.

Nothing!

"What do you mean, you got over me?"

Catherine turned around to see *him* standing in the doorway. His face awash with shadows, she could feel his angry glare more than see it.

Go ahead and seethe, Mr. O'Callahan. Stew in your rage until your entire body becomes pruney from it.

It was terrible to take such delight in a man's misery, but delight in it she did. Catherine kept her face from betraying her glee. She'd known he couldn't resist her words. That was why she'd left the door unlocked. The last thing she wanted was for him to break it down. And knowing him, he most certainly would have done it had she tried to bar him from her house.

Come into my parlor, said the spider to the fly. He wouldn't escape her clutches until she had exacted five years of rejection from his rotten hide.

"Did you need something?" she asked coolly.

O'Connell forced the emotions from his face as he swept his hat from his head. How could she stand there so all-fired calm and dismiss him like an old shoe?

Well, he wasn't some old shoe, to be cast aside and forgotten. They had been more than merely intimate. The woman had actually touched his unrepentant soul. And after all the years he had tortured himself with guilt over his actions, she had forgotten him?

Oh, he wasn't about to leave here until he made her remember what they'd shared. Stepping into her house, he closed the door behind him.

"What do you mean, you got over me?" he asked again as he closed the short distance between them.

She shrugged casually. "It's been five years, Mr. O'Callahan."

As if *he* needed her reminder. It had been five long, gut-wrenching years of missing everything about her. Of feeling her presence, smelling her scent. Of longing to hear her voice, feel her tender caresses on his flesh.

Like an arrogant fool, he had assumed she'd missed him as well. Obviously, he'd been wrong.

Well, he wasn't going to let her know how much it bothered him. If she wanted to play this with a cool hand, he was certainly one to give it right back to her. He could hide his emotions better than anyone else alive. Indeed, how many times had that trait made her loco?

"You're right, Mrs. O'Callahan," O'Connell said in a deceptively calm voice. "It has been five long years. For the sake of old times, could you at least tell me where I might find a doctor for my foot?"

A becoming pink stained her cheeks as she glanced down to his injured member. "I'm afraid Dr. Watson died a few months back and as yet we have no replacement. But since I'm the one who burned you, I'll tend it."

"Well *it* would definitely appreciate that since it is throbbing."

And now that he mentioned it, the other *it* was

throbbing, too. Especially as his gaze dipped of its own volition to her succulent breasts. His body grew even hotter and stiffer as his palm itched to caress the firm round mounds, and his mouth watered to suckle the soft pink tips until they hardened into rippled buds under his tongue.

And she felt nothing for him.

Nothing.

Stifling his growl, he vowed that that would soon change. If it was the last thing he did, he would make her remember how good they were together.

How much pleasure he could give her.

And if any other man had dared enter her bed in the last five years, the law could add the crime of murder to his wanted poster.

"If you're through ogling me," she said, "I keep my medicinal basket in the back."

"I wasn't ogling you," O'Connell muttered, unwilling to admit to her what he'd been doing.

She headed down a narrow hallway toward the back of the house. "Then please forgive me," Catherine said over her shoulder. "I guess after five years, I've forgotten what an ogle looks like."

Biting back his response, O'Connell limped his way down the narrow hallway, past the stairs. He looked around at the burgundy walls and the paintings lining the hallway. She had a beautiful home. He just wished he'd been the one to give it to her.

Even worse, a homey feel enveloped her boarding-house.

There had been a time once, long ago, when he had

dreamed of having such a place to call home. And the thought of sharing such a place with Catherine had been his idea of paradise.

But fate had turned her back on him and he had long given up that delusion. He could never have a life with her. He knew that.

"Nice place you have here," he said.

"Thank you. I made the down payment on it with the money you left behind."

"See?" he said defensively as he limped. "I wasn't all bad."

"Which is why I don't hate you."

O'Connell cursed under his breath. Back to square one. That hadn't helped his case the least little bit.

He wanted her anger, her hatred. He wanted . . . no, he corrected, he *needed* her to feel something for him. Something other than apathy.

There had to be some way to stir her up.

He paused in the doorway of the kitchen as she crossed the floor to put the apron and glass in a wooden trash receptacle. "If you'll sit at the table and remove your boot, I'll be right back with the burn salve."

She disappeared into a room off the kitchen.

O'Connell crossed the floor to the table. He set his hat down on the table, shrugged off his duster, then straddled the wooden bench seat and did as she ordered.

Grimacing in pain, he removed his scorched sock. He had to admit his foot had looked better. And it had most definitely felt better.

He blew air at his throbbing toes, noting the reddish skin that was already showing signs of blistering.

Damn, but it hurt. Even more so than his nose had when she'd accidentally smacked him in the face with a broom handle because of some spider web she couldn't stand being in the corner of the room. Personally, he'd have much rather suffered the spider than the broken nose.

Being around Catherine could be quite dangerous to one's health. Though, to be fair to her, he'd never seen her clumsy around anyone but him.

Then again, he'd never really minded her clumsiness, since she had such wonderful ways of making amends for it.

His breath caught in his throat at the memory of how she had made amends for his nose. Closing his eyes, he could still see her lowering herself down on him, feel her mouth teasing his flesh. Her teeth nibbling him all over.

And his body grew harder, hotter, until he could barely stand it.

Lord above, but she had such a sweet little mouth that tasted like honey and felt like hot silk as it slid over his flesh.

It really was true a body couldn't feel pain and pleasure simultaneously. Because when she teased his flesh with her tongue and teeth, all his pain evaporated like dew on a hot July morning.

Catherine returned to the kitchen, carrying a small wicker basket in her hand. She placed it on the table beside his hat, then leaned over to examine his foot.

A stern frown drew her brows together. "Did I do all that?"

"Yes, you did," he said petulantly.

"I'm sorry," she said. "I'd best get some butter for it." As she reached for the porcelain butter jar on the table, she accidentally brushed the wicker basket off the side.

It landed straight on his injured foot.

O'Connell sucked his breath in between his teeth as pain exploded up his leg.

"I'm sorry," she repeated as she bent over to retrieve the basket.

His gaze feasted hungrily on the site of her round bottom as she fished for the basket under the table. Oh, but she had such a nice, round bottom. One that felt incredible under his hands, or against his loins.

He forgot all about his foot until she straightened, teetered ever so slightly, then grabbed his injured foot to steady herself.

This time he cursed out loud.

Color exploded across her face. "I'm—"

"Don't," he snapped, cutting her off. "I know you didn't mean to, just please give my foot time enough to recuperate before you do anything else to it."

Her cheeks darkened even more as she set the basket back on the table. "It's your own fault, you know."

"How is that?"

"You make me nervous," she confessed.

"I make *you* nervous?" he asked in disbelief. If anyone had a right to be nervous, it should be him, since he never knew what injury she might inflict on him next.

"Yes, you do. The way you sit there and stare at me like I'm some prime roast and you haven't eaten anything in a week. It's quite disconcerting, Mr. O'Callahan. If you must know."

He stopped fanning his foot and looked up at her. "Why did you never tell me that before?"

"I used to not mind the way you looked at me."

"And now?"

"I mind it and I wish you'd stop."

O'Connell locked his jaw at her words. There had to be some way to chisel away the ice around her.

Of course, he'd never in his life had to practice chiseling ice away from a woman. Women had always melted in his presence. They had only shown a token resistance before lifting their skirts to him.

Catherine had been the only one he'd ever courted. But then, she'd always been different in his book. Her shy innocence had been what captivated him. The way her smile carried all the warmth of the sun in it.

Pete had mocked him for his love of her: "The woman's as plain as yesterday's bread."

But to him, she'd always been beautiful.

Catherine leaned over him and gently spread the butter on his foot. Her light touch shook him to his core, and a thousand needles of pleasure tore through him.

In spite of himself, he smiled. Her ministrations on his foot reminded him of how they first met.

He'd just turned nineteen and had only been working for her father a few weeks. The main gate to her house had been damaged by a storm and he'd been trying to patch it when all of a sudden she had come riding up over the hill like the Devil himself was chasing her. He had barely ducked out of the way before her horse leapt over him.

The post he'd been hammering into the ground slipped sideways and as he tried to grab it, the hammer had fallen from his hand and crashed down on his toes, breaking the little one. If that hadn't been painful enough, the entire post had also fallen on him.

She had instantly turned around and come back to check on him. Even now he could see her in the dark green riding habit that had no doubt cost more than a year's worth of his pay as she helped him push the post off his legs. Without any thought to her dress, she had knelt down on the muddy ground, carefully removed his boot, and checked on his toe even while he told her not to.

She had insisted that since she broke it, she should tend it.

That had been the first time in his life anyone had ever truly been kind to him without expecting something back in return.

Later that night when she brought out a tray of steak, potatoes, and biscuits to the bunkhouse he shared with the rest of the ranch hands, he'd known he was in love.

She had looked like an angel coming through the door with that large silver tray in her hands.

And that stupid daisy she'd put on it . . . The other men had mocked him for weeks after that. But he hadn't cared.

Nothing had mattered to him, except her smile.

"You're doing it again," Catherine snapped, drawing his attention back to the present as she reached for her burn ointment. Her touch even more gentle, she spread it over his burned toes.

"Doing what?" he asked.

"Ogling me."

O'Connell smiled at her. "Do you know why I'm ogling you?"

"I can't imagine."

"Because you're still the most beautiful woman on earth."

Disbelief was etched onto her face as she straightened and looked at him. "Is that why you left me?"

"No."

"Then tell me why."

THREE

O'Connell barely caught himself before he spilled the truth out. Now as then, he couldn't stand the thought of her knowing what he'd been.

What he'd become.

He'd never been proud of what desperation and family obligation had led him to. He knew he should have walked away from Pete and his crazy schemes years ago. But every time he thought about hurting Pete, he remembered his childhood, when Pete had been the only thing that stood between him and starvation.

The world was a harsh, cold place for two orphans alone, and filled with unscrupulous people who would quickly take advantage of them. But Pete, who was seven years older than him, had always kept him safe.

If only Pete could let him go. Unfortunately, his big brother saw them as inseparable twins joined at the hip.

And no matter what he did to escape, his brother managed to track him down like some possessed bloodhound.

No, there was no way he could ever have her while Pete trailed him. Sooner or later, his brother would show up and use her as leverage against him—just as he'd done five years ago in Nevada.

O'Connell could only stand strong against Pete

when just the two of them were involved.

Catherine made him weak. Vulnerable.

Besides, she was a good woman, with a good heart and he would rather she think him a sorry good-for-nothing lowlife, than ever learn she'd married an outlaw. No good could come of her knowing the truth.

So he answered her question with the first stupid answer that occurred to him. "I don't know."

She arched one dark brown brow at him as she lifted her gaze from his foot to his face. "You don't know?"

"It just seemed like the right thing to do," he offered as a consolation.

By the irate look on her face, he realized too late he should have just kept his mouth shut.

Catherine narrowed her eyes on him. "Why don't you just go and . . ." her voice trailed off.

He waited for her to finish.

She didn't. Instead, she stared strangely at his right arm.

"And?" he prompted.

She stepped around the bench until she rested by his side. She grabbed at the sleeve of his black shirt, and bent down to look closer at it. The contact brought her head right up under his nose. His gut wrenched. She still smelled like springtime. Her hair held that same delectable scent of fresh flowers and warmth.

And right then, all he wanted to do was lay her down on the kitchen table, lift her skirt up, and bury himself deep inside her warm body.

It took all of his willpower not to yield to that

desire as the scent of her circled him, making him dizzy. Hungry. Inciting him beyond thought or reason.

A full minute passed before he realized she was staring at his blood on her hand.

"You're bleeding?" she asked.

Unwilling to explain to her that Pete had shot him as he ran off with the stolen money, he rose to his feet. "I probably should be going now."

"Sit!" The sharp tone coming from her was so unexpected and out of character that he actually obeyed.

"Take your shirt off and let me see what you've done now."

"Yes, ma'am," he murmured sarcastically as he unbuttoned his shirt and obliged her.

Catherine opened her basket, then made the mistake of glancing back to him.

His slow, languid movements captured her gaze as those long, strong fingers of his worked the buttons through the black cambric. She had always loved those hands. The way they felt laced in hers, the pleasure and comfort they had always managed to give her.

Her throat dried at the memory.

He opened his shirt, then set to work on the buttons of his white union suit. And with every white button that opened, she saw more and more of his perfect, tawny flesh.

She had forgotten just how nerve-wracking the sight of his bare skin could be. The years had done nothing but make his muscles leaner, more defined. And all too well she remembered what it felt like to slide her hand over those taut ripples. The way his hard stomach felt sliding against her own as he held himself above her and drove her into paradise with long, luscious strokes.

Her body growing hot, it took all her concentration to force herself to reach for the makeshift bandage on his right biceps. His arm flexed seductively as her fingers brushed his skin, and a jolt of molten lust tore through her. There were few things on earth that felt better than those hard, strong biceps flexing beneath her hands.

Catherine clenched her teeth in frustration. How could he make her so breathless after what he had put her through?

Why was her body so determined to betray her? And right then, she wished desperately for an off switch to stop the overwhelming desire coursing through her veins.

Tend his wound, tend his wound—she mentally repeated the words over and over, hoping to gain some control over herself.

I will not succumb to him!

By all that was holy, she wouldn't.

Untying his bandage, Catherine immediately saw the bullet wound. "You've been shot?"

"And can you believe it wasn't by you?"

She stiffened at his playful tone. "You're not funny."

"Not even a little?"

"I told you, Mr. O'Callahan, I'm immune to your charms."

Don't you wish! If only she could live up to those brave words.

"I wish you'd stop calling me that," he snapped at her. "I have a name and you used to use it."

She didn't dare use it right then, because if she did, she had no doubt she would be his to do with as he pleased. Just the sound of those syllables on her tongue would be enough to finish her off.

She struggled to bring herself under control. "I used to do a lot of things with you that I don't do anymore."

"Such as?"

"Use your imagination."

That silver-gray gaze dipped to her breasts, which drew tight and heavy at his heated perusal. "Oh, I'm using it, all right. And I can *well* imagine the sound of your sighs of pleasure in my ear as I nibble the flesh of your neck. Do you remember?"

"No," she lied, her voice amazingly calm.

But in spite of her denials, she felt her body melt against the heat of that silver-gray stare. Even worse, she could smell the warm, uniquely masculine scent of him. It was all she could do not to bury her face in the crook of his neck and inhale the intoxicating scent.

Tend his wound, tend his wound! She forced herself to concentrate on the task at hand.

"Is the bullet still in there?" she asked as she examined the hole in his arm.

"Woman," he said huskily, his gaze never leaving her breasts, "right now I have a loaded gun just waiting to . . ." his voice trailed off.

He finally looked up and met her gaze, but she couldn't read anything in the smoldering depths of his eyes except the raw hunger that scorched her through and through. "Did I just say that out loud?"

She nodded.

He cleared his throat and looked across the room. "No," he said quickly. "The bullet passed clean through."

Disregarding his answer, she gingerly examined the wound to see for herself. As he predicted, it looked to be clean. "It needs to be stitched."

He met her gaze again. Only three inches separated their faces and she could feel his breath on her face as he spoke. "Then by all means, have at it. I'm sure nothing would give you greater pleasure than to take a needle to my hide."

She should take pleasure in it, but she knew she wouldn't. How could she ever delight in hurting the man who had stolen her heart?

But she would never let him know that. Not after he'd hurt her. No, she'd never let him know just how much power he still held over her.

Never.

"Actually, I won't feel anything," she said, reaching for her basket.

O'Connell clenched his teeth in repressed frustration.

I won't feel anything, he mocked silently as she reached for a needle and thread.

You stitch the wound, and when you're finished, I promise you you'll feel something, all right. She was going to remember his touch if it was the last thing he did.

O'Connell felt himself harden even more as she

placed the thread between her lips and licked it. The tip of her tongue poked out as she threaded the needle.

I can't stand this! his mind screamed from the needless torment. If he didn't know better, he would swear she did it on purpose.

When she set to work on his wound, he felt no pain, only the pleasure of her soft hands against his bare flesh. Her breath fell against his shoulder as she leaned so close to him he could smell the fresh sunshine of her.

Over and over he could envision letting her hair down and burying his hands in the thick waves. Feeling it fall across his chest as he placed her above him and feasted on those plump, luscious breasts.

Catherine could barely steady her hand as she closed the wound. Her memory of touching his hard, hot muscles couldn't compete with the reality of her hand against him now.

Her head swam at the contact. Worse, she could feel his heat surrounding her, feel his breath against her neck. His shoulder pressing against her right breast.

A thousand chills shot through her. It was all she could do not to moan and demand he take her right then and there. Oh, it was torturous. Especially after all the years she had yearned to see him again, all the years she had lain awake remembering the feel of him lying against her. The feel of him sliding inside her.

After what seemed an eternity, she finished the four tiny stitches that closed the wound. She had barely tied the knot off when he reached up, cupped her face in his hand, and took possession of her lips.

Catherine sighed at the contact.

He'd been the only man who had ever kissed her and the taste of him had been branded into her memory long, long ago.

He pulled her to him possessively and sat her down on the bench before him as he plundered her mouth.

Catherine buried her hands in his silken hair and pressed her breasts against his hot, naked chest. She should stop him, she knew it. But for her life she didn't want to. All she wanted was to savor him like she'd done all those years ago.

Volcanic heat poured through her body, pooling itself between her legs as she ached for him in the most primitive of ways. She wanted him desperately. And only he could pacify the aching heat that demanded his body inside hers.

He was her husband and the part of her that still loved him came rushing to the forefront. Under the assault of his scorching kiss, that part of her took possession of her common sense and forced it to flee her mind.

Before she knew what was happening, she felt her hair fall down around her shoulders and it was only then that he pulled back from her lips to kiss her cheek, her eyelid, the tip of her nose. His lips were hot and moist as they branded a fiery trail over her face.

"My precious Catherine," he whispered in her ear. "Let me love you the way you deserve to be loved."

She felt his hands unbuttoning her shirtwaist. She wanted to tell him no, but in truth she couldn't. The words lodged in her throat because deep down she wanted him. She had always wanted him, and no matter how badly he had hurt her, there was still a part of her that needed him.

And she gave herself over to that part.

He opened her shirtwaist, then buried those hot lips against the tops of her breasts as his hands reached around back to unlace her corset. She sighed in pleasure as she buried her face in his hair and inhaled the wicked, warm scent that was her husband.

O'Connell's head swam from the scent of her as he buried his face between the soft mounds of her breasts and licked her salty skin. It had been so long since he tasted her, felt her, and he knew that he would spend the rest of this night making up for the five years they had been apart.

The five long years he had been without a woman.

In her arms, he had always felt that anything was possible. That he could do anything, be anything. No other person had ever lifted him to the heights of goodness and pleasure that she did.

She was the one truth in his life that he could depend on. The one person he truly needed.

He ran his tongue over the tops of her breasts, delighting in the way she shivered in his arms as he struggled with the corset laces.

And at that moment he despised whoever had invented the cursed thing. It had to be some old, doddering matron seeking to preserve her daughter's virtue, for no man would ever design so inconvenient a contraption.

At last he loosened it to where he could free her breasts to his hungry mouth.

Catherine cupped his head to her as she stifled a moan of pure pleasure. His hand caressed her swollen breasts, drawing the taut nipples so tight she could barely stand it. Heat tore through her body as an ache started deep in the center of her. It was a familiar long-ing that she only felt in his presence.

No other man had ever aroused her the way he did. No one. And she doubted if anyone ever could.

And then his hands were under her skirt, stroking and teasing as they skimmed over her calves and thighs. One hand cupped her buttocks as he wrapped his other arm around her and drew her up tight against him.

He reclaimed her lips for one hungry, pulsating kiss, then pulled back.

He cupped her face in his hands and tilted her head to look at him. His lips were swollen from her kisses and he stared at her as if he were dreaming.

The need and hunger in that silver-gray gaze mes-merized her. Her breathing ragged, she could do noth-ing but stare up at him in wonderment.

"Say my name," he demanded, stroking her swollen lips gently with his knuckles.

She hesitated.

But what was the point? She had already surren-dered herself to him. And for some reason she couldn't fathom, she wanted to please him.

"Michael," she breathed.

He smiled, then returned to torture her mouth with sweet bliss.

He rose with her in his arms. "Where's your room?"

"In there," she said, pointing to the back hallway and the room on the left.

Limping all the way, he carried her to it, then shut the door with the heel of his burned foot. "Where's the lamp?"

Catherine squirmed out of his arms and moved to find her chest of drawers to the left of the door. Too dark to see, she groped along the smooth top as he came up behind her and cupped her breasts in his hands.

She moaned as he toyed with her and heat swept through her body.

"You're making this difficult," she said, then sighed at the feel of his lips on the back of her neck as he pressed his swollen shaft against her hip.

He gave one last possessive squeeze to her breasts, then released her. "Light the lamp," he said, his voice ragged. "I want to see you. All of you."

Quickly, she found the glass lamp. Lifting the globe, she took one of the matches beside it and lit it. She turned the wick down to a low, warm glow that made their shadows dance on the far wall.

Michael came up behind her again and placed a kiss on her shoulder as his arms wrapped around her waist to pull her close to his chest. She leaned her head back, savoring the feel of him. The strength and warmth in his powerful arms. His deep groan echoed in her ears and she sighed contentedly.

Slowly, he began undoing her clothes.

"Michael, what—"

"Shh," he said, placing a finger to her lips. "I want

to savor you like a wrapped gift. Slowly. Carefully and with relish."

And so he did. She didn't move as he took her shirt-waist off, then her skirt and petticoats. Her corset went next, exposing her upper body to him. She shivered from the cool air against their skin, but his hot gaze warmed her as he untied her pantaloons, then dropped them to the floor.

She swallowed as she stood naked before him.

O'Connell thought he'd go mad as he stared at her bare body. Not even his memory had been able to hold on to the true beauty that was his Catherine.

And for this one night she was his.

All his.

He reached out and ran one hand over her right breast, delighting in the way her nipple hardened to his touch. Then, he trailed his hand over her abdomen to the curls at the juncture of her thighs. She moaned as he slid his fingers against her.

His mind reeled at the hotness of her body, at the sleek wetness in his hand. She was as ready for him as he was for her, but he didn't want to rush this.

He wanted this night to last a lifetime.

"I am going to savor you," he told her. "Every single inch of you."

Catherine couldn't respond verbally. Her mind numb, she could do nothing more than watch him watch her.

He picked her up again and carried her to the bed, where he removed her shoes, then carefully rolled down her stockings, nibbling her legs as he went.

As she started to sit up, he held her in place with

one hand and shook his head. "Let me look at you lying there. I want to see you naked in your bed."

And look he did. His gaze traveled from the top of her head down to her breasts, to her stomach, her hips and legs, and then it returned to the center of her body, which thrummed with a hot, demanding need.

He lifted his hands to her thighs and spread her legs wider.

"Michael—"

"Let me look at you."

So she did, and his look burned even more than his touch. He leaned his head down and placed a tender kiss just below her belly button. His hot breath scorched her as his teeth tormented her flesh. He trailed his kisses lower, down to the inside of her thighs. Catherine closed her eyes and moaned as his lips brushed up against the center of her body.

Then he pulled back.

As if sensing how she ached for him, he quickly shed his own clothes, then climbed up between her legs. His entire body caressed hers in a long, luscious stroke.

She moaned at the erotic pleasure it delivered as her body arched to meet his. She felt him from the tips of her toes to the tips of her aching breasts, all the way to her forehead, where he placed a tender kiss.

His hot, stiff shaft rested on her belly.

Wanting him too badly to wait, she reached down between their bodies and stroked the velvety hardness of him. He hissed in her ear as she cupped him gently, then sought to guide him into her.

But he would have none of it.

Without entering her, Michael rolled to her side before his mouth returned to hers. He skimmed his hand over her body, then buried it between her legs.

Catherine hissed in pleasure as her hips lifted instinctively toward his hand.

He pulled back to stare down at her. "So," he whispered as his fingers toyed with the sensitive flesh between her thighs. He plunged one finger deep inside her, swirling it around and teasing her with pure, unadulterated pleasure. "Do you remember me now?"

"Yes," she gasped as his fingers did the most wicked things to her body.

He teased and toyed, his fingers circling and delving, faster and faster, until she was breathless from her aching need.

"And do you remember this?" he asked as he circled the core of her body with his thumb.

"Yes," she gasped again as her entire body throbbed.

He smiled a tender smile. "Now tell me what you want."

"I want to feel you deep inside me. Now."

He released her.

Catherine whimpered until he picked her up and moved her yet again. "What are you doing now?"

He led her to where her mirror stood in the corner. "You'll see," he whispered in her ear, raising chills on her arms.

He stood her before the mirror, where she could watch his hands as they caressed her body, kneaded her breasts, and masterfully stroked the flesh of her stomach.

He brushed her hair over her right shoulder to where it covered most of her and buried his lips in the curve of her neck.

Reaching up over her head, she buried her hand in his hair and groaned in pleasure.

"You still smell like sunshine," he whispered in her ear before swirling his tongue over the sensitive flesh. And when he plunged his tongue inside her ear, she melted and moaned as her entire body erupted into flames.

Catherine trembled all over as she watched his hands cup her breasts possessively. He pressed them, kneaded them, caressed them until she could barely stand it.

"I want to touch you," she said hoarsely, trying to turn around in his arms.

He stopped her. "You will," he said. "But not yet. Not until I *devour* you."

"Then devour me."

His rich laugh echoed in her ear. "Yes, ma'am," he whispered. "I'm more than happy to oblige you."

And then he trailed kisses down her spine. Slowly, methodically, covering every tiny inch of her flesh. She didn't know how her legs managed to keep her standing, for they trembled until she was sure she would fall.

His warm breath caressed her flesh as his hot, wet mouth teased her skin. He paused at the small of her back, his tongue gently stroking her buttocks. His hands circled around in front of her as he knelt on the floor at her feet.

Then his lips kissed the backs of her thighs, her knees, her calves, and when he got to her ankles, she jumped in erotic pleasure.

He laughed, then nudged her legs farther apart.

Fevered and hot, she did as he wanted and watched in the mirror as he positioned his body between her legs and kissed the front of her knees, her thighs.

He paused at the juncture of her thighs.

Her gaze transfixed by the sight of him in the looking glass, Catherine's entire body pulsed as his hot breath scorched her skin. He ran his left hand through her dark, short curls, kneading her erotically. Then, using both hands, he gently separated the tender folds and buried his mouth at the center of her body.

Tremors of ecstasy shook her.

O'Connell wanted to shout in victory as he tasted the most private part of her. She was his and this part of her was for him alone.

He would never share her! Never.

He ran his tongue over her, delighting in her moans and sighs. In the taste of her body, hot and moist against his starving tongue.

"Please," she begged. "I can't stand any more."

He nipped her tender flesh. "Oh, yes, you can, my love. I've only started with you."

Deciding he had tortured the two of them enough for the moment, he moved to nibble the sensitive flesh of her hip. She buried her hand in his hair. He delighted in the feel of her hands on his scalp.

More hurriedly than before, he kissed his way up

her body until he could bury his lips in the hollow of her throat.

He held her tightly against him, reveling in the feel of her naked flesh against his, the feel of her tight nipples burning into his chest.

Catherine lifted one leg up to cup him to her as she arched her body against him, needing desperately to be closer to his heat. His lips burned her throat. She rubbed her hips against his in a silent plea for him to have mercy on her and to squelch the fire scorching her from the inside out.

To her chagrin, he pulled back. Then he took her hands in his and braced them on the frame of the mirror as he moved to stand behind her.

She met his lustful, hot gaze in the mirror. Never had she seen such a look of love and lust intermingled. His breathing ragged, he whispered to her, "I want to see you see me take you."

And then with one powerful stroke he drove himself up inside her. She sucked her breath in sharply at the feel of his fullness stroking her.

"Oh, yes, Michael, yes!" she cried out.

O'Connell thought he would perish at the sound of his name on her lips while she surrendered herself to him.

At that moment, he knew what paradise meant. Nothing could ever be more pleasurable than being with the woman he loved, hearing her sighs, and feeling her body from the inside out.

"Show me," he said in her ear. "Show me that you remember me."

She hesitated only an instant before she lifted herself on her tiptoes, drawing her body up to the tip of his shaft. Just as he was sure she'd drive him out, she dropped herself back against him, wringing a deep-seated moan of pleasure from him. He ground his teeth in the bittersweet torture of her milking his body with hers.

To hell with dreams! he thought rabidly. They were nothing compared to this reality. To the true feeling of her body sliding against his.

Catherine smiled at the look of ecstasy on his face as she watched him in the mirror. Unabashed, she gave him what he wanted and took what she needed. Perspiration broke out on his forehead as he met her gaze in the glass.

She could feel her body starting to teeter, to spiral to the pinnacle only he had ever shown her.

But before she would go there, she wanted something else from him. She delivered one last, long stroke to him, then paused.

He arched a questioning brow.

"Did you ever remember me?" she asked.

"Every minute of every hour. I've never stopped wanting you."

The sincerity in his gaze told her he spoke the truth. Joy spread through her as she again rocked herself against him, then pulled away.

He looked at her questioningly.

"I want to hold you when it happens."

Unwilling to make the short distance to the bed, he laid her down on the floor and again entered her.

Catherine moaned at the sensation of him thrusting between her legs as she encircled his body with hers.

Wrapping her legs around his waist, she ran her hands down his spine and cupped his buttocks to her, urging him on. Her pleasure mounted higher and higher until she felt herself slipping again.

This time she let herself teeter over the edge.

Crying out, she shook as tremors of pure pleasure tore through her.

Still he thrusted, deepening her ecstasy until he threw his head back and cried out as well.

With a contented sigh, he collapsed on top of her and she reveled in the weight of him.

It had been too long. Far too long.

O'Connell couldn't breathe or move. Not until the throbbing returned to his arm and foot. "Ow," he breathed.

"Ow?" she repeated.

"My foot," he said as he rolled off her. "It's hurting again."

A blush stained her cheeks. She rose slowly from the floor and reached her hand out to him. "I think I know a way to make you forget about that."

He smiled and rose to her invitation. She took him to the bed and laid him back against the soft, feather mattress.

Surrendering himself to her whims, he watched as she crawled up his body like a naked wildcat. She wriggled her hips and then straddled his body.

O'Connell moaned at the feel of the hairs at the juncture of her thighs caressing his bare flesh as she sat down upon his stomach. She leaned forward, spilling her breasts across his chest as she wiggled that delectable bottom against him.

"Now let's see how much I remember," she whispered before burying her lips just below his ear. "Does this help the pain?"

"A little," he moaned.

She trailed kisses over his skin until she got to his chest. She stroked his nipple with her tongue and he hissed in pleasure. She nibbled him ever so gently.

"And that?" she asked.

"A little better than before," he said.

"Still not gone entirely?"

He shook his head.

"Well, then, let's see what it takes."

She moved to his side and as she bent over him her hair fell against his flesh, raising chills all over him. She lashed his chest with her hair, over and over, and he arched his back against the pleasurable beating.

"Better?" she asked.

"Somewhat."

She arched a brow. "Somewhat?"

He shrugged.

Her smile was wicked and warm. "In that case . . ."

She lowered her head and took him into her mouth. O'Connell pressed his head back into the pillows as his entire body jerked in pleasure.

"Catherine," he said hoarsely. "Next time, you can set fire to my entire body if that's the cure for it."

She laughed against him. "Don't tempt me," she said, looking up an instant before she returned to the part of him that was steadily growing larger. Harder.

Before he could move, she straddled him again and lowered herself on his shaft. "How's that?"

"Hot and wet, just like I like it," he said.

And this time when they came, it was in unison.

O'Connell didn't know what time they finally fell asleep. All he knew was that for the first time in five years, his body had been fully sated. He couldn't remember the last time he had felt this good. This free.

He cradled Catherine's slumbering form against his chest and buried his face in her hair. If he could, he would die right then and there.

Because with the dawn that would invariably come, he knew he would have to leave her. And he would rather be dead than walk out on her again.

But he had no choice.

FOUR

Catherine awoke to the sound and feel of Michael's breathing in her ear, to the warmth of his body pressed against her own. It had been so long since she last had the pleasure of him sleeping by her side.

How could she have told him she didn't remember, when all she did was remember the feel of him? The smell of him? The *essence* of him?

And how could she ever reject a man she loved so dearly?

Catherine opened her eyes and saw him lying on his side, facing her. His left leg snuggled between hers, he had his left arm draped possessively across her body.

Impulsively, she brushed the brown wisps of hair off his forehead and placed a tender kiss to his brow.

"I still love you," she whispered, knowing he couldn't hear her. That was one thing about Michael— once he slept, it would take the end of the world to wake him.

She heard footsteps outside in the kitchen. Afraid it was one of the children or Rebecca, someone who might enter her room to wake her, she quickly got up and dressed.

With one last look to savor the sight of him sleeping naked in her bed, she drew her quilt up over his sleeping form and tiptoed from the room.

Entering the kitchen, she didn't see anyone.

How strange.

She had definitely heard someone a moment ago.

With a frown, she walked into the parlor where they had placed the Christmas tree and toys. To the right of the tree, hidden in the shadows, she found her daughter, Diana, cradling the doll St. Nick had brought her.

Catherine paused, staring at the product of her love for Michael. Diana was a bit small for her four years. She had Catherine's long, wavy dark hair and Michael's silver-gray eyes. It never failed to amaze Catherine that something so pretty and smart had come from her.

Smiling, she approached her daughter who looked up, her eyes brimming with tears.

"Diana, what is it?" she asked, instantly concerned as she knelt by her side. She brushed the dark bangs back from her daughter's face.

"He didn't come," Diana whimpered as a solitary tear fell down her face.

"Of course St. Nick came, sweetling. You have the doll and everything."

"No, Mama, *he* didn't come," she repeated, hugging her doll even closer as more tears fell. "It was all I wanted for Christmas and he didn't come."

"Who, baby?"

"Daddy," she sobbed.

Catherine's breath caught in her throat at the unexpected word. Diana had only started asking about her father a few short months ago, and the fact that he *had* shown up in the night . . .

It was enough to give one the shivers.

"What are you talking about?" Catherine asked her daughter.

"You told me St. Nick could make miracles, remember, Mama?"

"Yes."

"And I told you I wanted a *special* miracle."

"I thought you meant the doll."

Diana shook her head. "I wanted St. Nick to bring me my daddy. I wanted to see his eyes like mine."

Catherine wrapped her arms around her small daughter and held her close. She wasn't sure what she should do. Part of her wanted to take Diana into the bedroom to meet her father, and the other part of her was too terrified of how Michael might react.

She should have told him last night, but she had turned coward.

It was one thing for him to abandon her. She could deal with it. But hurting Diana was another matter.

No, it would be best to wait and tell him about their daughter when Diana wasn't around. That way only she would be hurt if he ran for the door. Again.

With the edge of her shawl, Catherine wiped Diana's eyes. "No tears on Christmas, please?"

Diana sniffed them back.

She kissed the top of Diana's little dark head and squeezed her tight. "I'll talk to St. Nick after breakfast and see what I can do."

"But he's already gone back to the North Pole."

"I know, sweetling, but didn't anyone ever tell you that mommies have a special way of letting St. Nick know what their babies want?"

Diana wiped her tears with the back of her hand. "After breakfast?"

Catherine nodded. "Keep your fingers crossed and maybe he can manage something."

"I will. I promise."

She smiled at those silver-gray eyes that shone with innocence. "Good girl. Now go check your stockings and see what else St. Nick might have left while I go start breakfast."

Diana scooted out of her arms and Catherine rose slowly to her feet.

In truth, she felt ill. Her stomach knotted. How would she break the news to Michael?

Would he even care?

Taking a deep breath for courage, she knew one way or the other she had to tell him. Even an irresponsible scoundrel deserved to know he had fathered a beautiful little girl who wanted nothing more than to meet him.

"Just don't hurt her," she whispered. "Because if you do, I'll kill you for it."

O'Connell came awake slowly to the smell of bacon and coffee, and the sound of children laughing outside his door. At first he thought it was a dream.

How many times had he yearned to experience just such a morning?

Many more times than he could count.

"Catherine, do I need to set extra plates for whoever was at the door last night? I didn't know if he, she, or them stayed, or what."

He heard Catherine's mumbled reply through the

walls, but couldn't make out any of her words.

All of a sudden the memory of the night before came crashing back through him.

It had been real. All of it. This was no dream. He was, in fact, sleeping in Catherine's bed on Christmas morning.

O'Connell leaned his head back into the pillow as an overwhelming joy ripped through him. He felt like shouting or singing or doing something. Anything to celebrate such a glorious event!

Impulsively, he pulled Catherine's pillow to him and inhaled the fresh sunshine smell of her. Intoxicated, he listened to the children sing "God Rest Ye Merry Gentlemen" as someone jingled china and silverware.

"It's not a dream," he whispered.

He laughed softly as raw euphoria invaded every piece of him. He had his Christmas miracle.

Smiling, he rose from the bed and dressed, then made the bed up. Catherine had always complained he twisted the sheets into knots and she hated a messy bed.

This would be his gift to her.

He left the room warily and made sure no one spied him lest Catherine have some serious explaining to do. The last thing she needed was a tarnished reputation, and the last thing he needed was nosy questions he couldn't answer.

He saw the stairs behind him and made like he was coming from one of the rooms upstairs.

As he drew flush with the kitchen door, he saw Catherine standing in front of the stove, frying eggs.

He delighted at her trim form. She'd left her hair long in the back with a braid wound about the top of her head to keep it out of her eyes. Her dark green dress hugged every one of the curves he had feasted on the night before. And a white shawl draped becomingly over her shoulders.

Never had he seen a more glorious image, and he wished he could stay here forever.

"Rebecca?" Catherine called, stepping back from the stove and looking out the doorway on the opposite side of the room. "Are the children still outside?"

"Making snow angels, last I saw," a woman called as she came into the room. The petite brunette stopped dead in her tracks as her gaze fell to him.

Catherine caught the woman's gaze and turned to face him.

"Morning," he greeted them.

Catherine blushed, and he didn't miss the light that came into the short brunette's eyes.

"Morning," the brunette said warmly, suggestively.

Catherine cleared her throat. "Rebecca, this is our visitor from last night."

"Pleased to meet you," Rebecca said. "Mister . . . ?"

"Burdette," he said, falling into his most recent alias. "Tyler Burdette."

He glanced to Catherine, who took his name in with a frown.

"I'll just go set another place at the table for you, Mr. Burdette," Rebecca said.

As soon as they were alone again, Catherine approached him, waving a spatula dripping with hot grease dangerously near his nose. "Tyler Burdette?" she asked in a miffed tone. "Is there something you need to tell me?"

That was a loaded question and he wasn't sure how to answer it. Luckily another visitor, a man, spared him a few moments to think.

But to be honest, all he thought about was the fact that the distinguished-looking, gray-haired man spent a little too long staring at *his* Catherine.

"Miss Catherine?"

"Marshal McCall," she said, stressing the title, no doubt for his benefit.

And it worked. O'Connell was immediately on guard.

By the look on the man's face, it was obvious he wanted to ask Catherine something of a personal nature. Worse, the man stuttered and shifted nervously before he came out with, "I just came for my morning cup of coffee."

O'Connell's gaze narrowed. The damn man was infatuated with *his* wife!

He flinched as an image of her in the marshal's arms tore through his mind.

Would the insults never cease?

As Catherine moved to fetch a cup of coffee, the marshal glanced to O'Connell. "How do?" he asked amiably enough.

"Just fine, Marshal," O'Connell returned, trying to remain pleasant in spite of the urge he had to choke the man. "And you?"

The marshal frowned as he looked him up and down. "Don't I know you from someplace?"

Probably from about a dozen or so wanted posters, but he didn't dare say that. Instead, O'Connell shook his head. "I don't know any marshals." He made it his habit to avoid them at all costs.

"No?" the marshal asked. "You sure look familiar to me. You got any family in Reno?"

O'Connell shook his head. "Not that I'm aware of."

He seemed to accept that. But still he took a step forward and extended his hand. "Dooley McCall."

"Tyler Burdette," he said, shaking his proffered hand.

"Burdette," the marshal repeated. "Nah, I don't reckon I do know you after all."

Catherine handed the marshal his coffee.

"Thank you, Miss Catherine. I keep telling my deputies no one on earth makes a better pot of coffee than you do."

"Thank you, Marshal."

O'Connell didn't miss the blush staining her cheeks. For a moment, he had to struggle to breathe. How dare she blush at another man! So what if he had been gone five years, it still didn't give her the right to do *that* for someone else.

She was *his* wife, not the marshal's.

The marshal nodded, then took his coffee and left.

O'Connell wasted no time sneaking to the doorway to see the marshal sitting in the parlor with a paper, sipping his coffee as if everything were right in the world.

"What the hell is a marshal doing here?" he asked Catherine in a low voice.

She gave him a haughty glare. "He *lives* here."

"Lives here?" he repeated.

"I run a boardinghouse, remember? He's one of my regular tenants."

"Why would you let him live *here*?"

"I don't know," she said sarcastically. "Maybe I like having him here because it keeps out the riff-raff," she said with a pointed stare, "and he pays two months' rent in advance."

Catherine didn't miss the heated glare Michael gave her. Licking her lips, she felt a wave of misgiving run up her spine. Michael was entirely too interested in the marshal.

Something was wrong.

"Are you wanted?" she asked all of a sudden.

He stared at her with those clear silver-gray eyes. "It depends," he said in a serious voice. "I was hoping you'd want me."

Her breath caught. Did she dare hope that he might actually be able to settle down with her and Diana?

"And if I did?" she asked.

He looked back at the marshal. "This is a bad time. I really need to leave."

"Leave?" she gasped. "You can't."

"Why not?"

"Because you just got here. You can't just show up on my doorstep, roll around in my bed, and then take flight as soon as the sun comes up. I thought we had shared something special last night. Or were they all lies again?"

He winced as if she'd struck him. "I've never lied to you, Catherine."

"No. But you lied to my boarder and housekeeper. Is that not true, Mr. *Tyler Burdette*?"

"I—"

"Miss Catherine, Miss Catherine?" An excited boy came bursting through the kitchen with Pete's saddlebags in his hands. The blond head bobbed as the kid jumped up and down. "I just found these outside by the front door, and look," he said, flipping one open. "They're filled with money! Can I keep it?"

O'Connell went cold as everything came together in his mind.

"I found this little orphanage in a town called Redwood," Pete had said. "You'd probably like it a lot, Kid. It had a real *homey* feel to it."

O'Connell cursed as his stomach drew tight. Pete knew! He had sent him purposefully to find Catherine.

Panic swept through him. That meant Pete wouldn't be far behind. He had to get her to safety before his brother showed up and used her to drag him back into robbery.

But how? She'd never leave her business or her orphans.

"This is bad," he whispered. "Real bad."

Catherine looked into the saddlebags. "Where did this come from?" she asked the boy.

"I was told it was stolen from you," O'Connell said as he double-checked where the marshal sat.

Looking up at him, Catherine frowned. "By whom?"

"Is it yours?" O'Connell asked, seeking to delay the inevitable explanation of how he'd come by her money. "Were you robbed?"

"Yes, we were. But how did you get it?"

So much for delaying the inevitable.

She looked at him sternly. "Did *you* take it?"

"No!" he barked. "How could you even ask that?"

"Well, what am I to think?" she asked as she set the saddlebags on the table and excused the boy.

She moved to stand just before him, hands on hips. "I thought I knew you, and yet every time I blink I learn something about you that scares me. Now tell me how it is you have my money."

O'Connell didn't have a chance. Before he could say a word, the back door opened to show Pete holding one of Catherine's little girls in his arms.

"Knock, knock," Pete drawled. He flashed an evil grin to O'Connell, then lifted the little girl's face to where O'Connell could see her tear-streaked eyes. "Look what old Uncle Pete found out in the yard."

FIVE

O'Connell felt the air leave his lungs as he gazed into a pair of eyes indistinguishable from his own. They were set in a face that looked identical to Catherine's, right down to the dark brown curls spilling over Pete's arm.

In an instant, he recognized his daughter.

Sobbing uncontrollably, the girl looked to Catherine. "Help me, Mama! Make the mean man let me go."

Catherine took a step toward the girl, but O'Connell grabbed her arm and pulled her to a stop.

No one approached his brother. If Catherine tried to take the girl, there was no telling what Pete might do to her.

"Let her go, Pete," O'Connell said, his calm voice belying the volatile state of his mind and body.

Pete gave an evil smile. "I told you in Oak River, you can't escape me, Kid. Now I ask you again, are you coming with me or what?"

"Oak River?" he heard Catherine repeat under her breath.

That was the town where he'd left her. Only then, Pete had used Catherine as his leverage. It was either go with Pete to rob another bank or see his wife hurt.

After the robbery, O'Connell had lacked the heart to go back to her. He couldn't face her after what he'd done for Pete. Worse, he knew that sooner or later Pete would show up again with the same threat.

And the last thing he wanted was to kill his brother for hurting his wife.

So long as there was life in his body, he would protect his Catherine.

You're my second chance. That's what O'Connell had told her on their wedding night. Catherine hadn't known what he'd meant by it. But he had.

For a time, he had been stupid enough to believe it. But second chances were for fools.

And Catherine could never again be his.

"I'll come with you, Pete. Just put her down."

Pete nodded. "Good boy. I knew you'd see things my way once you saw them again." Pete squeezed the girl's cheeks and tilted her head up to where he could look into her face. "She is kind of cute, isn't she?"

Rage infused every cell of O'Connell's body. "Take your hands off her, Pete, or I'll kill you for it."

His brother met his gaze and for several seconds they stared at each other in mutual understanding. "You know, Kid, I believe you would."

"You can count on it."

O'Connell didn't breathe again until Pete set the girl on her feet, and she ran to Catherine's outstretched arms.

Pete glanced to Catherine and the little girl. "Since it's Christmas and all, I'll give you five minutes with them. I'll be waiting outside by the horses."

O'Connell waited for him to leave before he turned to face Catherine, who cradled the little girl to her chest.

His daughter.

He felt so much pride and delight, he thought his heart might burst. But the joy died as he remembered his brother waiting for him outside.

O'Connell reached a hand out to touch the dark brown curls. The softness of his daughter's hair reached deep inside him, carving a place in his heart.

"She's beautiful," he breathed.

Catherine saw the pain deep inside him and she noted the tenseness of his hand on Diana's hair. "Her name is Diana."

He gave a bittersweet smile. "Named for your mother?"

She nodded.

"Why didn't you tell me about her in Nevada?" he asked, his eyes misting.

"I didn't know I was pregnant until after you left." She narrowed her gaze on him as she finally understood everything that had happened. "You left because of him, didn't you?"

"He's my brother," he said simply. "I had no choice."

"We always have choices."

He shook his head. "No, we don't. You don't know what kind of man my brother is, but I do. I know he's cruel, but I owe him. If not for Pete, I'd have never survived after the death of our parents. He's harsh because that's the way the world made him."

"He's harsh because he's—"

O'Connell stopped her words by placing his fingers on her lips. His heart tearing apart, he leaned over, kissed her gently on the mouth, and whispered, "Until the day I die, I'll always remember you."

He touched Diana's hair one last time, then he turned and walked away.

O'Connell met Pete by his pinto, which Pete must have saddled. His brother was as fair-haired and fair-skinned as O'Connell was dark. The two of them had always been opposites in most everything. Even Pete's eyes were a brownish green.

And never before had O'Connell felt so much resentment and hatred for the brother who had once protected him.

"Why can't you just let me go?" he asked Pete. "I've paid my debt to you a thousand times over."

Pete gave him a hard glare. "You're my family, Kid. Like it or hate it, it's just you and me." Pete smiled wickedly. "Besides, you're the only man I know who can blow a safe and not destroy half the money with it."

"You're not funny."

Pete shucked him on the shoulder. "Now, don't get sore on me, Kid. You can do better than her. I told you that years ago. She ain't nearly pretty enough for you."

He grabbed Pete by his shirtfront. "I'm not a kid anymore, Pete, and I'm no longer scared of you. Catherine is my wife and she deserves your respect. If you ever say anything else against her, as God is my witness, I'll tear your hide apart for it."

For the first time in his life, he saw a glimmer of fear pass through Pete's eyes. "All right, Kid. Whatever you say."

O'Connell let him go. He had barely taken a step when he heard the front door of the boardinghouse open.

The marshal strode out across the porch with two men in tow. And all three of them carried shotguns in their arms. By the grim, determined looks on their faces, he knew what they wanted.

Him and Pete.

His blood went cold.

The marshal stared at Pete as he leveled the shotgun on them. "Pete O'Connell," he said slowly. "Never did I expect to receive such a great Christmas present. Imagine the bounty of *both* O'Connell brothers."

Pete swore, then went for his gun.

O'Connell didn't think. He merely reacted. He was tired of his brother's schemes, and tired of the lives Pete had taken for no reason.

It was time for it to end.

He grabbed his brother's gun, and the two of them struggled for it.

Catherine watched the men tussle from the parlor window. She had sent Diana upstairs with Rebecca, then immediately sought out the marshal to let him know there was a possible outlaw outside.

She pressed her hand to her lips as terror sliced through her as she watched the two men fighting for possession of the gun. What had she done?

A gunshot rang out.

Catherine stopped breathing. Michael and Pete

froze and locked gazes. Time seemed suspended as she waited.

Who had been shot?

Then Michael staggered back, and she saw the red stain on his shirtfront right before he collapsed on the ground.

"No!" she shouted as tears stung the backs of her eyes. It couldn't be Michael! It couldn't be.

Pete just looked down at him, his face indecipherable.

Dropping her shawl, Catherine ran for the door, down the steps, and across the yard to Michael's side.

His brother stood coldly to the side as the marshal and his men put irons on his wrists.

Sobbing, she knelt by Michael's side. Terrified and shaking, she touched his cold brow.

"Michael?" she breathed.

He opened his eyes and looked up at her. In that look she saw the love he had for her. He opened his mouth to speak, but she pressed her fingertips to his lips.

"Save your strength," she whispered. She looked up to Marshal McCall, who stared angrily at Pete.

"I always heard you were mean, but damn, to shoot your own brother on Christmas? You're a sick man, O'Connell," the marshal said to Pete.

His face blank, Pete glanced down to her and Michael, then back at the marshal.

"What are you, stupid? Do we *look* like brothers?" Pete drawled slowly. "My brother got killed in Shiloh last month during our last holdup. That there's just some stupid cow-poke thinks he's a bounty hunter.

Bastard's been trailing me for weeks. I don't even know his name." Pete locked gazes with her, then shocked her with his words, "But I think the lady over there knows him. Ask her who he is."

The marshal gave her a probing stare. "That true, Miss Catherine? You know this man?"

A tremor of panic shook her as she realized Michael's entire fate was in her hands.

What should she answer?

She looked down at Michael's calm, deliberate stare. He expected her to betray him. She could read it plainly in his eyes as he waited for her to denounce him.

But she couldn't. She didn't know everything yet, but before she handed him over to the marshal, she wanted some long-overdue answers. Answers he couldn't very well give her locked up in jail.

"He's my husband," she answered honestly. "Michael O'Callahan."

The marshal gave her a hard stare. "I thought you said your husband ran off."

"He did," she said, looking back at Michael. "But he came home to me last night."

"Farley," the marshal shouted to his deputy. "Help me carry Miss Catherine's husband inside while Ted locks up O'Connell."

The marshal helped her to her feet.

"Where you want us to take him?" the marshal asked.

"To my room," she said, leading the way back into the boardinghouse.

* * *

Michael O'Connell didn't say anything for the rest of the day. His head swam with what had happened.

Why had Pete lied?

Why had Catherine protected him, when she could have easily seen him in prison for the next ten to twenty years?

None of it made any sense to him, and worse, Catherine had avoided coming into the room for him to question her. If he'd been able to, he would have gone after her himself, but he was too weak to do much more than just breathe.

The door to his room creaked open. He glanced over to see a tiny dark head peeking in.

He smiled at the sight of his daughter in the doorway.

When Diana saw him look her way, the little girl smiled from ear to ear.

She fanned the door back and forth as she twisted in the door frame. "Are you really my daddy?" she asked.

"What did your mama say?"

"She said St. Nick brought you to me last night."

O'Connell gave a half laugh at her words, but he couldn't manage any more than that, since pain cut his breath off. Pete had been called a lot of things over the years, but this was the first time anyone had ever referred to his brother as St. Nick.

"Yeah," he said with a grimace. "I guess maybe he did."

Releasing the doorknob, she ran across the room and scrambled to sit next to him on the bed. He winced at the pain she caused by dipping the mattress, but in truth he didn't mind it at all. To have his daughter near him, he would suffer a lot worse than that.

"You sure are pretty for a man."

O'Connell smiled at her words. No one had ever said *that* to him before.

She reached out one little hand to touch his eyelid. "You do have eyes like mine. Mama told me you did."

He cupped her soft cheek, amazed at what he saw in her face. It was so strange to see parts of him mixed in with parts of Catherine.

Never in his life had he seen a more beautiful little girl. "We get them from my mother."

"Was she pretty, too?"

"Like you, she was as pretty as an angel."

"Diana!"

He started at Catherine's chiding tone.

"I told you not to disturb him."

"I'm sorry, Mama."

"She's not disturbing me," he said, dropping his hand from her face.

Catherine shooed her out anyway. At first he thought she'd leave as well, but she hesitated in the doorway.

"Why didn't you tell me who you really were?" she asked.

He stared at her. "I liked the man you saw me as. To you, I was a decent man, not some no-account outlaw drifter. The last thing I wanted was for you to change your mind about me and hate me."

"So you lied to me?"

"Not really. I just didn't tell you everything."

She shook her head. "I always knew you were hiding *something* from me. I was just never sure what. Funny, I used to think it was another woman you loved, not a lunatic brother."

He gave her a hard, meaningful look. "I could never love anyone but you."

"Do you mean that?"

"On my life."

And then she gifted him with one of those loving smiles that had kept him warm on the coldest days. "So tell me, Michael, where do we go from here?"

EPILOGUE

CHRISTMAS EVE, TWO YEARS LATER

"Hey, Pa, where do we go from here?"

Michael looked up at nine-year-old Frank's question. After Catherine had given him his second chance, the two of them had decided to adopt the orphans she'd been keeping. And every day of the last two years, he had spent every minute making up to her for the time they had been apart.

She would never again have cause to doubt him, and he reveled in the blessing of his family and home.

"I think you'd best be asking your mother that question," he said to Frank. "Catherine?"

"It's the big white house at the end of the street," she said as she waddled up to them beside the train station.

Michael grinned at the sight of her pregnant body. He'd missed seeing her carry Diana, but he was definitely enjoying her now.

The way Catherine figured, they had two more months before the baby would join them. Just enough time to visit her parents with their passel of children in tow, and then make it back home in time for the little one's birth.

Four of the orphans still lived with them. Five children total with Diana. Michael smiled as he watched all of them climb aboard the wagon he had rented.

He'd always wanted a big family.

"You nervous?" he asked Catherine as he draped a comforting arm over her shoulders. She hadn't seen her parents since the day they had eloped almost seven years before.

"A little. And you?"

"A little."

Even so, he was too grateful for his life to mind even a lengthy visit at his in-laws'. He still found it hard to believe Pete had lied to save him.

"I've ruined your life enough, Kid. This is one place I think I'd best go to alone," Pete had told him.

Pete would be in prison for a long time to come. Maybe it would make his brother a better man.

All he could do was hope that one day his brother would find the peace that had always eluded him.

Michael placed a tender kiss on Catherine's brow as he took Diana's hand in his and helped her up into the wagon.

Every day for the last two years, he had been grateful that his wife had stood by him, even though it was the last thing he'd deserved.

"Thank you, Cathy," he breathed as he helped her climb into the wagon seat.

"For what?" she asked.

"For making my life worth living."

Her smile warmed him to his toes. "It's been my pleasure, Mr. O'Callahan. Merry Christmas."

And a Merry Christmas it would be, too. For in this life, there were second chances, and this time, Michael wouldn't waste the one he'd been given.

CHRISTMAS BONUS

Lori Foster

ONE

Eric Bragg heard the even staccato clicking of her designer high heels coming down the polished hallway. He straightened in his chair as anticipation thrummed through him, matching the quickened beat of his heart.

He knew the sound of Maggie's long-legged, purposeful walk with an innate awareness that exemplified his growing obsession with her. He could easily identify the sound of her stride apart from that of all the other employees. Mostly because when he heard it, he felt the familiar hot need, mixed with disgruntled dismay, that always seemed to be a part of him these days wherever Maggie Carmichael was concerned.

He remembered a time not too long ago when her footsteps would have been muted with sneakers that perfectly matched her tattered jeans and oversized sweatshirts. A time when she was so anxious to visit the office, she wouldn't have bothered to measure her stride and she would have forgotten her now-impeccable good manners in her excitement at the visit. She used to hurry up and down the hallways with all the enthusiasm of a nineteen-year-old woman-child, almost old enough, almost mature enough.

Eric shifted, trying to settle himself more comfortably in his large chair while his muscles tightened and his pulse quickened.

Unfortunately for Eric, Maggie had stepped right out of college and into the role of boss, a circumstance he had never foreseen. Perhaps if he had, he wouldn't have bided his time so patiently, waiting for the differences in their ages to melt away under the influence of experience and maturity. Ten years wasn't much, he'd always told himself, unless you were tampering with an innocent daydreamer still in college. *The boss's daughter—and now the damn boss.*

But who would have guessed that her father would pass away so unexpectedly with a stroke? Or that he would have left Maggie, fresh-faced and uncertain, in charge of his small but growing company, rather than Eric, who'd served as his right-hand man for many years?

Deliberately, Eric loosened his hold on the pen he'd been using to check off items on a new supply order and placed it gently on his cluttered desk. Every other year, at just about this time, Maggie had visited him. She'd be out of school on Christmas break and she'd show up wearing small brass bells everywhere. They used to be tied in the laces of her shoes, hanging from a festive bow in her long, sinfully sexy hair, on ribbons around her neck. She loved Christmas and decorating and buying gifts. Eric reached into his pocket and smoothed his thumb over the engraved key ring she'd given him the year before.

This year, everything was different. *This year, he'd become her employee.*

Sprawled out in his seat, pretending a comfort he didn't feel, Eric waited for her. But still, he caught his breath as Maggie opened his door without knocking and stepped in.

There wasn't a single bell on her person. No red velvet ribbons, no blinking Santa pins. She was so damn subdued these days, it was almost as if the old Maggie had never existed. The combination of losing her father and gaining the responsibility of a company had changed her. Her glossy black hair had long since been cut into a chic shorter style, hanging just to the tops of her breasts. When she'd first cut it, he'd gotten rip-roaring drunk in mourning the loss of a longtime fantasy. Her slender body, which he'd become accustomed to seeing in sporty, casual clothes, was lost as well, beneath a ridiculously boxy, businesslike suit. It was drab in both color and form—but it still turned him on.

He knew what was beneath that absurd armor she now wore, knew the slight, feminine body that it hid.

And her legs . . . oh, yeah, he approved of the high heels Maggie had taken to wearing. They'd helped him to contrive new fantasies, which he utilized every damn night with the finesse of a masochist, torturing himself while wondering about things he'd likely never know. He went to sleep thinking about her, and woke up wanting her.

He was getting real used to surviving with a semi-erection throughout the day.

He felt like a teenager, once again caught in the heated throes of puberty. Only now, groping a girl in the backseat of his car wasn't about to put an end to his aching. Hell, an all-night sexual binge with triplets wouldn't do the trick. He wanted only Maggie, naked, hot, breathless, accepting him and begging him and . . .

Damn, but he had to get a grip!

"Maggie." He ignored the raw edge to his voice and eyed her still features as she stared at him. There was a heated quality to her gaze, as if she'd read his thoughts. "You're flushed, hon. Anything wrong?"

Maggie looked him over quickly, her large brown eyes widening just a bit as her gaze coasted from the top of his head to the toes of his shoes. Unlike Maggie, he hadn't trussed himself up in a restricting suit. But then, he never had. From the day he'd been hired, he'd made do with comfortable corduroy slacks or khakis—a true concession from his preference of jeans—and loose sweaters or oxford shirts. Ties were a definite no-no. He hated the damn things. Her father had never minded, and evidently, neither did she.

Maggie shut the door behind her and lifted her chin. She was a mere twenty-two years old, yet she managed to imbue her tone with all the seriousness of a wizened sage. "We need to talk."

Eric smiled the smile he reserved just for Maggie. The one with no teeth showing, just a tiny curling at the corners of his mouth, barely noticeable, while his eyes remained intent and direct. He knew it made her uneasy, which was why he did it, cad that he was. Why should he be the only one suffering? Besides, seeing Maggie squirm was like refined foreplay, and he took undeniable satisfaction in being the one who engineered it. These days she was so set on displaying confidence, on proving herself while fulfilling the role her father had provided, it was a major accomplishment to be the one man who could put a dent in her facade.

He relished the small private games between them, the subtle battle for the upper hand. He wanted the old Maggie back, yet was intrigued by her new persona.

Eric leaned forward, propping his elbows on his desk amid the scattered papers. He did his job as well as ever, and managed to contain his nearly uncontainable lust. There surely wasn't much more she could ask of him. "What is it you think we need to talk about, Maggie?"

Her indrawn breath lifted her delicate breasts beneath the wool jacket. When he'd first met her several years ago, he'd thought her a bit lacking in that department. Then she'd shown up one hot summer day, braless in a college T-shirt, and the air-conditioning had caused her nipples to draw into stiff little points— which had caused various parts of him to stiffen— and since then he'd been mesmerized by her delicacy. He wanted to hold her in his hands, smooth her nipples with his thumbs, then his tongue, tease them with his teeth. . . .

Her jaw firmed and she pushed herself away from the door, catching her hands together at the small of her back and pacing to the front of his desk in a grand confrontation. "I want to talk about your attitude and lack of participation since I've stepped into my father's position."

Eric eyed her rigid stance. She was such a sweet, inexperienced woman that she'd at first misinterpreted his lust for jealousy. She'd assumed, and he supposed with good reason, that he resented her instant leap into the role of president of Carmichael Athletic Supplies. Most men would have. Eric had worked long and hard for Drake Carmichael, and under his guidance, the close personal business had grown. It was still a friendly company with a family atmosphere and very loyal employees, but the presiding stock Maggie inherited had doubled in worth from the year before—thanks to Eric. Because of that, Eric wasn't the only one who had assumed he was next in line for the presidency.

But in truth, Eric didn't give a damn about his position on the corporate ladder, except that he didn't like the idea of having Maggie for his boss. It put an awkward slant to the things he'd wanted with her, throwing the dynamics of a relationship all out of whack. Maggie wasn't a woman you messed around with; she was the marrying kind. Only now, if he pursued her for his wife, some might assume he was still going after the company in the only way left to him. That not only nettled his pride, it infuriated his sense of possessiveness toward her. He wouldn't let anyone shortchange her worth.

So he'd assured her immediately that he had no desire to be president, no desire to usurp her new command. She'd looked equally stunned by his declaration, and bemused.

Still, he had hoped Maggie might tire of being the boss. She had always seemed like a free spirit to him, a woman meant to pursue her interests in the arts and her joy of traveling. She was a very creative person, fanciful, a daydreamer who had only learned the business to please her father, or so he'd assumed. Eric thought she'd merely been going through the motions when she worked first in the stock room, then briefly on the sales floor, before eventually making her way all the way to the top—at her father's request.

But he had to give her credit; she knew what she was doing. Like all new people, she needed a helping hand now and then in order to familiarize herself with how operations had already been handled, but she was daring enough to try new things and had enough common sense not to rock too many boats at one time. The employees all respected her, and the people they dealt with accepted her command.

He'd do nothing to upset that balance, because contrary to his predictions, she hadn't gotten frazzled and bored with corporate business. She'd dug in with incredible determination and now, within six months of taking over, Maggie had a firm grasp of all aspects of the company.

Eric, in the meantime, suffered the hellish agonies of unrequited lust and growing tenderness.

Shoving his chair back, Eric came to his feet and circled his desk to stand in front of Maggie. This close, he could inhale her scent and feel the nearly electric charge of their combined chemistry. Surely she felt it, too—which probably explained why she'd begun visiting his office more often. Eric got the distinct feeling that Maggie *liked* his predicament.

Tilting his head, he asked, "Why don't you drop the president aura and just talk to me like you used to, Maggie?" Six months ago, when her father had first passed away, Maggie had clung to him while she'd grieved. Eric had settled her in his lap, held her tight, and let her cry until his shirt was soaked. The emotions he'd felt in that moment had nearly brought him to his knees.

Nothing had been right between them since.

Eric crossed his arms over his chest and watched a faint blush color her cheeks.

He loved how Maggie blushed, the soft rose color that tinted her skin and the heat that glowed in her eyes. She blushed over everything—a good joke, a hard laugh, a sly smile. He could only imagine how she'd blush in the throes of a mind-blowing climax, her body damp with sweat from their exertions. . . . *Down, boy.*

"How long," Eric asked, trying to distract himself, "have I known you, honey?"

A small teasing smile flitted across her mouth. "I was seventeen when Daddy hired you."

"So let's see . . . that's five years? Too damn long for you to traipse in here and act so impersonal, wouldn't you say?" If he could only get things back on a strictly friendly basis, maybe, just maybe, he could deal with the powerful physical attraction between them.

"Yes." She sighed, letting out a long breath and clasping her hands together in front of her. "I'm sorry, Eric. It's just . . . well, since taking over, so many people have been watching me, waiting for me to fall on my face. I feel like I'm under constant scrutiny."

"And you think I'm one of those people?"

She met his gaze, then admitted slowly, "I don't know. Despite what you've said, I know you thought—*everyone* thought—that you'd be the president, not me." There was an emotion in her face that seemed almost . . . hopeful. No, that couldn't be.

"I already explained about that, Maggie."

"I know." She gave a long, dramatic sigh. "But you've been so . . . I don't know, *distant,* since I took over."

And she'd been so damn beguiling.

Eric had done his damnedest to come to terms with a radical chink in his plans. He wanted her. Looking at her now with her hair pulled sleekly to one side by a gold clip, her clothes too sophisticated for her spirit, her heels bringing her five-foot-eight-inch height up enough to make her within kissing level to his six-foot-even length . . .

God, but he wanted her. She had her back to the desk and he could have gladly cleared it in an instant, then lowered her gently and parted her long sleek thighs. The thought of exploring her soft female flesh, of coaxing her to a wet readiness, made him shake. He knew without the slightest doubt how well they'd fit together.

He cleared his throat as he thrust his hands into his pockets and tried to inconspicuously adjust his trousers. "It's the holiday season, hon," he said with a nonchalance he didn't feel. "Lots to do, not only at work, but at home, too. You know that. If you need anything—"

She waved that away. "You've been very helpful here, Eric. I never could have made the transition so smoothly if you hadn't been giving me so much assistance."

That made him frown. "Nonsense. The transition was smooth because you worked hard to make it so. Don't shortchange yourself, Maggie. Drake would have been damn proud if he could see how you've filled his shoes without a hitch."

A short laugh escaped her, even as she began to relax. She stared out the window to the left of his desk. A gentle swirl of snowflakes softened the darkening day. "Daddy's wishes," she said quietly, while sneaking a somewhat shy peek at him, "might not have been as clear as you think."

Eric frowned at those cryptic words, sensing she meant to tell him something, but having no idea what it might be. "You want to explain that, Maggie?"

"No." She shook her head, determination replacing the vulnerability he'd witnessed. "Never mind."

"Maggie . . ." he said, making it sound like a warning.

She sighed again. "There've been plenty of hitches, Eric. Believe me."

A feeling of menace invaded Eric's muscles, making him tense. "Has someone been giving you a hard time?" He stepped closer, willing her to meet his gaze. He'd specifically warned everyone that if they valued their jobs, they'd better work with her, not against her, or he'd personally see them out the door.

"No!" She reached out and touched his biceps in a reassuring gesture. Her touch was at first impersonal, and then gently caressing. God, did she know she was playing with fire?

She drew a shuddering breath. "No, Eric, it's nothing like that. We have the very best employees around."

Eric barely heard her; his rational mind stopped functioning the moment her small hand landed on his arm. She was warm and soft and her scent—that of sweet innocence and spicy sexuality—drifted in to him. He inhaled sharply, and she dropped her hand, tipping her head to study him.

"The problem," she said, now watching him curiously, "is that I've been ultra-popular since taking over."

A new feeling of unease threatened to choke him. "What the hell does that mean?" He propped his hands on his hips and glared. "Have the guys here been hitting on you?"

"Yes, of course they have." Her simplistic reply felt like the kick of a mule, and then she continued, oblivious to his growing rage. "Not just the guys here, but the men we deal with, men from neighboring businesses, men from—"

"I get the picture!" Eric paced away, then back again. It was bad enough that the female employees had, for some insane reason, decided he was fair game and had been coming on to him in force. But the males were hitting on Maggie, too? Forget the holiday spirit of generosity—he wanted to break some heads!

"You realize," he growled, deciding she could do with a dose of reality, "that it's not your sexy legs and big brown eyes they're after?"

She blinked at him and that intriguing blush warmed her skin. "You think I have sexy legs?"

Eric drew back. Damn, he hadn't meant to say that.

Just as he didn't mean to glance down at her legs, and then not be able to look away. Her legs were long and slender and shapely and they went on forever. He'd seen her in jeans, in shorts, in miniskirts. He'd studied those long legs and visualized them around his hips clasping him tight, or better yet, over his shoulders as he clasped her bottom and entered her so deeply. . . .

"Eric?"

He shook his head and croaked, "You have great legs, sweetheart, really. But the point is—"

"And my eyes?"

She watched him, those big dark eyes consuming him, begging for the words. "You have bedroom eyes," he whispered, forgetting his resolve to keep her at a distance. "Big and soft. Inviting."

"Oh."

His voice dropped despite his intentions. "A man could forget himself looking into your eyes."

Her face glowed and she primped. "I had no idea."

Eric locked his jaw against the temptation to show her just how lost he already was. "The point," he said in a near growl, "is that many of the men hitting on you are probably only after the damn company."

"I'm not an idiot. I know that already."

"They think if they . . . What do you mean, you know?"

"That's what I was talking about," she said with a reasonableness Eric had a hard time grasping. "I've been in or around this business for ages—as I already said, since I was seventeen. Most of the men ignored me. I mean, I realize I'm kind of gangly and people saw me as a little too flighty. No," she said when he started to argue with her, appalled by her skewed perceptions of herself. "I'm not fishing for more compliments. I'm a realist, Eric. I know who and what I am. But the point is that men who have always ignored me or only been distantly polite suddenly want to take me to the Bahamas for a private weekend winter getaway, or—"

"What?"

"—or they want to give me expensive gifts or—"

"Who the hell asked you to the Bahamas?"

"It doesn't matter, it's just—"

"It most certainly does matter!" Eric felt tense from his toes to his ears. He was forcibly keeping away from her, refusing to involve her in an affair, and equally opposed to making her the object of speculation and office gossip. He'd be damned before he let some other bozo—especially one with dishonorable intentions—cozy up to her. "Who was it, Maggie?"

She touched him again, this time on his chest. "Eric." Like a sigh, she breathed his name, and once again her eyes were huge. "I appreciate your umbrage on my behalf, really I do. But I don't need you to play my white knight."

His tongue stuck to the roof of his mouth. Ridiculous for a thirty-two-year-old man to go mute just because of a simple touch. And on his chest, for God's sake. Not anyplace important. Not where he'd really love for her to touch him.

But he'd wanted her for five long years, and then been denied her just when he'd thought his waiting was about over. He mentally shook himself out of his stupor and framed her face in his hands. Her skin was so warm, so smooth, his heartbeat threatened to break his ribs. "If anyone—and I do mean anyone—insults you in any way, Maggie, I want you to promise to tell me."

Her eyes darkened, and she stared at his mouth. "Okay."

"Your father was one of my best friends." *Good,* he thought, *a tack that makes sense, a reason for my unreasonable reaction.* "Drake would have expected me to help take care of you, to watch out for you."

Just like that, the heat left her eyes. She gave him a withering half smile, patted his left hand, and then pulled it away from her face. Stepping back, she put some space between them and propped her hip on the edge of his desk.

She once again wore her damn professional mien that never failed to set his teeth on edge.

"I appreciate the sentiment, Eric, but I'm a big girl. I know that even though you don't want the company, others do and they're not above trying to marry me for it. But I can take care of myself."

Goddamn it, *he* wanted to take care of her. But he couldn't very well say so without running the risk of sounding like all the others. If only he hadn't been so noble, if only he'd told her from the beginning how much he wanted her. But she had been so young. . . .

Eric nodded his head, feeling incredibly grim. "Just keep it in mind."

Her smile was a bit distracted. "It's almost time to call it a day, so I'd better get to the point of my visit, huh?"

"All right." Eric watched her as she stood and began edging toward the door.

"The annual Christmas party. I heard from Margo that you don't plan to attend?"

Margo had a big mouth; he'd have to talk to her about that. "I haven't decided yet," he lied, because he had no intention of forcing himself into her company any more than he had to.

"Margo said you turned her down."

Eric rubbed the back of his neck. "Yeah, I didn't . . ."

"I understood that you'd turned everyone down. Margo, Janine, Sally . . ."

"I know who I've spoken with, Maggie. You don't need to remind me." Hell, half the female employees had asked him to the party. He wondered how Maggie knew that, though.

She stared him in the eye. "You, uh, aren't dating anyone right now, are you?"

Eric frowned at her, wondering what she was getting at. It wasn't like her to get involved in his personal life. "No, I'm not dating anyone right now." Despite the female employees' efforts, there was no one he wanted except Maggie, so he'd been suffering a self-assigned celibacy that was about to make him crazed.

"Excellent." She lifted her chin with a facade of bravado and announced boldly, "Then you can go with me. I . . . I need you, Eric."

TWO

Maggie watched as Eric gave her his most intimidating frown. Good Lord, the man was gorgeous. Her father had accused her of an infatuation, calling her obsession with his right-hand man *puppy love*. Granted, at seventeen, it could have been nothing else. But she was twenty-two now, and there was nothing immature or flighty about her feelings for Eric Bragg.

She was getting downright desperate to get his attention, and her New Year's resolution, made a bit early out of necessity, was to seduce him. It would be a Christmas present to herself. At least an office fling would give her something, if not what she really wanted. And perhaps, with any luck, once she'd made love to him he'd begin to see her as a woman, rather than the boss's daughter.

Eric looked dazed. His broad shoulders were tensed and his legs were braced apart as if he had to struggle for his balance. Hazel eyes narrowed, he rasped, "Come again?"

Being cowardly, Maggie inched a tiny bit closer to the door and escape, should Eric's response prove too humiliating to bear. Admittedly, she lacked experience. But she felt certain that he'd been giving her mixed signals. Sometimes he patted her head like she was still seventeen, and then every so often he'd throw her for a loop, like his comment on her legs, accompanied by a certain hot look in his eyes. . . .

"I need you," she blurted again. It was easier saying it the second time, but not much. "I want to attend the party. As the boss, I'm pretty much obligated to go. But so many of the male employees and associates have asked me, and I wasn't sure how to refuse them without causing a personal rift—so I lied and said I already had a date. You."

"Me?"

Nodding, she added, "It's just for pretend. I mean, you won't be expected to spend any money on me or dote on me or anything. But I might as well come clean and tell you that everyone also assumes you're helping me organize the Christmas party."

"Maggie . . ."

He sounded choked and she didn't know if it was anger or not. If he was mad, she'd have to scrap the second step of this evening's plan. That is, if her lack of courage didn't cause her to scrap it anyway. She reached behind her and felt for the doorknob. "Don't worry about it. I've got everything under control, so you don't have to really do much for the party. Except make others think you're helping me." Which she hoped would force them into some isolated time together. She bit her lip with the thought. "I'll give you a . . ."—she had to clear her throat—"Christmas bonus for helping out."

"I don't want a goddamned Christmas bonus from you," he growled, and started toward her with a dark frown.

Maggie felt her mouth drop open when he stopped a mere inch in front of her. Her entire body was zing-

ing with awareness, the way it always did whenever
Eric was close. His hazel eyes were intent and probing
and they made her feel like he could see right into
her soul.

She'd often wondered if he looked at a woman like
that while making love to her.

She swallowed audibly with the visual images filling her brain.

"You're mad?" She wanted it clarified before she
went any further.

"With your assumption that you need to reward me
for helping. You're damn right."

"Oh." Well, that was good, wasn't it? Definitely.
"Okay, so you *will* help?"

He gave an aggrieved sigh. "Yes."

So far, so good. "Will you also accompany me to
the party?"

Flattening one hand on the door, Eric leaned toward her. Despite his dark frown, there was something
else in his eyes, something expectant. He looked at
her mouth, and his jaw clenched. "Yes."

She licked her lips, saw his eyes narrow, and shivered. "The thing is," she said, sounding a bit breathless, "I have to give you a bonus. I'm giving everyone
a bonus, so if I don't, the employees might begin to
talk."

He stilled, then leaned away from her again, shoving his hands deep into his pants pockets. He scowled.
"That would bother you? If they talked, I mean?"

She didn't want anyone to say anything negative
about Eric! Her possessiveness over him had amused

her father, but he'd promised never to say a thing to
Eric, and as far as she knew, he hadn't.

What her father had done instead was worse, because it had backfired in a big way. "I just think we
should avoid gossip whenever possible."

Looking resigned, Eric nodded. "What do you want
me to do for the party? Hell, I don't even know what
goes into planning a party. I've never done it before."

Maggie tried a nervous smile. "As I said, most of
it is taken care of. But I had those offers from the
guys . . . so I said you were helping. That's okay?"

He gave a sharp nod, distracted by some inner
thought.

"The hall and caterers are taken care of. And I've
already started to . . . well, decorate the offices a little."

Some of the rigidness left Eric's shoulders. She
loved his body, how hard it was, how tall and strong.
He did nothing to emphasize his muscular bulk, but
his leisurely attempts at style managed it anyway. He
always rolled his shirtsleeves up to his elbows, displaying his thick wrists and solid forearms. Even the
look of his watch on his wrist, surrounded by dark
crisp hair, seemed incredibly sensual and masculine.
And his open shirt collar, which showed even more
hair on his chest, made her feel too warm in too many
places. She imagined he was somewhat hairy all over,
but she wanted to know for sure. She wanted to touch
him everywhere.

His walk was long and easy, his strength something
he took for granted. His corduroy slacks appeared soft

and were sometimes worn shiny in the most delectable places—like across his fly.

She forced herself to quit staring and met his gaze. "Why are you smiling?"

"Because I like seeing you enthused about something again."

Her eyes nearly crossed in her embarrassment. He knew how enthusiastic she was about his body?

Eric chuckled at her startled expression. "I remember how excited you used to get over Christmas." He reached out and touched her gold barrette with one long, rough finger. "What happened to those cute little bells you used to wear, Maggie?"

Cute? She'd assumed that she was far too immature for Eric, what with her silly holiday dressing. So she'd tried to look more sophisticated, more mature, in order to get his attention. But every day it had seemed like additional distance had come between them.

Her father had thought the lure of the company would be enough to get Eric to notice her. The letter he'd included to her in his will had stated as much. He was giving her a chance at the man she wanted, and she loved him so much for his well-meaning efforts. But instead of having the desired result, Eric wanted less to do with her than ever.

He'd said he didn't want the presidency. Evidently he didn't want her, either. Yet. But she was working on it.

Maggie pulled the door open and prayed he wouldn't notice the mistletoe until it was too late. "I'm not eighteen anymore, Eric. And I'm the boss. I can't be caught dashing up and down the hallways, jingling with bells and disturbing everyone."

He stepped into the doorframe with her. "You never disturbed me, hon." His eyes darkened and his mouth tilted in a crooked, thoroughly endearing smile. "At least, not the way you think."

Maggie had no idea what he meant by that, and besides, she needed all her concentration to screw up her daring. She drew a deep breath, smiled, and then said, "Oh, look. We're under the mistletoe."

Eric faltered for just a heartbeat, but she moved too quickly for him. Grabbing his neck with both hands, she pulled him down as she went on tiptoe. She heard his indrawn breath, felt the heat of his big body, and then her mouth was smashed over his and lights exploded behind her eyelids.

She moaned.

Eric held very still. "Uh, Maggie?" he whispered against her lips.

"Hmmm?" No way was she letting him go yet. This was very, very nice.

She felt the touch of his right hand in her hair, then his left was at her waist and he said in a low, rough rumble, "If we're going to do this, baby, let's do it right."

Maggie's eyes opened in surprise, but slowly sank shut again as Eric drew her so close that their bodies blended together from hips to shoulders. Her breasts, feeling remarkably sensitive, flattened against the hard wall of his chest. Her pelvis cradled his, and she became aware of his erection, which literally stole her breath away.

He wanted her? He liked kissing her?

His large hand opened on the small of her back and urged her closer still, until she felt his every pulsing heartbeat in the most erotic way possible. With a subtle shifting of his head, his mouth settled more comfortably against hers and he took control of the kiss. And wow, what a kiss it was!

He left her mouth for a brief moment to nuzzle beneath her ear. "Relax, Maggie."

What a ludicrous suggestion! She felt strung so tight, her body throbbed. "Okay."

She gave him all her weight and sighed as every pleasurable sensation intensified. His open mouth left a damp trail from her throat to her chin to her lips. She shivered. His tongue slid over her lips, teasing, and then into her mouth. *Oh, God.* She tried to stay calm, but it was so incredible, so delicious, that her breath came faster and her nipples tingled into hard tips and a sweet ache expanded low in her belly.

Eric growled low, a primitive response that thrilled her. His tongue, damp and hot, stroked deeply into her, over her own tongue, tasting her, exploring her.

Her hands knotted in his shirt, she arched into him, and then—she heard the tiny twitter of a feminine laugh.

Stunned when Eric suddenly pulled away, Maggie would have stumbled if he hadn't kept her upright with one strong arm wrapped around her waist. He glared over his shoulder, and there stood his secretary and two male employees.

Mortified heat exploded beneath Maggie's skin, making her dizzy. Everyone stood in heavy silence.

She was the boss, Maggie told herself, she had to take control of this small turn in events. Clearing her throat even as she stepped out of Eric's reach, Maggie said, "Well. I thought everyone had gone home already." She raised a brow, silently asking for an explanation.

"We were just about to leave," his secretary, Janine, informed them.

Eric dropped back to lean against the doorframe and crossed his arms over his chest. He seemed either oblivious or unconcerned with the fact that he had a very noticeable erection. Despite the impropriety, it thrilled Maggie, because at least that meant he was interested.

Of course, she had been rubbing up against him rather thoroughly, and that could account for the physical reaction. Mere friction?

Maggie stepped in front of him, shielding him with her body, and pointed up. "Mistletoe," she explained to her audience.

The secretary smiled like a damned cat and glided forward, her intent plain. "So I see. How . . . fortunate."

Not about to let anyone else touch Eric now that she'd gotten him revved up, Maggie stationed herself in front of him like a sentinel. When the secretary merely looked at her, Maggie made a shooing motion with her hands. "Go on home, Janine. I'm not approving any overtime today. Go on."

Janine barely bit back a smile. "But . . ."

Eric, sounding on the verge of laughter, said, "I

think it's just the mistletoe she's after, Maggie, not
more pay."

Maggie sent him a quelling glance over her shoulder, before addressing the woman again. "There's
more down the hall," Maggie assured her, trying to
shoo her on her way. "I put some in all the doorways.
You two," she added, pointing to the men, both of
whom had been pursuing her earlier, "go with her.
Find some mistletoe. Go."

The men, displaying a sense of discretion, hid their
amusement and escorted the willing secretary out.
Maggie glared at them until they were completely
gone from sight, mumbling under her breath about
pushy women.

"You want to explain that?" Eric asked.

"Hmmm?" Maggie turned to face him. "Explain
what?"

"Why you turned into a ferocious amazon just because Janine wanted to kiss me. I mean, kissing is the
purpose of mistletoe, right? And you're the one who
hung it in my doorway."

"Well." Of course kissing was the point, but she
wanted to be the only one taking advantage of it with
Eric.

Maggie couldn't quite look at him as she tried to
figure out how to get things back on track. Which
meant getting his mouth back on hers, his hands
touching her again. "I put you in that awkward situation by kissing you," she muttered, thinking it out as
she went along, "so I didn't want you to feel . . . obligated . . . to kiss anyone else. I was . . . protecting
you."

"So you don't personally care if Janine kisses me? I mean, if the mistletoe stays there, I assume she'll take care of it in the morning."

It was hard to speak with her teeth clenched. "No," she ground out, nearly choking on the lie. "If you want to kiss Janine, that's certainly your business."

His eyes narrowed. "I see." In the next instant he surprised her by plucking the mistletoe down and shoving it into his pants pocket.

Maggie gave a silent prayer of relief. But when she peeked up at him, she felt doubly foolish for the confusion and annoyance on his face.

"I don't want to kiss Janine," he explained.

"Good." *Get it moving, Maggie.* "I mean, then since that's settled, perhaps . . ."

"Maggie?" When she pretended a great need to straighten her jacket, Eric reached out and tilted up her chin. "Why did you kiss me, sweetheart?"

She gulped. He wanted explanations? Good grief, she hadn't expected that. She'd planned on carrying things through should he prove agreeable, or slinking away if he rebuffed her. But not once had she considered an interrogation, for crying out loud.

Men, in her limited experience, were either interested or not, but they never wanted to talk about it!

"I . . . ah, I was trying to get you into the Christmas spirit."

Eric released her and frowned thoughtfully. "You're embarrassed?" She denied that with a shake of her head, so he pointed out, "Your face is red."

She was horny. Turned on. Aroused. All hot and bothered. "I'm not embarrassed."

He quirked one brow.

"It was just a simple kiss, after all." And at twenty-two, she'd had as many kisses as any other woman her age. *But none like that. None with Eric.* Oh, it was different, all right, just as different as she'd always known it would be. "We've both been kissed plenty, right? No big deal."

His frown turned fierce, and she figured she'd managed to tick him off after all. "All right, then." She clasped her hands together and gave him a beatific smile. "Since you agreed to help me with the Christmas party, I guess we're all settled."

She started away, bent only on retreat before she blew it completely, but Eric's voice stopped her. "When do we start, Maggie?"

She hesitated. "Uh . . . how about tomorrow? At my place? That is, if you don't already have a date for the weekend. . . ."

"I'll be there at two o'clock."

Two? In the afternoon? She'd really been hoping for something toward the evening, when she'd be able to light some candles, put a fire in the fireplace, set the mood for seduction. . . .

She realized Eric was waiting, staring at her in speculation, and she smiled as if she had not a care in the world. If he got suspicious, if he guessed at everything she wanted to do to him, he might not come at all. "Two is just fine. I'll see you then."

Eric managed to wait all of five minutes before curiosity got the better of him and he made his way to Maggie's office. If he'd read her right—and he was fairly certain he had—she wanted him. Not as much as he wanted her: that was impossible. But while he'd made a resolution not to seduce her, he hadn't figured on her trying to seduce him!

Despite everything he'd told himself about how disastrous a relationship would be, he knew damn good and well he wouldn't be able to resist her now that she'd shown some interest. She was lucky he'd let her walk away at all, much less promised to wait until two the next day. If he'd been thinking clearly, he'd have pulled her back into his office, locked the door, and made use of the desk as he'd envisioned earlier.

He told himself it didn't matter that all they could have was an affair. Maggie had already made it clear what she thought about someone chasing her for the company. If he tried to take things beyond an affair, she'd forever wonder what he'd really wanted. And then, too, there'd be the jokes about him trying to screw his way to the top. The idea was intolerable. Especially since she didn't want any gossip. Marrying the boss, which was what he really wanted to do, would certainly stir up the speculation.

Damn, he didn't have many choices.

When Eric opened her office door, he knew right away that she was already gone. All the lights were out and, as usual, her desk was neatly cleared of all the day's work. Maggie was tidy to a fault.

Then he noticed a paper on the floor.

Evidently she'd been as rattled as he after that killer kiss. Perhaps she'd left in a hurry, anxious to get home to the same cold shower he now anticipated. Although actually, looking out the window toward the

frozen winter landscape, he realized that just getting
to his car was liable to cool down his lust.

Knowing he was condemned to a lonely night of
erotic frustration made Eric want to howl. Unlike
Maggie, he wasn't in a hurry to head home, where
the solitude would cause him to dwell on all the sensual things he wanted to do to Maggie Carmichael,
and all the explicit things he wanted her to do to him.

But the cleaning crew, who came by every Friday
evening, would be arriving soon. He had no choice
but to be on his way. He stepped forward to retrieve
the piece of paper in case it was anything important,
meaning to simply place it on her desk.

One typed word, about midway through the text,
seemed to leap right out at him. *Thrust.* He leaned
against the edge of her desk and read the sentence:
*She was hot and wet and his fingers thrust into her
easily, eliciting a cry from deep in her throat.* Eric
nearly dropped the paper.

He locked his knees as his pulse quickened and his
body reacted to that one simple sentence. Quickly, his
gaze flicked up to the header on the paper and he read:
Magdelain Yvonne, Heated Storm, pg. 81. Magdelain
Yvonne? That was Maggie! Magdelain Yvonne Carmichael.

Maggie had written this?

Numb, moving by rote, Eric pulled out her desk
chair and sank into it, his eyes still glued to the paper
in his hand. A small lighted ceramic Christmas tree,
situated at the corner of her desk, provided all the
illumination he needed. He started at the top of the
page and began reading.

It was by far the most sensual, erotic, explicit passage he'd ever read outside of porn. But porn was unemotional and there was nothing unemotional in the deeply provocative love scene his Maggie had written.

When the paper ended—right in the middle of the female protagonist experiencing a gut-wrenching orgasm thanks to the guy's patience and talented fingers—Eric nearly groaned. His own hand clenched into a fist as he considered touching Maggie in just that way, watching her face while he made her come, feeling her body tighten around his fingers, feeling her wetness, her heat, and hearing her hoarse cry.

Where the hell was the rest of it?

Frantically he looked at her desk, moving papers aside and lifting files, but it was all business-related things. He opened a drawer and peeked inside, feeling like a total bounder but unable to stop himself. The drawer had only more files and notations in it. So he tried the others. Finally, in the drawer at the bottom of her desk, hidden beneath a thick thesaurus, he found the rest of the manuscript.

With no hesitation at all he slipped page 81 into place and settled back in the chair to read from the beginning. He was still there when the cleaning crew arrived. He'd just reached the end—which wasn't the end at all. Maggie needed several more chapters to finish the story, but already Eric could tell that she was very talented. He'd gotten so absorbed in the story he'd almost forgotten it was written by Maggie, and simply began enjoying it.

When he had remembered it was written by Maggie, he'd been hit with such a wave of lust he broke out in a sweat.

He'd never read a romance. He'd had no idea they were so good, so full of fast-paced plot and great characterization. Just like his mystery novels, only with more emphasis on the emotional side of the relationship. And lots more sex. *Great sex.* He liked it.

The only problem, to his mind, was the physical descriptions of the characters. The blond female was voluptuous, with large breasts and generously rounded hips and a brazenness that Eric had to admit was sexy as sin. She in no way resembled Maggie.

So why the hell did the male character so closely resemble him?

Maggie had given him the same height, same eyes, same dark hair. Even some of the things the guy said were words right out of Eric's mouth. And his wardrobe . . . well, he had the exact same clothes hanging in his closet at home.

The only major difference was that the guy in the story had finally gotten the heroine naked and in the sack for some really hot action. Hell, not only that, but he'd come three times thanks to the heroine's enthusiasm, something Eric wasn't even sure was possible.

Yet Eric was going home each night to an empty bed.

Well beyond the crazed stage, Eric was highly affronted, and jealous, that his fictitious character could take what he'd denied himself.

Was this, perhaps, what Maggie really wanted?

His heart pounded with both excitement and resentment. Ha! He was on to her now. It made his insides clench to realize she wasn't nearly as inexperienced as he'd always let himself believe. No way could she have devised such graphic sex scenes out of the depth of imagination.

In hindsight, he admitted Maggie was too sexy, too vivacious, to have stayed inexperienced for long. His nobility in attempting to wait had come back and bitten him in the ass. But that was over with now. She wanted him, had made love to him in fiction, and no more would he play the gallant schmuck, giving her plenty of time and space.

If Maggie wanted to write about sexual satisfaction, he'd show her sexual satisfaction! She'd started this tonight with her damned mistletoe and her teasing and her invitations.

His little Maggie was in for a hell of a surprise.

Despite Eric's heated plans, it bothered him immensely to put the book back in her drawer, where anyone might be able to find it. He'd have to talk to her about that—after he showed her that no fictitious character had anything on him when it came to reality.

He buried the manuscript under books and papers, just as she'd had it, then piled in a few more things, trying to be extra cautious. He was aware of a fine tension in his muscles, a touch of aroused excitement.

Eric glanced at his watch, saw that it was seven o'clock, and by the time he could reach Maggie's, it'd likely be eight. But that wasn't so late, and now he had a damn good reason to call on her tonight. He felt for the mistletoe he'd put in his pocket, and grinned when his fingers closed around it.

Maggie was a writer. A very talented, very erotic writer. And she wanted him; he had no more doubts about that. If he couldn't have Maggie for a wife, at least he could have this, and if all went as planned, she'd be his, not in matrimony, but in a basic, physical way that was even more binding.

For the first time in six months, things seemed to be getting back on track.

THREE

Maggie hurried out of the shower when she heard the doorbell peal. The pizza she'd ordered must have arrived early, so she trotted out of the room even as she pulled on her oldest, thickest robe. Her wet hair was wrapped in a towel, turban-style, and her bare feet left damp indentations in the plush carpet.

On the way to the door she made certain her cloth belt was securely tied and grabbed money for a tip. She ordered so many pizzas that the owner of the small restaurant let her run a tab, which she paid at the end of each month.

She wrenched the door open just as the doorbell chimed again. "Sorry, you got here quicker than . . . I . . . thought. . . ."

Eric stood there, snowflakes clinging to his midnight hair, his cheeks ruddy from the cold, his gaze blazing with some emotion that she couldn't begin to decipher. At the sight of her, his eyes narrowed and did a slow study of her from head to toe. She felt it like a tactile stroke, flesh on flesh. Ignoring her mute surprise, he stepped in, which forced her to step back. Holding her gaze, he pushed the door shut.

Maggie shivered. A cold blast of winter air had preceded Eric, but that wasn't what caused the gooseflesh to rise on her damp skin. No, Eric brought with him the scent of the brisk outdoors, his delicious co-

logne, and his own unique smell, guaranteed to make
her melt. She never failed to react to it with a delicate
shudder and a hungry tingling inside.

He looked so good, and here she stood looking her
worst! Her makeup was gone, her hair in a towel, and
her robe was so ratty it would had been generous to
describe it as broken-in.

"You expecting someone?"

There was a growled undertone to his words that
Maggie didn't understand. She pressed her hands to
her warm cheeks even as she began to explain. "I
thought you were the pizza guy."

The frown disappeared. With a small predatory
smile, Eric looked her over once again, and there was
so much heat, so much satisfaction in his gaze, she
suddenly felt too warm for the thick robe. "Do you
always greet deliverymen dressed like this?"

"No." She pulled the lapels of her robe together at
her throat, a five-dollar bill clenched in her fist. "I
thought he was early. Usually I have plenty of time
to shower and change. I could have just let him leave
the pizza outside the door, but I wanted to tip him. It
is almost Christmas, and the weather isn't the
best. . . ."

Eric reached out and slowly plucked the money
from her hand. In the process his knuckles grazed
lightly over the top of her breast, across her chest and
throat. "Sweetheart, if you answer the door that way,
you won't need any further tip, believe me."

Mouth hanging open, she blinked at him, dazed by
what she assumed—*hoped*—was a compliment. Eric
gazed briefly at her mouth before abruptly turning

away. Maggie watched as he laid the money on the entry table and then looked around her home with frank interest. She cleared her throat. "I . . . I didn't expect you tonight."

"I know." He said the words gently, and with some great, hidden meaning. "I changed my mind about waiting until tomorrow. Am I interrupting any plans?"

None that she would mind having interrupted. She'd hoped to work on her book for a few hours, which was why she'd ordered the fast food. Whenever she typed, she ate. The two just seemed to go hand in hand, which, because she was always pressed for time since taking over for her father, was a blessing. Heaven knew she rarely had time for a sit-down meal. "I was just going to get some . . . work done."

"Ah." He gave her a wicked, suggestive grin. "Maybe I can help?"

She got warm with just the thought. Eric help her with her writing? She didn't think so. For now, she was still a closet writer, not telling any of her non-writing friends. As the president of the company, she couldn't imagine how her business associates might react to the fact she wrote very racy romance novels. She wasn't ashamed of what she did, but she simply didn't need the added hassle of speculation. At various conventions, she'd heard all the jeers and jokes about how a romance writer researched. For her, research on the love scenes was simply daydreaming about Eric. There were parts of him in every hero she created; there had to be, for her to consider the men heroes.

Until she resolved the issue of her new position in

the company, she wouldn't breathe a word about her
need to create characters and romances.

"It's nothing that can't wait." Belatedly, she realized they were still standing just inside the door. She
blushed again. "Come on in."

His hand lifted to trail along a looping pine gar-
land, fastened in place around her doorframe with
bright red and silver bows. He seemed intrigued by
her Christmas decorations, examining the dancing
Santa on the table where he'd placed her five-dollar
tip, before gazing across the room to her collections
of candles displayed on the fireplace mantel and the
corner of the counter that separated her kitchen from
her living space.

Every tabletop held some sort of Christmas para-
phernalia, old and new. Eric was right that she loved
the holidays and rejoiced in celebrating them.

Her small, freshly cut tree, heavily laden with ornaments and tinsel and lights, blinked brightly at the
opposite side of the room. It fit perfectly in the small
nook just in front of her desk and work space.

Eric nodded in satisfaction. "This is more like
you."

She raised a brow, questioning.

"The holiday spirit," he explained, but his voice
trailed off as his gaze lit on her laptop computer and
the piles of paper littering her scarred antique oak
desk.

Good grief, she'd all but forgotten about her newest
chapters sitting out! From this distance, there was no
way Eric could tell what it was, but that didn't reassure her overly. Trying to look nonchalant, Maggie

crossed the room and closed her laptop quickly, then stacked the papers and shoved them in a drawer.

Eric watched her so closely, she flinched. "Bringing work home?" he asked.

As he spoke, he pulled off his shearling jacket and hung it on her coat tree beside her wool cape. And just that, the sight of the two garments hanging side by side, made her wistful. It would be so nice if he hung his coat there every night.

"Uh, nothing important." She preferred working on the computer at her office during her lunch breaks, since the monitor was much bigger and easier to see than the laptop. But she also worked at home whenever she could. Finishing up a book on deadline while working a fifty-hour-a-week job was grueling. Once she finished this book, she planned to buy a new computer for her home. But the idea of getting things set up and functioning at this particular moment, with the rush of the holidays, the pressure of a deadline, and her escalating sexual frustration, was more than she could bear. The past six months had been adjustment enough. She didn't need the aggravation of breaking in a new computer.

Eric started toward her with a slow, deliberate stride.

She cleared her throat, gave one last glance at her desk to make sure nothing obvious was still out, then said, "Why don't I get us something to drink?"

She hoped to escape to the kitchen, thinking to divert Eric from his path. Though everything was now put away, she'd feel better if he kept plenty of distance between himself and the desk.

Before she could take two steps, Eric stopped her with a large hand on her elbow. Her living room was small and cozy, but how he'd moved across it so quickly, she couldn't imagine.

"Your place is nice. I haven't seen it before."

Until her father's death, she'd lived in their family home with him. Eric had been to that house many times. But since then, he'd been avoiding her for the most part, despite her efforts to get closer to him.

"After Daddy died," she whispered, "I couldn't quite take living in the house. It seemed too big, too cold, and I missed him too much. So I moved here." Her home was now a moderately sized condominium that suited her perfectly. She had her own small yard, complete with patio and privacy fence, a fireplace, and a balcony off her bedroom.

The space where her desk and various office equipment sat had been intended as a breakfast nook, but she'd commandeered the space for her office.

Her bedroom, a spare room, and the bath were all upstairs. Eric was looking at the heavy desk and she said quickly, "I kept Daddy's desk from home, and some of his furniture."

Maggie watched as Eric made note of the two straight-backed armchairs flanking the fireplace. They were antique also, repadded with a soft velvety material that complemented the subtle striping in her own overstuffed beige, rose, and burgundy sofa. Marble-topped tables that had been in her family for over fifty years were situated at either end of the sofa and each held an array of framed photos and Christmas bric-a-brac. On the matching coffee table was a large glass dish filled with candies, and two more fat candles. Over the warmly glowing parquet floor was a large thick area rug that had once decorated her father's library.

Nodding, his hand still cupped securely around her arm, Eric said, "You and your father were very close, weren't you?"

The warmth of his hand made casual conversation difficult. "I think more so than most daughters and fathers, because my mother had passed away when I was so young." She shrugged, but the sadness never failed to touch her when she thought of her father. "It was always just Dad and me, and he was the best father in the world."

Eric tugged her closer and stood looking down into her face. Memories flitted through her mind, the way he'd held her on his lap and let her cry the day her father had passed away. Eric had been the only other person she'd wanted to grieve with. When she'd come to him, he hadn't questioned her, hadn't hesitated. He'd held her, and she'd been comforted.

Eric lifted his free hand and smoothed her cheek. The touch was intimate and exciting. "I'm sorry you've caught me looking so wretched," she blurted.

He smiled and his hand slipped around her neck, his rough fingertips teasing her skin even as he bent his head. "You look adorable."

Maggie barely absorbed the absurd compliment before the feel of his mouth on hers scattered her wits. But this kiss was gentle and fleeting, his warm mouth there and then gone, leaving her lips tingling, her breath catching. Making her want so much more. She leaned toward him, hoping he'd take the hint—and her doorbell rang.

"You go get dried off," he whispered as he teased the corner of her mouth with his thumb, "and I'll get the pizza."

Flustered, she stepped back and retightened her belt. "It'll just take me a few minutes to change and get my hair combed out."

Eric straightened her chenille lapels, letting the backs of his hands glide over her upper chest, then lower. His knuckles barely fell short of actually coming into contact with her nipples. She gasped, waiting, in an agony of anticipation.

He met her encouraging gaze and ordered in a low voice, "No, don't change. I like this. It's sexy."

"It is?" She looked down at the faded peach robe, threadbare in some spots where the chenille had fallen out from too many washings. Bemusement shook her out of her stupor. "*This* is sexy?"

"Are you naked beneath it?"

She gulped. "Yes."

His hazel eyes glowed with heat. "Damn right it's sexy."

She turned on her heel and stumbled out of the room. Eric appeared to be here for a reason, and her heart was racing so fast she could barely breathe. "I'll be right back," she called over her shoulder.

"Take your time," he answered on his way to her front door, but within five minutes she had her hair combed out and nearly dry, a touch of subtle makeup on, and her best perfume dabbed into the most secret places.

Eric didn't stand a chance.

*   *   *

Eric had set the pizza in the kitchen and was studying Maggie's colorful tree when he felt her presence behind him. He turned slowly and was met with the sight of her bright, expectant gaze. She watched him so closely, he felt singed. Anticipation rode him hard.

Maggie might enjoy writing hot love scenes, but he intended to see that she enjoyed experiencing them even more.

The idea of getting Maggie Carmichael hot made blood surge to his groin, swelling his sex painfully and making his heart race. He wanted everything from her, but he'd take what he could get.

"Come here," he whispered.

Lips parted, her pulse visibly racing, Maggie padded toward him on bare feet. She moved slowly, as if uncertain of his intent. Good. She had teased him at work, tempting him with that killer kiss beneath the mistletoe and then darting away. Did she sense her teasing had come to an end?

When she got close enough, Eric casually looped his arms around her waist. His hands rested on the very top of her sweetly rounded behind. Though his fingers twitched with the need to cuddle her bottom, to see if it was as soft and resilient as he'd always imagined, he didn't give in to the urge. That would be too easy, for both of them.

Nuzzling her cheek, he asked, "Do you know why I'm here, sweetheart?"

Her small palms opened on his chest and she nodded. "I think so."

He lightly bit her neck, making her gasp, then

laved the small spot with his tongue. Fresh from her
bath, her skin tasted warm and soft and was scented
by something other than Maggie herself. That disappointed him. Why did women always try to conceal
their own delicious smell with artificial scents?

"You're wearing perfume," he noted out loud.

"I . . . yes."

"Where all did you put it, Maggie?"

Maggie's breath deepened, came faster. She shook
her head, as if she didn't understand.

"When I'm this close to you," he said softly, "I
want to smell *you.*"

Eric let his hand glide up her waist to the outer
curves of her breast. "When I kiss you here," he said,
holding her gaze as his thumb brushed inward, just
touching the edge of a tightly beaded nipple, "I don't
want to be distracted with the smell of perfume. Do
you understand?"

Her whole body trembled with her repressed excitement. "Yes."

"And," he added, trailing his fingers slowly downward, watching her, judging her response, "when I
kiss you . . . here—"

"Oh, God." Her eyes drifted shut and she shivered.

"I want to know your scent." His fingers brushed,
so very gently, between her thighs. Her lips parted,
her head tilted back. The robe was thick enough that
his touch would only be teasing, but still she jerked.

Eric took the offering of her throat and drew her
tender flesh against his teeth, deliberately giving her
a hickey. He wanted to mark her as his own—all over.
She moaned and snuggled closer to him.

"Damn, you taste good." He waited a heartbeat, letting that sink in, then added in a whisper, "I can't wait to taste you everywhere." His fingers were still between her thighs, cupping her mound, and he pressed warmly against her to let her know exactly what he meant.

Her hands curled into fists, knotting in his shirt. He waited for her to get a visual image of that, already planning his next move while he had her off balance.

Her eyes opened, hotly intent. "I'd like to taste you, too," she answered, and Eric barely bit back his groan.

"Damn." If she got him visualizing things like her mouth on him, he'd never last! He gave a half laugh at her daring, which earned him a startled expression. Maggie never failed to amaze him. "I want this to last, you little tease. Don't push me."

She didn't deny the teasing part, and simply asked, "This?"

"Mmmm." He slipped his hand under her collar and rubbed her nape, feeling the cool slide of her damp, heavy hair over the back of his hand. "I want you so much I'm about to go crazy with it."

"Eric." She breathed his name, attempting to wiggle closer to him.

He held her off. "No, not yet. I need you to want me as much, Maggie."

With her hands clenched in his shirt, she attempted to shake him. He didn't budge, and her brown eyes grew huge and uncertain. "But I do!"

"Shhh." He pressed his thumb over her lips, silencing her. "Not yet. But you will. Soon."

Wind whistled outside the French doors behind her

desk, blowing powdery snowflakes against the glass. The twinkle lights on her tree gave a magical glow to the room. Eric stepped away from her, amazed at how difficult it was to do. "You need to eat your pizza before it gets cold."

Maggie's breathing was audible in the otherwise silent room. With a quick glance, Eric saw that her hands were folded over her middle, as if to hold in the sweet ache of desire, and her nipples were thrusting points against the softness of her robe. His testicles tightened, his cock throbbing at this evidence of her arousal, but he refused to make this so easy. He'd been suffering for a hell of a long time, wanting her, yet not wanting to make her unhappy. Now he knew that she was as physically attracted as he. But if that was all they could have, he wanted it to be the best it could be. And that meant being patient.

"Forget the pizza," she said. "I'm . . . I'm not hungry anymore."

Eric noted her stiff posture, the color in her cheeks. "Is that right?"

She lifted her chin in that familiar way that made his heart swell. "I'm hungry for *you*. So stop teasing me."

Against his will, Eric felt his mouth curling in a pleased smile. Maggie liked giving orders, further evidence that she fit the role of "boss" to perfection. He nodded slowly, keeping his gaze locked to her own, and said, "All right, sweetheart."

She accepted his hand when he reached out to her, her slender chilled fingers nestling into his warm palm. Eric turned them toward the sitting area and led

Maggie to a single straight-backed chair. The Christmas tree with its soft glow was behind her, lending the only illumination other than the faint light from the kitchen.

Maggie looked at the chair, then at the very soft, long couch, but he could tell she wasn't brazen enough to insist they sit side by side, which he'd been counting on. If they settled together on the couch, she'd end up beneath him in no time and all his seduction would be over before it had really started.

That wouldn't do.

With a soft grumble, more to herself, though he heard her plain enough, Maggie slid into the chair and then fussed with her robe, making certain it folded modestly over her legs. A futile effort on her part, but for the moment he let it go.

Hiding his grin, Eric walked behind Maggie. She stiffened, alert to his every move. Eric touched her hair.

"Do you have any idea how much I loved your hair long?"

Tipping her head back, she looked at him upside down. "No."

Eric smoothed his hands over her throat, and when her lips parted, he leaned down and kissed her lightly. "I used to imagine your hair all spread out on the pillow, *my* pillow."

"But . . ." She started to twist around to face him more surely, and he held her shoulders to still her movements.

"I used to think about the fact that your hair was long enough and thick enough to hide your breasts.

You could have stood topless in front of me, and I wouldn't have been able to see a thing. But now"— he slid his hands over her shoulders and cupped her small firm breasts completely—"there's no way you can hide from me. Can you, sweetheart?"

Her back flattened hard against the chair and she held herself rigid, not in fear or rejection, but in surprise. The erratic drumming of her heart teased his palm. God, she felt good. Soft, round. Moving lazily, he chafed her nipples with his open hands until she gripped the arms of the chair in a death hold and her every breath sounded like a stifled moan.

Impatient, Eric loosened the top of her robe and parted it enough to see her pale breasts and her taut pink nipples. He caught his breath.

Just that quickly she jerked away and turned to face him, yanking her robe closed in the process. There was so much vulnerability in her face, he felt his heart softening even as his erection pushed painfully against his slacks.

Her bottom lip quivered and she stilled it by holding it in her teeth. Both hands secured her robe, layering it over her throat so that not a single patch of her soft flesh showed.

Eric slowly circled the chair, never releasing her from his gaze. When he was directly in front of her, her face, as well as her fascinated and wary gaze, on a level with his lap, he laid one large hand on top of her head. Her hair was cool in contrast to the heat he saw in her cheeks. "What is it, babe?"

She squeezed her eyes closed.

"Maggie?" Using one finger, he tipped up her chin.

Was he moving too fast, despite her bravado of wanting him to get on with it? He frowned slightly with the thought. "I am going to look at you, you know."

She winced. "It's just that . . . I'm actually sort of . . . small."

Ah. Biting back his smile, Eric knelt in front of her and covered her hands with his own. Carefully wresting them away from their secure hold on fabric and modesty, he said, "You're actually sort of perfect."

She trembled, but met his gaze. "You like big-breasted women."

He remembered the woman in her story, with her full-blown, overripe figure. Was this why she'd put that particular female with his fictional counterpart? He ran this thumb over her knuckles, soothing her, then loosely clasped the lapels of her robe. "What makes you think so?"

She held herself in uncertain anxiety. Did she expect him to rip the robe away despite her wishes? Never would he deliberately push her or make her uneasy. He cared far too much about her for that. No, his plans were for sensual suspense, not embarrassment.

A small sound of frustration, or maybe more like resignation, escaped her. "*All* men like big breasts."

Perched on the edge of her seat, she looked ready to take flight regardless of the fact that Eric was on his knees in front of her, blocking her in. To prevent her from trying to do just that, he leaned forward until her legs parted and he was able to settle himself between them. Her eyes widened and her hands automatically clasped his shoulders for balance.

He released her robe to wrap his long fingers around her hips, then snugged her that small distance closer until their bodies met, heat on heat. He pushed his hips against her.

In a low growl that was beyond his control, Eric asked, "I've had a hard-on since I walked in the door. Does that feel like disinterest to you?"

Mute, she shook her head while staring into his eyes.

He cupped her breasts again, still outside the robe, and closed his eyes at the exquisite feel of her. "Beautiful. And sexy."

"But . . ."

"I want to see your pretty little breasts, Maggie. I want to see all of you. Will you trust me?"

She stared at his mouth. "Will you kiss me again first?"

He liked it that she wanted his mouth.

Leaning forward, he said, "I'll kiss you everywhere. In time." Her lips parted on a deep sigh as their breaths mingled and he took her mouth. So soft, he thought, amazed that a kiss could feel so incredible, taste so good. He devoured her with that kiss and relished her accelerated breathing. His tongue sank inside and was stroked by hers, hot and damp and greedy. It went on and on and when she relaxed completely, when her open thighs gave up their resistance and she slowly sank back in the chair, half reclining with her legs opened around his hips in a carnal sprawl, he lifted his head.

Watching her, caught by the sight of her velvety dark gaze and swollen mouth, he touched her lapels again. She swallowed, but didn't stop him when he slowly parted the material. As his gaze dipped to look at her, his heartbeat punched heavily inside his chest.

He couldn't imagine a woman more perfectly made. Her rib cage was narrow, her skin silky and pale. Her soft little breasts shimmered with her panting, nervous breaths. Pale pink, tightly pinched nipples begged for his mouth as surely as she had. "Oh, Maggie."

Her hands fell from his arms and flattened on the seat beside her hips, as if she needed to steady herself. She inhaled sharply, then held her breath as he moved forward to nuzzle against her. Her body, softened only moments before, quickly flexed with tightened muscles and churning need. Teasing, he circled one nipple with tiny kisses, driving himself insane as he resisted the urge to draw her into the damp heat of his mouth, to suck her hard, to sate himself on her.

"Eric . . ."

"Shhh." He flicked her with the very tip of his tongue. "We've got all night."

"I won't last all night."

He chuckled soothingly and switched to the other breast. Deliberately taking her by surprise, he closed his teeth around her tender flesh and carefully tugged. Her whole body jerked; her hands clasped his head, trying to urge him closer.

From one second to the next, his patience evaporated. Wrapping one forearm around her hips, he anchored her as close as he could get her, pelvis to pelvis, heat to heat, then suckled her into his mouth.

Her groan, long and intense and accompanied by

the clench of her body, nearly pushed him over the edge. He drew on her, his head muzzy with the reality of what he was doing, of who he was with. The mere fantasy couldn't begin to compare.

Openmouthed, he kissed his way to her other nipple, greedy for her. She guided him, squirming and shifting, and sighed when he latched onto her breast again as if she needed it, needed him, with the same intensity he felt.

"Do you see," he muttered around her damp nipple, "just how perfect you are?"

She hitched one leg around his hips and hugged him closer. Instinctively, she moved against his rigid erection, seeking what he wouldn't yet give.

Eric slowly pulled away from her, determined on his course.

"Eric . . ." She started to sit up, reaching for him while her legs tightened.

Pushing the robe down to her elbows, trapping her arms; his position between her thighs, combined with her movements, had parted the material over her legs, which now left her virtually naked. The robe framed her body, with the silly belt still tied around her middle. Her belly was adorable, and he kissed it even as he remonstrated with her for her small lie.

"You're not naked, sweetheart." He touched the waistband of her white cotton bikini panties. "Not that I'm complaining, because this is very cute."

"Don't . . . don't make fun of me, Eric."

He managed a grin in spite of the hot throbbing of his body. "Why would I make fun of you? Because of your conservative underwear? I like it."

"Like you like small breasts?"

His gaze met hers. In the pose of a confirmed hedonist, she lounged back, face flushed, body open to the pleasure he'd give her. Her dark hair was mussed, her eyes soft, her lips swollen. He absorbed her near nudity, her innate sexuality, and said gently, "Like I like you."

Her eyes closed briefly, then opened when he dipped one rough fingertip beneath the waistband of her panties and teased her stomach, low enough to just brush her glossy dark curls, high enough to keep her on a keen edge of need.

Her breath came in hungry pants. "Are you going to make love to me, Eric?"

"Absolutely."

"When?"

Situated as he was between her thighs, he could smell her desire, the rich musk of arousal. His nostrils flared. It was a heady scent, mixing with the perfume she'd put on, making his cock surge in his pants, his muscles quiver. "When I think you're ready."

"I'm ready now."

"Let's see." Slowly, he lifted each of her legs and draped them over the arms of the chair. The position left her wide open in an erotic, carnal posture. Eric trailed his rough fingertips up the insides of her thighs, seeing her suck in her stomach, hearing her gasp. Her breasts heaved in excitement and anticipation.

She looked so damn enticing he couldn't resist her. Without warning, he kissed her through the soft damp cotton, his mouth open, his tongue pressing hard. He breathed deeply and felt himself filled with her. He could taste her—and quickly grabbed her hips to hold her steady when she would have lurched away from sheer reaction.

She said his name in a breathless plea.

Her response thrilled him, drove him. He wanted to pull her panties aside so his tongue could stroke her slick naked flesh, heated by her desire, silky wet in preparation for much more than his tongue.

He gave her his finger instead.

Leaning back to watch her, he wedged his large hand inside her panties, stroked her once, twice, then pressed deep. The instant, almost spastic thrust of her hips, her coarse groan, the spontaneous clasp of hidden muscles, told him she liked that very much.

"Jesus, you're tight," he ground out through clenched teeth, struggling to maintain control. "And wet."

"Eric . . ."

He stared at her through burning eyes. "Am I hurting you, babe?"

She groaned, whispered something unintelligible, and her sleek, hot flesh squeezed his finger almost painfully.

"That's it," he encouraged softly, feeling himself near the edge. "Hold on to me." He stroked, slowly pulling his finger out, then thrusting it back in, deep, teasing acutely sensitive tissues, mesmerized by the sight of his darker hand caught between her white panties and pale belly, her glossy black curls damp with excitement.

Eyes closed, body arched, she gave herself up to him as he fingered her, stretching her a bit, playing with her a lot. He pressed his finger deeper, measuring her, then pulled out slowly to tease her taut clitoris, making her entire body shudder.

He wanted all of her at once; he wanted her to feel all the same desperate need he felt. And maybe, just maybe, if he did this well enough, if he made her feel half of what he felt . . . what? She'd give up the presidency of her father's company just to marry him?

Eric hated himself for letting the selfish thought intrude for even one split second. He didn't want her to give up anything. He didn't want her to be forced into choices.

He loved her. *Goddamn it.*

To banish those thoughts, he pulled his hand away and stripped her panties down her thighs. She blinked at him, grabbing the chair arms for balance as he re-adjusted her and then once again settled himself close. Those long luscious legs of hers looked especially sinful lying open, leaving her totally vulnerable to him, displaying her pink feminine flesh, swollen and slick. Her hips lifted, seeking his touch again. He had to taste her, and leaned forward for one leisurely, deep stroke of his tongue.

Maggie cried out, her entire body jerking in response. Eric was lost.

With a harsh groan he covered her with his body, kissing her mouth deeply, consuming her, taking what he could because he couldn't have it all. Her small body cradled his larger frame perfectly. "I want you so fucking much," he rasped.

"Yes!"

He cupped her breast with a roughness he couldn't control and rocked his hips hard against her, feeling her pulsing heat through his slacks. She was silky soft, warm and female everywhere, and he wanted to absorb every inch of her. With one hand he lifted her soft bottom, grinding himself against her.

"Eric!"

Stunned, he looked at her face and watched her climax, her teeth clenched, her throat arched, her breasts flushed. His heart seemed to slow to a near stop as love consumed him, choking out all other emotions.

She whimpered as he continued to move her against him, more slowly now, carefully dragging out her pleasure, his fingers sinking deep in her soft bottom, letting her ride it out to the last small spasm until finally she stilled and her muscles relaxed.

Limp, eyelashes damp on her flushed cheeks, her lips still parted, she was even more than he'd ever imagined. Eric gathered her close and rocked her gently, attempting to regain control of his own emotions—which were far beyond sexual.

As if each limb were made of lead, Maggie struggled to resettle her legs, locking them around his hips. So slowly he couldn't anticipate what she wanted, she got her arms around his neck, one hand tangled in his hair. Finally her sated, dazed eyes opened.

"Sorry," she muttered in such an endearingly drowsy and somewhat shy voice, he couldn't help but smile with a swell of satisfaction and tenderness.

His hand still held her small backside and he gave her a gentle, cuddling squeeze. "For what, sweetheart?" His tone was soft in deference to the moment.

She studied his face, her own pink, then managed a halfhearted shrug. "Okay. I'm not sorry." She yawned. "Now will you please make love to me?"

How humor could get him while he was so rock hard he could have driven in railroad spikes, he didn't know. But the chuckle bubbled up and he tucked his face into her breasts as he gave in to it.

"Are you laughing at me?"

She didn't sound particularly concerned over that possibility, which made the humor expand.

"Eric?"

Her hand tightened in his hair, causing him to wince. He lifted up, kissed the end of the nose, and grinned. "I'm just happy."

"Why?"

Tenderly, he smoothed a tendril of dark hair behind her ear. "Well, now, I just made Maggie Carmichael come. Why else?"

She snorted, but her face was so hot she looked sunburned. Her hand loosened its grip, her fingers threading through his hair, petting him. "I've wanted you so long, it wouldn't have taken much. Except you kept playing around. . . ."

"Look who's talking."

She raised a brow, but the effect was ruined by another yawn.

"Never mind, sleepyhead. Have I put you out for the night?"

"Absolutely not." She shifted subtly, then whispered, "I'm just dying to feel you inside me, Eric."

"Jesus." He didn't feel like laughing now. Though

his legs were shaky, he managed to loosen her hold and stand. He didn't want to make love to her in a damn chair. He wanted her in bed, under him, accepting him.

He reached a hand out to her and when she took it, he hauled her up—and then over his shoulder.

"Eric!"

Flipping the robe out of his way, he pressed his cheek to her hip and kissed her rounded behind. "The bedrooms are upstairs?"

She had both hands latched on to his belt in back, hanging on for dear life. "Yes, but don't you dare. . . . Eric, put me down!"

Instead, he stroked the backs of her thighs with his free hand as he started up the steps. Using just his fingertips, he teased her with light butterfly touches, getting her ready again, keeping her ready.

"Eric . . . *Eric.*" She groaned as he explored her.

FOUR

"I'm done playing, Eric. Make love to me."

As if he hadn't heard her, Eric strolled into the bedroom and slowly brought her around in his arms. His strength amazed her, not that she was a heavyweight, but considering how boneless she felt right now . . . Of course, he hadn't climaxed.

And she wanted to remedy that as soon as possible.

The second her feet touched the floor, she reached for his belt. Thankfully, he didn't stop her. Instead he began emptying his pants pockets, putting his wallet, a condom, and the sprig of mistletoe he'd removed earlier from the office doorway, onto her nightstand. Seeing the condom and the mistletoe so close together, Maggie shivered.

As she hurriedly worked on his clothes, Eric calmly unknotted the fabric belt still caught around her waist. He finished first and tossed her robe aside. His hands, so incredibly large and warm, settled on her waist, holding her loosely, allowing her to slide his leather belt free and then waiting patiently while she unbuttoned and unzipped his slacks.

"Your hands are shaking," he noted.

She peeked up at him. "I'm excited. I've wanted you . . . well, longer than you can imagine."

"Try me."

To distract him from her words, she abandoned his

slacks and quickly began unbuttoning his shirt. The promise of his nudity gave her incentive and her fingers literally flew until his shirt was hanging open.

With a type of reverent awe, she bared his chest. Fingers spread, she ran her hands over his upper torso, absorbing the feel of crisp dark hair, solid muscle, and manly warmth. "I've wanted you since the first time I saw you."

The breathless words took him by surprise, then skepticism narrowed his eyes. "You were barely seventeen, sweetheart. A child."

"Mmmm. And so creative." With the edge of her thumb, Maggie brushed his right nipple and heard his intake of breath. His knees locked. "I got so tongue-tied around you," she whispered, "because at night, alone in my bed, I imagined this very thing. Touching you, having you touch me."

She looked up, saw his flared nostrils, the dark aroused color high on his cheekbones, and she went on tiptoe to kiss his chin, now rough with beard stubble.

Eric caught her wrists as she began a downward descent to his slacks. "You're saying you fantasized about me?"

"From the very beginning." She pulled her hands free and sank to her knees in front of him. She felt like a sexual supplicant, kneeling before him, naked, hot. His erection was a thick ridge plainly visible through his slacks. She leaned forward and pressed her cheek to him, nuzzling. "There's nothing I haven't done to you in my imagination."

"Maggie." One large hand cupped around her head, trembling.

"Lift your foot." He obliged and she tugged off first one shoe and sock, then started on the other. Her face close to his groin, deliberately tantalizing herself— and probably him, given how heavy his breathing had become—she knotted her hands in his slacks and pulled them down.

Eric didn't move as she reached for his snug cotton boxers. More slowly now, savoring the moment, she bared him.

Her breath caught. She'd never seen a fully grown man naked, up close, personal. She'd seen photos, which didn't do the male form justice.

Tentatively, she touched him with just her finger-tips and then smiled as he jerked, his erect flesh puls-ing, hot. A drop of fluid appeared on the broad head, and she used the tip of one finger to spread it around, testing the texture, exploring him.

Breath hissed out from between his teeth. "That's enough."

Maggie paid him no mind. In her novels, the men always pleasured the women with their mouths; the very idea of it excited her incredibly. But now she wondered why the reverse had never occurred to her. The idea of taking Eric into her mouth, licking him, tasting him, flooded her with heat and doubled her own desire.

"Tell me if I do this wrong," she whispered. And even as he cautioned her to stop, his voice a low, harsh growl, she wrapped one small hand around him to hold him steady. Amazingly, she could feel the beat of his heart in her palm, could feel him growing even more. Her tongue flattened on the underside of his hot, smooth flesh, slowly stroked up and over the tip—and Eric shattered.

She'd barely realized the taste of him, the velvety texture, before he went wild, shaking and gasping. He roughly pulled her to her feet and she found herself tossed on the bed. Before she'd finished bouncing, Eric had kicked his pants off and donned a rubber.

She opened her arms to him and he came down on top of her. Using his knee, he spread her legs wide, then wider still. "I wanted this to be slow," he said through his teeth, reaching down to open her with his fingers, "but I can't wait now."

She started to say she was glad, that she didn't want to wait, but then he thrust hard, entering her, filling her up, and she lost her breath in a rush.

It wasn't at all as she'd imagined, smooth and easy and romantic. Instead, Eric anchored a hand in her hair and held her face still for an all-consuming, wet kiss that made it impossible to breathe, impossible to think. He stroked into her fast and hard. *Deep.* And though she was aware of her own wetness, her own carnal need, the tight friction was incredible.

Her senses rioted over a mix of heated perceptions. There was discomfort, because she was small and inexperienced, but also building pleasure, too acute to bear, because this was Eric and she'd wanted him forever.

Not romantic, but so wonderful, so real and erotic and . . .

Her climax hit suddenly, making her clutch at him,

her fingers digging deep into his shoulders, her heels pressing hard into the small of his back. Eric lifted his head, jaw locked tight, eyes squeezed shut, and gave a raw groan as he came.

Through the haze of her own completion, Maggie watched him. She loved him so much, and she wanted him, in every way, always. Seeing his every muscle taut and trembling, his temples damp with sweat, left her feeling curiously tender, softened by the love and the depletion of physical strength.

Eric slowly, very slowly, lowered himself back into her arms. His heart beat so hard against her breast, she felt it inside herself. Threading her fingers through his warm, silky hair, she said, "Eric?"

He gave a small grunt that she supposed might have been a response.

"Will you stay the night with me? Please?" If he refused, if he left now and this was all she'd ever have, her heart would simply crumble, leaving her empty.

But he didn't refuse her. Instead, his arms tightened and he rolled to his side, bringing her with him. Long seconds led into longer minutes before his breathing ultimately evened out. Idly, he stroked her, her shoulder, her hip, her back. "I'm not going anywhere," he finally said in a rough whisper.

She snuggled closer, letting out the breath she'd been holding.

Eric kissed her forehead and, with a sigh, moved to leave the bed. Enjoying the sight of his naked backside, Maggie watched him go into the bathroom, heard running water, the flush of the toilet, and then he came back. The condom was gone and Eric, in full frontal nudity, his sex now softly nestled in dark hair, was more appealing than she'd ever imagined a man could be. Amazingly, she wanted him again. She licked her lips.

Eric smiled at her as he climbed back into bed. "You little wanton, you," he whispered, and she heard the amusement in his tone. Tucking her into his side and covering them both, he affected a serious tone. "Maggie, this was your first—"

"Yes." She felt a little embarrassed over her inexperience. "I didn't want anyone but you. Not ever."

He absorbed that statement with a heavy silence, then kissed her temple with a gentleness that brought tears to her eyes. "I want you to tell me about this long-hidden admiration you have for me."

Maggie knew her time had come. It took her several seconds to screw up her courage before she could force herself to look up and face Eric. When she did, his hand cupped her cheek and there was a softness in his expression she'd never seen before.

She swallowed hard. "Not an admiration, Eric. Love."

He remained quiet, waiting.

"I've loved you," she declared, "since the first time I saw you. My father knew it, and that's why he left me the company. He believed you wanted it, and he had hoped . . . that is, he thought that perhaps the company would be a lure, to get you to notice me."

Eric stared at her as if someone had just hit him in the stomach. She felt him tense and prayed he'd at least hear her out.

Rushing, hoping to get it all said before she chickened out, she explained, "I don't want the company, Eric. I never have. I wish I'd known what my father was going to do, because I would have stopped him. Not only did it not lure you in, you've been distant since I got the damn controlling stock."

Eric sat up, his expression dumbfounded. Feeling suddenly naked, Maggie clutched the sheet to her throat and came up to her knees. "Eric, I swear we didn't mean to manipulate you. That is, I didn't even know until it was too late—"

"Shh." Eric put a finger to her lips, silencing her. He looked thoughtful, with a frown that wasn't quite annoyance, but rather confusion. "You don't want to run the company?"

Since his finger was still pressed to her mouth, she didn't try to reply. Instead, she shook her head.

Eric left the bed to pace. That was enough of a distraction to make her regret the damn topic. She wanted him back in bed with her. She wanted to do more exploring.

"Now that we're involved," he said, and he looked at her, daring her to challenge his statement, "there's going to be some gossip."

Maggie scrambled off the bed and stood before him, the sheet held in front of her. "I won't let anyone insult you, Eric, I swear!"

A grin flickered over Eric's firm mouth. "Ready to defend me, huh?" He touched her chin. "I can handle gossip, sweetheart. I just don't want it to hurt you."

Heart pounding, she said, "I can handle it—as long as you can."

"Then we're agreed." He cupped her face and kissed the end of her nose. "Now, about the company . . ."

"You don't have to worry that I'll make you responsible. I'm going to sell my shares. I don't want to be tied to the business so much. I have . . . other interests right now. And Daddy was only trying to make me happy—"

"You're not selling the shares."

Her brows lifted. "I'm not?"

"No. I'll run things for you." His expression was so intent, she squirmed. "If . . ." he said, emphasizing that one word beyond what was necessary, "if you'll marry me."

Maggie caught her breath. Slowly, to make certain she understood, she asked, "You're willing to take the extra shares off my hands—"

"No. The company will remain yours."

"But . . ."

"I won't have people saying you were part of a bargain, Maggie, that I married you for the company. I want it clear that I want you for *you,* not for the added benefits."

"Do you . . . see the company as a benefit?"

He shrugged. "I always assumed I would one day be in charge."

"But you don't want that." Maggie felt swamped in sudden confusion.

"Not true. It's just that I wanted you more." His voice dropped, became seductive. "Much, much more than any damn company."

"Oh."

Eric sat on the bed and pulled her into his lap—after he tossed the concealing sheet aside. Cupping her breast and watching intently as he thumbed her nipple into readiness, he said, "Just as you say you used to daydream about me, I sure as hell dreamed about you. I planned to make my intentions known after you graduated, except so many things happened then. You lost Drake and inherited a company. Everything got confused. You were missing your father, and I assumed, judging by your competence, that you enjoyed running the company. I thought if I came after you then, you'd never be certain what it was I wanted."

Maggie searched his face, almost afraid to believe. "But you wanted . . . me?"

"God, Maggie." Eric squeezed her tight, and his voice sounded raw with emotion. "I wanted you to the point I about went crazy." He kissed her, then kissed her again.

Big tears gathered in her eyes and she blinked hard to fight them off. "I was so afraid you'd never ever notice me. I tried everything. I thought if I was more sophisticated, if I showed you I wasn't a kid anymore, you'd stop ignoring me."

Eric riffled a hand through her hair. "I love you, Maggie. Exactly as you are, any way you want to be."

Maggie wanted things clarified about the company, but Eric returned to her mouth, and his hand on her breast was lightly teasing, and she felt him hardening against her bottom. She decided further discussion could wait.

*   *   *

Eric rolled over and reached for her, but she wasn't there. A heady contentment had him smiling even before he was completely awake. *Maggie was now his.* Once his eyes were fully open, he saw that it was still night. Where had Maggie gone?

He left the bed, shivering as the cool night air washed over his naked body. Before leaving her bedroom, he pulled on his slacks, but didn't bother buttoning or zipping them.

Creeping silently down the steps and into the living room, he found Maggie at her desk, writing by the lights of the Christmas tree and her laptop. Her beautiful silky hair tumbled around her face, and she'd donned the same soft robe, though sloppily, so that one shoulder was mostly exposed. The twinkling lights of the tree reflected in her big dark eyes while the eerie glow of moon-washed snow outside the French doors framed her in an opalescent halo.

She was absorbed in her writing, oblivious to her surroundings, and didn't notice him. Eric lounged against the wall watching her. So precious. A grin tugged at his mouth as he wondered exactly what scene she was working on now.

The sprig of mistletoe that he'd brought from the office lay on the desk beside her.

"Getting the facts down while they're still fresh in your mind?"

With a yelp, she jerked her head up to stare at him. "Eric! What are you doing down here?"

He strolled toward her, still smiling, filled with contentment and masculine satisfaction. "I was going to ask you the same thing."

She pushed her chair back and stood, then glanced at her laptop. Nervously she began to tidy her desk. She picked up the mistletoe. "I was just . . . too excited to sleep. I figured I might as well get some stuff done."

"Mm-hmm." Eric closed in on her and she turned her back to the desk, her hands clasped at her waist. The mistletoe crushed against her belly. "Ah, now, there's an idea," he said.

Maggie blinked. "What?"

He traced her stomach with one finger, edging underneath her robe. "I read part of your book at the office."

Her mouth fell open, then snapped shut and she scowled.

"You're incredibly talented."

The scowl disappeared. "I am?"

He nodded. "I can't wait to read the rest of it." Eric met her eyes and asked, "Have you been using me for research?"

"Oh, for crying out loud," she blustered, "I don't—"

"Because I wouldn't mind. At all." He kissed her lips, her throat. Pressing his palm against her beneath the mistletoe, he said, "I kind of like the idea."

A tad breathless, she said, "If you read the book, then you know we haven't done all the things that the characters did."

"But I'd sure like to." His fingers searched her through the chenille. "And the guy in your book reminded me a lot of me."

"Yes." She closed her eyes and sighed. "I've sold

three books, Eric. This one will be my fourth. I've written about a doctor, a Navy SEAL, a car salesman, and now a businessman."

Eric froze. "So who were the other guys?"

He watched her lips twitch into a smile. "They're all you, at least in part." Her beautiful brown eyes opened and she stared up at him. "They may not all look like you, but the qualities they have that make them interesting, that make them heroes women want to read about—those I get from you. Those are the things that are most important."

Her words touched his heart. "I do love you, Maggie."

With a crooked smile, she said, "And you like the way I write?"

"I think you're incredible." Slowly, deliberately teasing her, he dropped to his knees. "Will you let me read the rest?"

It took her a breathless moment to say, "When . . . when I'm finished with it."

Eric parted the robe and pressed a kiss to her naked belly, just beneath the mistletoe now crushed in her hands. "And you'll let me run the company for you?"

She dropped the mistletoe. It landed beside Eric's knee. Bracing her hands on the edge of her desk at either side of her hips, she said, "Yes, thank you."

Eric grinned. He used his thumbs to gently part her so he could kiss her where she'd feel it most. "And will you," he asked against her hot flesh, "marry me, sweetheart?"

Her groan was long and loud and unselfconscious. *"Yes."*

"I've got to hand it to you, Maggie," he said, feeling her legs tense. "This is the best Christmas bonus I've ever gotten."

EPILOGUE

Eric stood beside Maggie at the Christmas party as she called for everyone's attention. He had no idea what she might do, but he intended to be beside her regardless.

She positively glowed, he thought, watching her dark eyes as she laughed and held up a hand——a hand that sported an engagement ring she'd picked out yesterday. Her hair was pulled back by a red and green headband and she had tiny Christmas bows as earrings. Over her left breast, a miniature Santa head with a blinking red nose drew his attention. He loved it that she'd quickly given up her frumpy suits, and that she was every bit as energetic and enthusiastic as he remembered.

She was especially enthusiastic in bed. Eric had to chase those thoughts away, or be damned with a hard-on for the entire staff to see. He cleared his throat and concentrated on what Maggie was saying.

"This year," she called out, "besides getting the Christmas bonus bucks and a ham, I'm giving everyone a share of company stock."

Eyebrows lifted in surprise and a buzz of hushed conversation filled the hall. Eric stared at Maggie, floored by her declaration.

"It's not much," she explained, "but I didn't want controlling shares, and Eric refused to take them off my hands. So now, he and I are equal partners in the company, and all of you have a stake in it as well. I know my father would have approved."

Heads turned; everyone now staring at Eric. He chuckled, amused at Maggie's way of settling any thoughts of gossip.

"And just for fun, I wanted you all to know"—she flashed the ring, her smile wide—"we're getting married!"

A roar of applause took Eric by surprise. No one seemed the least surprised by her declaration, or suspicious of his motives. Maggie snuggled up against his side and he automatically slipped his arm around her.

Someone, he thought it might have been his secretary Janine, called out, "It's about time," and everyone laughed as if they all agreed.

Maggie put her hands on her hips and pretended to scowl. "How come none of you are surprised?" she asked, laughing.

Janine, accepting the role of leader, stepped forward at the encouragement of her fellow employees. "We've been taking bets," she explained with a smile, "on when the engagement would take place. Everyone could see you were both in love."

"You asked me out," Eric accused her.

"We all did." Janine shrugged, unrepentant. "We thought it might get Maggie moving. And that's why the guys asked Maggie out—"

Eric narrowed his eyes. "Yeah, who did that?" He scanned the crowd, but the men all started whistling and shuffling their feet, trying in vain to hide their humor. Maggie lightly punched Eric in the arm while laughing out loud.

The sound of her laughter never failed to turn him on. He wanted to get the party over with so he could take her home. "We're officially engaged," Eric stated, holding Maggie close, "so you can all keep your distance from her now. Understood?"

The men bobbed their heads, still grinning, while the women smiled indulgently.

Janine made a fist and waved it in the air. "A Christmas engagement. I win!"

Eric shook his head, then tipped up Maggie's chin. "No, I win." He didn't need mistletoe to prompt him. Right there, in front of everyone, he kissed Maggie until her knees went weak—and no one had a single doubt that love had brought them together.

A Night with Emily

Dee Holmes

ONE

He filled the doorway. Behind him, wind swirled the fresh dusting of snow through the winter night.

"Karen didn't tell me you would be here," he said in that slow, even tone he used when he was annoyed.

"Surprise." She gave him a bright smile, hiding the fact that she was indeed astonished.

"I hate surprises." He gave her a sour scowl.

"I remember."

His scowls got deeper. Her easy comebacks weren't working.

Johnny Cross remained standing in the doorway, looking cold and fierce and more sad than she'd ever remembered. His face was drawn and tight, shadowed by the December night, his black hair coated with snowflakes. He looked as if he wanted to back out and run far, far away.

Emily Madden had never thought of herself as a rescuer of the lost, nor did she now. She was a portrait artist and studying facial expressions and body language had become second nature. If she were to draw Johnny, she would have painted him in despair.

Shivering from the frigid air that blew in behind him, she said, "Why don't you come in and close the door?" Wearing comfy blue fleece, she sat on her haunches on the braided rug amid open boxes of Christmas tree ornaments wrapped in white tissue. In her hand she held a Victorian needlepoint stocking that had been made for her years ago by Johnny's mother. She laid it aside and rose to her feet.

Yet he didn't move, just continued to stare at her, contemplating, she guessed, a diplomatic way to tell her to leave. He almost looked frightened, which, of course, was ridiculous. Yet his demeanor aroused both her curiosity and her empathy.

"Johnny, are you coming in or not?"

"I've got stuff in the truck."

"Need some help?" She started forward when he shook his head.

"When are you leaving?" he asked abruptly.

Emily blinked at his bluntness. So much for giving him credit for tact. "Now, is that a nice way to talk to an old friend?"

"Screw nice. Old friends I don't need." He turned, heading back outside.

Determined not to be offended by his rudeness, she called after him, "Well, maybe I need you."

The moment she said it, she regretted it. Telling Johnny how she felt about him was a mistake she'd vowed four years ago to never repeat, but there was something about this ill-mannered side of him that begged for a response. The wind was howling and she hadn't said it too loud. Maybe . . . maybe . . .

No such luck. He came into the room and slammed the door closed. He angled his head, his eyes weary. "Emily, we don't want to go there. Not tonight. Not tomorrow. Not ever." He studied her as if pondering how specific he should be, but left the point unexplored. "You didn't answer my question. When are you leaving?"

This wasn't just bad manners, he really wanted to know. She sighed. How was it possible for one man to turn her insides into a bag of floating feathers while at the same time she wanted to kick him? On the other hand, she wasn't here like some vagrant or an intruder. She considered telling him that. She considered getting her coat and boots and mittens and sailing right past him. She considered saying she couldn't leave soon enough.

Instead she gave him her best above-the-fray smile. "Christmas is in a few days, but I'd planned to stay through the New Year. Karen didn't want to leave the house empty, so I volunteered." She walked closer to him and she could have sworn he tensed up.

"House-sitting . . . yeah, that figures. But I'm here now, so you can go on home."

She stood only a foot away, remembering the last Christmas they were together, remembering how the holidays had begun so filled with promise and then ended . . . She swallowed. *Stop it. That was four years ago. Don't think about it. Your relationship with him is over and finished.* He'd gone his way—off to work in a construction company partnership with his best friend, and she'd gone hers—pursuing her love of portrait painting. There was no reason why his unexpected appearance should do anything but make her curious.

And just because her heart was hammering with a tension that she hadn't felt since the last time he'd made love to her—get a grip, here. Leaving would be wise.

"I can't leave."

"Of course you can. I'll drive you where you need to go."

"Johnny—"

He gripped her shoulders, holding her away so that she knew he didn't want to be touched, while at the same time his hands on her managed to sap all the air out of her lungs.

"Let's do it this way, Emily," he said, slowly, calmly, as if she were three years old. "I'll bring in my stuff and you go and get yours." Then he turned her toward the stairs that led to the second floor. "I'll even start the truck so it stays warm."

But when he returned with his duffel she was back fiddling with the tree ornaments. Before he could say anything, she did. "You didn't let me finish. I can't leave. I don't have anyplace to go. My cousin from New Jersey and her husband are honeymooning in my apartment. There was some mess-up with their B&B reservations and they were stuck."

Undaunted, he said, "I'll get you a room in the village."

"Two days before Christmas?"

"What about friends? Janet or Betsy or Ginny?"

"Two have houses full of relatives and Ginny is on the verge of the flu, although she won't admit it."

"Terrific." He remained silent for a moment, then scooped up the duffel and slung it over his shoulder. "I'll find a place, then."

She hurried around him and blocked the doorway. He peered at her with raised eyebrows.

She folded her arms and didn't move. "This is silly and you're acting like a bratty kid."

"Bratty kid?"

"Absolutely. It's snowy and cold and there are no rooms in the village, and yet you're going to stomp out because you're irritated that I'm here."

He scowled, started to say something, then apparently changed his mind.

But Emily continued. "This is your house and at last count there were three bedrooms upstairs. Surely one of them would be suitable. And just to reassure you, I'll try mightily to not rush in all a-twitter and seduce you in the middle of the night."

"Very funny," he grumbled, looking genuinely perplexed by the stuck-with-an-old-girlfriend fix he found himself in. "If I didn't know better, I'd swear Karen had cooked this up like seasonal cheer, but she doesn't know—" He stopped himself, and she waited through five beats of silence.

"Doesn't know what?"

"Never mind. I just figured I'd have the house to myself."

It was clear that his disappointment was genuine. "I'm sorry, Johnny, really I am, but Karen never said you were coming. In fact, she said she was concerned about the house being empty over the holidays. Before I even knew about my cousin's dilemma, I had already told her I'd stay. It worked out perfectly for me."

"Not for me, it hasn't. You here with me is *not*

perfect." He seemed so amazed by that concept that she knew whatever was missing of the puzzle that was Johnny Cross, the pieces were major. "In fact, you here with me is a disaster."

Nevertheless, instead of stomping out the door, he carried his duffel into the den and then emerged a few moments later without his jacket and carrying a glass of whiskey. He walked over to the hearth, where birch logs crackled. His body was lean and tense in faded jeans and blue and red rugby shirt. Johnny had never been dignified or even suave, but he'd always been cool. A heartbreaker in his twenties, and by his mid-thirties, he gave the definite impression that he wasn't playing hard to get. He *was* hard to get.

No longer true, or so his sister had told Emily in October. He was engaged to a woman who worked for a Boston television station—Karen had been amazed that her rough-and-tumble brother would fall for such sophistication, but he seemed genuinely in love and happy.

Well, he sure wasn't happy now, Emily mused.

"I'll try not to be bowled over by your compliments," she said, deciding that putting up with his nastiness was not part of her agreement with Karen. "Look, since you're here to pout and grumble alone, I'll leave you to your crankiness. But I'm here to enjoy Christmas. Before your parents passed away, they always had festive and happy holidays that included their friends. I loved coming here and your mother made me feel like family. I just thought I'd try to re-create some of the joy they had in abundance." She rose and hung her stocking on one of the mantel hooks. "Instead of making the best of an unexpected situation, you're acting like you're afraid I'm going to make you even more unhappy than you are."

"Maybe you should be afraid of me," he muttered, sipping his whiskey.

It was all too much like some bad made-for-TV movie and she chuckled, then quickly covered her mouth, a final giggle escaping. "Sorry, but me afraid of you is just too silly."

Johnny set his glass down, took the few steps needed to stand over her. He remained still for a few seconds before reaching down and bringing her to her feet. Her eyes were wide when his mouth moved to within inches of hers.

"You always did have a smart mouth," he muttered before kissing her so hard that Emily felt him clear to her toes. She couldn't kiss back because she was stunned and dizzy and couldn't move, although she wanted to. It had been a long time since she'd been kissed like this and she'd forgotten how much she liked it.

He pulled back, his breathing rushed, eyes glittering so hot they made her cheeks flame red. When she said his name it sounded more like a caress and her eyes drifted closed.

He shook her lightly. "Damn it, Emily! Don't do that. Slap me or scream or threaten to call the cops."

"I don't want to slap you and no one but you would hear me if I screamed and a kiss is hardly worth a 911 call."

He let her go, swearing.

She touched his arm, grinning when he glanced at

her. "Actually, I kind of liked it. You always were
the best kisser."

He rolled his eyes. "Just what I need, stuck with
an old girlfriend with a droll wit and delusions about
the past."

TWO

Three hours after all the lights were out and the house had cooled down, Johnny was sprawled in a saggy old easy chair where his dad had held court about any hot family problems. While his problem wasn't a family one, it was definitely hot. Moonlight reached into the room, but it might as well not have bothered.

Johnny wasn't thinking about moonlight and the festiveness of the holidays; he wasn't even giving much thought to Emily, although knowing she was asleep upstairs unsettled him. No, Johnny wasn't thinking in some free-flowing manner. He was plotting revenge.

Beside him was a bottle of whiskey. There was also a bowl of untouched soup that Emily insisted he have. To Johnny, this was houseguest stuff, like the blanket and sheets she'd brought down to the den when he absolutely refused to sleep upstairs. She called him stubborn and ornery. He added it was his house and he'd sleep where he damn well pleased. She'd marched out and he'd slugged down a shot of whiskey—or was it two?

Nothing like a little back-and-forthing with an old lover, he concluded with a kind of guarded bemusement. He'd tried not to think her in terms of a onetime lover, with all the lusty charms and yesterday's passions. *Girlfriend* was better—neutral and homey and easily forgettable.

He rose and walked to the windows. The moon reflected the pristine whiteness blowing into shadowy, silvery mounds beneath the stars. It spread out before him, all pure and flowing and sterling. There'd always been a gentle peace and welcome solitude on a wintry night in this house. A place of memories and innocent times; a place for new plans.

Well, he was here and a helluva long way from innocent; tonight's memories of the past twelve hours were fierce and unrelentingly ugly. He'd come home to drink. He'd come home to piece the shards of his life together and he'd come home to plan.

Okay, hotshot, you know what you want. The issue is, can you pull it off? You caught them. You called them every foul name you could think of. You didn't want explanations or apologies or excuses. What you wanted was to kill them.

And the truth of the matter was, he'd gotten into his truck and driven home to Jepson, Rhode Island, because to stay in Massachusetts would have been disastrously sloppy.

And Johnny Cross didn't do sloppy. He could be a hothead and he could be a hard-ass, but he was never sloppy.

On the ninety-minute drive, he'd nursed his anger, his hurt, and his disillusion, and instead of finding the empty house that he'd craved and expected, he'd walked in on some bucolic Christmas scene complete with the lovely Emily Madden . . .

"Johnny?"

He whirled around, banging his shoulder on the window molding and wincing. She held two huge pillows that swamped most of her, but it was clear she was covered in a white flannel granny-sized robe that fell almost to the floor. Red socks were on her feet. How like Emily to keep appearing at unexpected moments. If he didn't have to figure out his own problem . . .

In a soft quizzical voice, he asked, "Are you here to seduce me?"

She came into the room, slanting a look at him with those sexy green eyes that always seemed to look right through him. "I promised I wouldn't, remember?"

"Damn," he grumbled pleasantly. "You always were too good at keeping promises." Even as he spoke the words, he realized this trait wasn't one she acquired, but was simply the way she was.

"Especially with men engaged to other women," she said airily. "I just brought you the pillows I forgot earlier." She glanced at the sheets and blankets that were still where he'd tossed them and then she focused on the untouched soup. "You didn't like it?"

"I wasn't hungry. Emily, about kissing you, I'm sorry—"

She pressed her hand on his mouth. "Don't. I should be the one apologizing for acting like any of it meant anything. Of course it didn't and I know that." She put down the pillows and tightened the sash on her robe.

Kissing you always means something to me, he concluded suddenly, as if the thought had been in cobwebs for years and had finally broken free. Nonsense. He didn't need or want conflict and complications

with Emily. He wasn't here to rekindle *anything* with
an old flame.

She flitted around shaking out the first sheet and
tucking it into the cushions, acting as if his silence
were irrelevant. Johnny felt like a two-bit heel because he could clarify all of his angst and nastiness
in about a minute, but dumping all the shit on Emily
in some all-purpose heart-baring wasn't what he was
about. Besides, he left her for the high-stakes career
challenges of the big city; she was hardly likely to be
sympathetic that he got royally screwed.

Then suddenly, as if using the tense stillness to
gather her thoughts, she arranged the second sheet,
then straightened and gave him her best tough-babe
look. He almost smiled.

"Just because in the past we teased and flirted, and
just because I acted flirty a few hours ago, doesn't
mean I put any credence in it. I mean, it wasn't for
real."

He nodded solemnly. "Okay, not for real. Got it."

But she continued, walking around the couch, tick-
ing off their past as if she were an accountant crunch-
ing numbers. "We broke up a long time ago. You
wanted to move to the big city and I didn't. Different
lifestyles, different ideas of what makes happiness.
But truthfully, it was deeper than something as elusive
as being happy. It was really about freedom and independence and both of us finding them in our own
way."

"And how did you find them?" he asked, while
telling himself he was nuts to be delving into this.

"But that was then and this is now and I shouldn't

have acted as if I just said good-bye to you two days ago—" She stopped talking and looked at him closely. "What did you say?"

"I asked you how you found them. You know, freedom and independence?"

She looked rattled. "I have both."

"I'm sure you do, but I asked you *how* you found them."

She glared at him. "I don't know. I just know I have them."

Johnny held his hands up in a peace gesture and backed away from her. "Hey, no argument from me." It wasn't his intent to back her into a corner. Besides, he wasn't supposed to be curious, fascinated, or even remotely interested in what was going on in her life.

"Why are we arguing about the past?" she said lightly. "It doesn't matter. Now is what is important. In fact, I should be congratulating you on your engagement and wishing you bushels of happiness. Allison is beautiful. I'm very happy for both of you." She turned away, clearing her throat.

He chuckled. "Emily, you are such a liar."

She sighed. "Well, maybe I did overdo the gushing a bit."

"Yeah, I think so."

"But Johnny, I want you to be happy. Honest, I do. Actually, I like Allison and she certainly is in love with you. When I met her last summer you were all she talked about, so the engagement this past fall wasn't a huge surprise."

"Lucky me," he muttered, then shifted the topic to Emily. He had an urgent need to draw her into his arms as if she were a place of safety. He clenched his hands to keep them to himself. "I haven't even asked about you. About your art? Boyfriends?" He grabbed the blanket before she could shake it out. "You don't need to wait on me."

"I wouldn't call it that. I just want to make sure you're comfortable. I mean, sleeping down here when you could be upstairs . . . well, I just feel as if it's kind of my fault for being here."

"Believe me, nothing is your fault."

"Sometimes I get a little nervous about unexpected changes."

And suddenly both knew they weren't talking about making a bed or being stuck with one another—this was about caring and missed opportunities and a onetime love. Being together now was just a bit scary. Their gazes held, their bodies separated by only a fuzzy green wool blanket. Both knew their unforeseen union on a snowy night had a value beyond simple questions and past memories. Both knew that old feelings could trigger new consequences.

"Talk to me, Emily," Johnny whispered. "What's been going on with you?"

"I'm working, dating once in a while, doing some work with the adopt-a-family program." Then she quickly changed the subject. "Tell me why you came home."

"I can't."

"Why?"

"Because it's dirty stuff and I don't want to lay it all on you."

"I have broad shoulders."

"No."

"We're friends. I want to help you."

"Trust me, you wouldn't have a clue what to do."

For a long moment those wily green eyes of hers studied him as if she might see into his soul. Finally she said, "I'm disappointed in you, Johnny."

"It won't be the first time."

She glanced at the clock on the Governor Winthrop desk. "I think we should both get some sleep. Maybe tomorrow will look better." She reached down and smoothed the blanket, patting the pillows, and then straightened. At the door she said, "I have to run some errands in the morning, but I'll leave the coffee plugged in, in case you're still asleep."

He didn't move, only nodding and mumbling a good night.

But it wasn't until he heard her bedroom door close that he relaxed. By some incredible mental turn, his thoughts were more confused now than before his disconnected conversation with Emily.

It had been about everything and nothing, but one lesson was clear. He had to stay clear of her. He'd come home to get his head straight and plan his revenge. He had no plan that included Emily.

THREE

"Emily, I'm sorry to have to call you at the last minute," Ginny Calhoun said amid coughing and sniffling. "I was a little sniffly yesterday, but this morning I feel like a dish rag."

"Of course you shouldn't go out. I can take care of getting things to the Warrens'."

"I just hate to miss it." She sighed and then sneezed. "Excuse me a minute while I get the box of tissues."

"Sure." Emily peered out of the kitchen window as the blowing snow whipped into swirls by the garage. She told herself it wasn't as bad on the main roads as it looked in the backyard. Besides, this was New England, and driving in snow was a given in winter. The driveway had been plowed before daylight, although by the looks of the falling snow, Eddie would have to come back before nightfall.

Johnny had parked his truck facing the road, and since he had four-wheel drive, drifts and clogged roads were not a problem. Hmmm, perhaps she should ask him if she could borrow his truck—but that meant awakening him. That meant going into the den to get his keys. That meant seeing him.

And after last night, she needed some time to get her bearings. Johnny Cross still affected her—he was sexy and more good-looking than she recalled and much less friendly. It was one of the first things she'd noticed. Where once he'd been open and fun and teasing, now he seemed closed and distant and angry. Whatever terrible thing had happened hadn't just hurt him, it had made him angry.

Stop trying to piece him together, she scolded. He wasn't home for her wonderful words of wisdom, even if she had some to impart. Which she didn't. Her own life was hardly a bubbling feast of experience beyond the village limits of Jepson. However strong her feelings or curiosity, he was engaged and she had no right to offer anything beyond friendship.

"Okay, I'm back," Ginny said.

"I'll swing by in about twenty minutes. Are the packages all wrapped, or do you need some help?"

"Nope, all wrapped. Damn. I really wanted to go with you to deliver them. The Warrens are going to be so happy and I love seeing those big shining eyes on the kids. It makes Christmas into what it should be—a time of giving and joy."

"Yes, it's wonderful to see, isn't it?" she said softly, recalling Mary Warren's tears when Emily went to tell her that the Warrens had been chosen. Mary's oldest and only son, Nicky, had submitted their name to the select committee without telling his mother, " 'cuz she'd be too embarrassed," he'd admitted with a refreshing forthrightness. Emily wasn't sure who had been more excited about the gifts and the food, she and Ginny or Mary and her family. "I have the food basket, too, and as soon as I get it into the car, I'm leaving." Emily finished loading the dishwasher as she and Ginny chatted about the Warrens.

The adopt-a-family program had been started by a small neighborhood church and over the years had grown to include other religious organizations. When Emily was a little girl, her family had been one of the first beneficiaries. She and her brothers had tried valiantly to ignore how poor they were. Their parents were heavy drinkers and despite too many promises that "this Christmas will be better," their holidays were mostly spent trying to keep their parents from getting drunk. When adopt-a-family chose the Maddens, Emily and her brothers received not only gifts and food, but a true sense that sometimes strangers care more than a family. She'd never forgotten that Christmas, and in later years she had become one the project's biggest boosters. She had volunteered since she was old enough to get a job and help contribute.

Mary and the three Warren children lived in a small cabin that was some distance from the village of Jepson. Their father had abandoned them, and Emily felt a particular kinship because of her own family's poverty. It made her sad that too many children had to deal with grown-up problems when their lives should be filled with love and lollipops and stories about courage and heroism.

"Emily? You still there?"

"Oh, I'm sorry." She blotted the moisture from her eyes. "I should hang up so I can get going."

"Wait. Before you go. What's this I hear about Johnny Cross being there with you?"

"Now how did you hear that?"

"Then it's true," Ginny said, the delight in her voice impossible to miss. "Actually, Eddie told me this morning when he was here to plow."

His truck, of course, with C&B CONSTRUCTION painted on the door, would be hard to miss. "Well, he's here, but he isn't exactly visiting for the holidays. Something's wrong, but he won't talk about it."

"Men. I've yet to meet the guy who willingly talks about what really is bugging him. Mark and I've been married seven years and the only time I can get him to talk is if he wants sex." She chuckled. "Guess it could be worse, couldn't it?"

"Yeah, I don't think you have a lot to complain about," Emily said, rejecting the wash of envy she had for Ginny and Mark. They had the kind of giving and loving marriage Emily had once imagined she'd have with Johnny. Once imagined before the Christmas four years ago when Johnny announced he was relocating in the Boston area. She'd had commitments here in Jepson—her mother's continual struggle for sobriety since her father had died was one responsibility, plus her art studio had finally shown real promise of success. Throwing it all away and moving like some wisp in the wind . . . well, she couldn't do it. Johnny's sudden decision struck her as more about rebelliousness than good sense.

Then again, she'd known for some time that Johnny was struggling with being his own man, making a life as Johnny Cross, not as Samuel Cross's son. Much was expected of the son of the man who had been the mayor of Jepson and who was given much credit for the village's growth and the attraction of tourists, which in turn brought cash into the hands of the local businesses.

Johnny was no slouch, but he wasn't a glad-hander or schmoozer like his old man. And in a village like Jepson, expansive friendliness was a necessity. His partnership in C&B Construction with his best friend, Gabe Barry, had been mostly local work—renovations, additions, and work on a low-income housing development.

Then he and Gabe had the low bid on constructing an office complex south of Boston. When the building was completed without going over budget, their business was suddenly hot. Big money, big operation, and big references.

Looking back after they'd agreed to go their separate ways, Emily concluded that he really wanted out of their relationship, and making a career move was easier than telling her he no longer loved her. While she hadn't liked it, she'd had no alternative but to accept it and get on with her life. And she had. Until last summer, when he brought Allison Fortes home. The engagement was announced the following October.

"Is Allison with him?" Ginny asked.

"No."

"Uh-oh."

"Hmmm. I wondered if they'd had a fight."

"Didn't you ask?"

"Well, it didn't come up in a way that I felt like I should."

"Oh, come on. You and Johnny were quite an item years ago. Why would you be shy about asking him anything?"

"Why would I care if he and his girlfriend had a fight?"

"Because you're still in love with him."

Emily took a deep breath. Ginny and she rarely discussed Johnny because Emily flat-out refused to be drawn into dissing Allison or playing the role of the woman dumped. "That's old news and all the more reason why I should keep my mouth shut."

"How long is he staying?"

"I assume not long. With Christmas so close, I'm sure he'll want to be with Allison for the day."

"And what if he doesn't leave?"

"Ginny, give it up. Johnny left me of his own volition. He has a life in Boston and a future with Allison. End of story."

"My, oh, my, but aren't we generously high-minded."

"So what do you want me to do?" she snapped, losing patience. The man had been in the house less than twelve hours and all she'd done was think about him. And now she was *talking* about him.

"Honey, you know the answer to that. If it were me, I'd seduce him. You never should have let him go off to Boston without you. He probably figured you didn't care since you didn't even squeak when he moved away."

"I didn't want him to hate me or resent me for clinging to him when he clearly wanted his freedom."

"Freedom? Freedom to get snagged by another woman."

Emily's head was beginning to ache. "I havc to go. I'll be there in about an hour." She didn't wait for

Ginny to add any more advice, but said good-bye and hung up.

She took the huge food basket out of the cool pantry. The only addition was the thawing fifteen-pound turkey. The basket had been filled with traditional foodstuffs plus ribbon candy and a huge tin of Christmas cookies from a neighborhood cookie swap. Emily checked to make sure nothing was forgotten, then took the turkey from the refrigerator and, with the basket, put them all on the counter by the back door.

She took her jacket from the downstairs closet, listening for any sounds coming from the den.

Nothing.

Quietly, she fished around the closet floor for her boots, scowling when she couldn't find them. She sat back on her haunches, mentally retracing her steps when she'd come home from the store yesterday. She'd taken her boots off in the kitchen, then when they were dry she'd taken them and . . .

Then she remembered.

She rose to her feet, wishing mightily she were home where she had two spare pairs, but of course she wasn't, and to go out into ten-plus inches of snow in sneakers was insane. Damn the man! If he'd slept upstairs she wouldn't have this problem.

At the closed den door, she slowly turned the knob, trying frantically to remember if this was one of the house's squeaky doors. She eased it open. A tiny squeak keened into the air, making her shudder. She held her breath, expecting it to get louder, and when it didn't she exhaled the breath she hadn't realized she was holding.

With the door open, the room was still and cool, with light spilling through the open drapes. She saw her boots on the fireplace hearth where she'd put them to finish drying. Now, if she could just get across the room and back out without waking him . . .

"Good morning."

FOUR

Emily jumped, her heart slamming up into her throat and then dropping back down to her toes. "I'm s-sorry. I left my boots in here and I . . . uh . . ." Her voice faltered as if she'd run out of oxygen. She took a few shallow breaths while glancing around the room. He wasn't on the couch or at the windows or seated in the old lounger.

For a few brief seconds she wondered if she'd imagined his voice. Then she saw him in the shadowed side of the room by the door. He was seated on a library table, feet bare, wearing jeans and an unbuttoned flannel shirt that did nothing to hide the lawn of chest hair. If she closed her eyes she could feel its softness on her fingers.

Her gaze lifted to find him watching her with assessing eyes. His cheeks were scruffy with whiskers, his mouth more bemused than annoyed by her unannounced entrance.

Then her attention bounced back down to his lap and a chill shuddered through her. Oh, God, what had she walked in on? Maybe she could just pretend she didn't notice that a very long black rifle rested against his thighs.

Talking rapidly, she said, "I just need to get my boots."

"Help yourself."

She walked quickly across the room, picked up the boots, and turned to leave.

"Any coffee left?" he asked.

"Uh, yes. I've got to go out for a little while." She continued to move toward the door. "There are cranberry muffins and cereal, and eggs and bacon in the refrigerator. There's plenty of milk and orange juice." She shut up before she started listing how many forks were in the drawer and what brand of marmalade was in the cabinet. *Good grief. Get a grip here.*

"Gee, and I had my heart set on waffles," he said so easily she wondered if she'd stumbled into a surreal time zone from the netherworld. Surely the scene must be stupidly comical. Him sitting there, looking buffed and as lazy as a retired gunslinger, and her standing frozen like some iced-over intruder.

Why did he have this ability to rattle her? Was it his calmness in the face of her own ricocheting feelings about him? Perhaps. She knew in her gut that she still cared a great deal for him, and while being in love with an old lover who now loved someone else wasn't wrong, it was certainly futile and potentially painful. She needed to keep her distance and her heart carefully protected.

"This isn't a restaurant," she snapped, narrowing her eyes. "You'll have to make do with the meager selection."

"That's my Emily."

"I am not your Emily!"

He winced and had no compunction about showing it. "Whoa. Sorry. I was merely commenting about the

quick-witted woman I remember too well." He
grinned. "Want to use my truck?"

"Your truck?" The moment she said it she wanted
to snatch it back. He was too quick and once upon a
time she'd prided herself on keeping up with him.
Quick-witted woman, indeed. She almost smiled.

"Yeah, the one I drove home. You know, black
with big tires? Eats snow the way a shark eats minnows? You said you're going out, and by the looks
of the snow you could· use something rugged and
tough."

Something rugged and tough? Like his truck or like
him? And wasn't it true that men drove vehicles that
they thought reflected them? She couldn't help but
wonder what minnows he planned to devour.

She stared at him, her gaze coming back to his lap.
Coming back to the weapon he held resting on his
thighs. She couldn't help but conclude that her initial
reaction last evening had been correct. Something
deeply troubled him.

Incredibly, she was impressed with the ease he ex-
hibited now; Johnny Cross, rugged and tough, could
handle just about any crisis that came his way.

Nevertheless, it was obvious he was enjoying her
trying to avoid asking about the gun. She drew herself
up and said evenly, "Thank you for the offer of your
truck. And yes, I would like to take it."

"It's yours."

"Terrific. That being settled, I have something to
say to you."

"Lay it on me, sweetheart," he murmured, a grin
beginning.

"I don't appreciate being startled, and damn it, don't you dare smile."

He didn't. But just barely. Then he straightened, appearing serious and thoroughly chastened. "Yes, ma'am."

"You have a hell of a lot of nerve sitting there with a rifle like it's some toy pop gun."

He glanced down at the weapon as though giving it a closer look. "Nope, it's definitely not a toy."

"Obviously. So why do you have it? Or maybe the better question is, what are you going to do with it?"

He shrugged. "I found it in the closet. Been about fifteen years since I'd even seen it. I figured Karen had junked it." Emily knew that Karen and Johnny had agreed to get rid of a lot of the clutter after their parents died. Since Karen lived in the house, Johnny had okayed her making the final decision on what to keep and what to discard.

"She probably didn't know what to do with it."

"Or thought I might want it."

Emily drew a little closer, her concern about him increasing. "Johnny, what's going on?"

"Relax. I wasn't planning on using it on you."

"What kind of answer is that?"

"The right one, since you're much prettier alive and yelling at me."

"Please be serious." She paused. "Johnny . . . ?" she asked softly. "You're not thinking about, uh, well, doing something to yourself, are you?"

"Killing myself?" He looked amazed that she would even have such a thought. "No way. Not even a possibility."

She sagged beneath an inner relief.

He laid the weapon aside and scooted off the desk, sauntering over to the couch, where the sheets and blanket from last night had been neatly folded and piled at one end. The pillows were on a nearby chair. Johnny pulled on socks and then boots. "Tell you what, I'll go get the truck warmed up for you."

Emily dropped her own boots on the floor, the clunk causing him to look up. She crossed her arms and gave him her most fierce look. Now that she'd been assured he didn't intend to commit suicide, her questions rushed back. "I want to know why you are here and why you are angry and how some old gun fits into it."

He stood, buttoning his shirt. "You just don't give up, do you?"

"I'm very worried about you," she said, baring much more of her heart than she wanted to.

Then, without his eyes leaving her, he unbuttoned his jeans. "I can take care of myself."

When he slid one shirttail inside and then the other, her mouth suddenly went dry. She swallowed, her voice husky. "All men say that."

She caught a glimpse of soft cotton underwear before he rebuttoned the fly. She knew she should look away. She should blush or at least act embarrassed that he felt such a freedom to practically undress in front of her. Then it occurred to her that of course he wasn't bothered about whether she had a reaction; she'd seen him do this many times before.

The truth was that she wasn't embarrassed but intrigued and attracted, and wished she had the guts to just tell him he still looked great in jeans.

Johnny slowly walked toward her, his boots making soft squishes on the carpet. She felt herself grow warmer the nearer he got. She watched him come closer and closer, her pulse rising and racing, her heart thumping and pounding so hard she could barely breathe.

When he slipped his hands over her shoulders and under her collar to enclose her neck, she almost sighed at the feel of his warm fingers. Then when he slowly settled his palms so that his thumbs tipped up her chin, Emily whimpered.

He lowered his head, his mouth mere inches from hers.

"Johnny, don't . . ." she whispered. It was the hardest thing she'd ever refused. She clenched her hands to keep them from climbing to embrace his cheeks and pull his mouth to hers.

"You're the kink in my plan, Emily." The words drifted through the air between them. "I hadn't planned on you being here. I sure as hell hadn't planned on wanting to take your clothes off and see if you still have that strawberry mark on your left breast."

"You shouldn't be saying these things." And inside her heart she wrestled with wanting him and wanting to hear every provocative word while knowing it was wrong. "You're engaged and anything between us would be inappropriate."

His thumbs rode the sides of her jaw like tiny pads of feathery heat.

"Ah, then, if I wasn't engaged, it would be okay."

It wasn't a question but a confident statement.

Her eyes widened. "What are you telling me? That you and Allison aren't engaged?"

"That's what I'm telling you." He brushed his mouth across hers, not lingering, and then stepped away so suddenly she almost lost her balance.

She stared at him in astonishment as he crossed over to where the rifle lay, lifted it, and put it back in the closet. He then locked the door and pocketed the key.

"She broke it off?" she finally asked.

"You could say that."

"You were okay with that?"

"Yeah, you could say that." He lifted her boots and handed them to her, then glanced out the window. "The snow is getting deeper."

Was the broken engagement the reason behind his sudden and unexpected appearance? But of all the emotions she'd seen in him, sadness hadn't been one of them.

"Emily? The snow?"

"Yes, yes, I need to get going," she muttered as a bundle of new questions flew through her mind.

He followed her out of the den, grabbing his sheep-skin jacket on the way. He went out the front door and she heard his truck rumble to life.

Emily hurried into the kitchen to get the basket. One thought turned over and over in her mind. *His engagement was over.* She returned for the turkey, slipping it into a red plastic bag and tying it closed with a gold bow. *His engagement was over.* She tugged on her down jacket and plunged her feet into her boots. Gloves and her scarf and earmuffs. She grinned widely. *His engagement was over.*

Johnny came back in, brushing snow from his hair and shoulders.

"Emily, it's a mess out there."

"You'd prefer to drive me." She settled earmuffs on and tied her scarf under her jacket collar.

"Uh, well, yeah," he said, seemingly amazed he didn't have to argue her into it. "It's not that I don't think you can handle it."

"Why should I want to even try when you're here and willing?" She gave him a stunning smile and handed him the basket while she took the turkey.

"Why do I have the feeling I missed something?"

Emily laughed.

It was going to be a wonderful Christmas!

FIVE

The faded gray Warren house appeared aged and feeble against the press of the freshly fallen snow. To Johnny, it looked more like a makeshift shanty that should have been used to store junk, not secure a family. A metal chimney, puffing wood smoke, elbowed out of one side of the dwelling while a young boy shoveled snow from the front door.

"Christ, this place looks as if a kid with a slingshot could level it," Johnny said, frowning at the scene before him. Because he was in the construction business, he was always conscious of structural deterioration. With this dump, the least of the problems were rotting beams and a huge heat loss evident by the iced-up windows.

"Mary Warren refuses to move," Emily said as if in defense of the woman's decision. "She doesn't want to go into public housing and there's a long list for subsidized, so she stays here and does the best she can."

Johnny scowled at the emaciated shack, but Emily's words brought back a jolt of reality about his own past. *She stays here and does the best she can.* That was exactly what he *hadn't* done.

He hadn't stayed and done his best; he'd left Jepson for the lure of some kind of workingman's Shangri-la—or so he'd once believed. He'd wanted independence from his old man and to make sure his success was shored up by his own abundance of ambition and not by paternal influence.

Well, he'd gotten it all—he'd harnessed success and made a disgusting amount of money. Yet despite the trappings of achievement, he'd struggled with a deep inner vacuum that he honestly believed Allison had filled. Instead, he discovered just how big a fool he'd been.

Curiously, this short time with Emily, although neither expected nor sought after, had distracted—and, more to the point, disoriented—him. Just the astonishing fact that he was sitting here and about to play Santa Claus to a desperately poor family was way out of sorts with his homecoming purpose. He'd expected to have a strategy by now, but instead he'd awakened this morning with a magnificent hard-on and too many sexy thoughts about Emily.

He glanced over at her and she had a puzzled look, as if delving into his thoughts might be a scary proposition. *Not scary, sweetheart, but definitely dangerous.*

"So," Johnny finally asked, "where's Mary's husband?"

"He abandoned her and the three kids years ago."

"Nice guy," he said cynically. "What about the owner? When I was a kid, this place belonged to Essie Beene."

"It still does. But she's not in good health and her kids are handling the property. The boys don't charge Mary a lot of rent, yet they don't do any improvements, either."

"And Mary doesn't complain because she's afraid that if they do some work, then they'll hike her rent."

"Something like that. It's just terrible. I found out a lot during the past month. I spoke with Mary a few times, and while she tried so hard not to sound as if she was complaining, the poor woman doesn't even have enough of the basics. The village has been wonderful in donating items, but Mary never seems to get ahead. Frankly, I think Essie would be appalled if she knew what was going on. But her mind isn't good and I don't know that she could understand all the ramifications if they were presented. Part of me feels like I'm being nosy and the other part makes me want to call Essie's sons and rag them out."

Emily to the rescue, Johnny thought, recalling her worrying about him, wanting to help, wanting, no doubt, to rescue him. "I vote for the rag-out. Give me their number and I'll make the call." He shoved the truck into park and added, "It's possible Mary isn't reading the Beene boys right. I knew them when I was a kid and they weren't weasels then."

"Well, they certainly aren't conscientious landlords. This place is falling down." Emily undid her seat belt. "Look, why don't you wait for me? I won't be long."

"Uh-huh. I sit here in a nice warm truck while you make four trips carrying stuff inside. Get real."

"I just don't want you to say anything. Mary knows that Johnny Cross is half owner of a construction business. She'd feel like you were noticing how bad the place is."

"I don't have to be inside for that. Let's go. I'll be on my best behavior."

It took them two trips from the truck to the house to carry in the bags of gifts they'd picked up at Ginny's, plus the turkey and the enormous basket that Johnny guessed must have weighed twenty-five pounds.

Mary, a small square woman with deep red hair, made no effort to hide the glisten of tears and gratitude in her eyes. The basket nearly covered one counter and the turkey barely fit in the old refrigerator. Her children, two girls who looked like first- and second-graders and a scrawny, gangly, early-in-his-teens boy, stood close to her.

Their eyes were huge and amazed when Emily took out the wrapped gifts and placed them under a small decorated tree. Their eagerness to shake and pinch the packages reminded Johnny of when he was kid and the guessing was as much fun as the opening.

He found it refreshing that so little could bring so much. He'd been at a friend's house a few days ago and their kids wanted all kinds of high-tech gifts with stratospheric price tags. The Warren kids were delighted and awed by gifts that more affluent kids would have scoffed at. What a concept, he thought, amazed at how taken he was with this simple scene of being grateful for what was given rather than whining about what was missing. He scowled when he realized the implication of that same concept in his own fucked-up life.

While Mary insisted they stay for coffee and Emily accepted, Johnny watched the boy go back outside

and return with an armload of wood for the woodstove.

The two girls were busy arranging the wrapped
presents beneath the tree. Arranging and shaking and
giggling. Mary passed out the mugs of coffee and
smiled. "It's good to hear them laugh."

The boy stacked the scraps of wood by the stove
and then went over to whisper something to his
mother. Johnny caught something about not much
wood. Then Mary's eyes darted to the meager pile.
"We'll talk about it later," she whispered to her son.
He wiped a forearm beneath a runny nose and nodded.

Then he passed Johnny, turned, and said in a low
voice, "Mister, is it okay if I go look at your truck?"

"Nicky, his truck isn't a toy," his mother admon-
ished.

"Jeez, Mom, I know that. I wasn't going to scratch
it, I just wanted to sorta look it over."

Johnny heard the depth of disappointment and despite knowing he should keep his mouth shut, he
didn't. "Mrs. Warren, I have an errand to run, and if
you don't mind, Nicky could come along and give me
a hand."

"You mean ride in your truck?" the boy asked as
if Johnny were truly Santa Claus in disguise.

Johnny nodded. "If it's okay with your mom."

Mary Warren looked unsure, glancing at Emily for
help.

When Emily didn't answer, Johnny realized that
she, too, might not be sure. First there was his unannounced arrival that he still hadn't explained to her,
then the incident with the gun that had clearly rattled

her. He guessed that she must be thinking, *This isn't the Johnny Cross I used to know*, and therefore she wasn't quite willing to vouch for him.

Beats of silence, no more than a few seconds, but endless in his mind, for as she looked at him, he could feel her assessment deep in his gut.

For reasons that made absolutely no sense he wanted Emily to trust him, to reassure Mary Warren, and to support him as the Johnny Cross she once loved.

Across the room the two girls scuffled over which package to shake. The small woodstove crackled. Nicky watched his mother, waiting for her answer, his eyes naked with longing to actually ride in the truck.

Johnny said nothing. This had to come from Emily and the time to plead his case was not in front of a mother rightfully concerned for her son.

"I think Johnny has some wood he wants to get rid of," Emily said so confidently that Johnny stared in astonishment. She continued, "His sister is away and Johnny will just be here for a few days. There's no reason for all the chopped wood to sit there and not be used. Isn't that what you were thinking, Johnny?"

"Uh, yes, that was part of it," he murmured, wondering how she had so easily read his mind. "I thought Nicky could help me load the truck."

"Oh my, I couldn't take wood after all you've done for me."

"Mrs. Warren, I haven't done anything except drive Emily over here and carry in the basket. As to the wood Emily mentioned, we have a lot of trees and every year they need to be thinned out and trimmed.

What happens is we end up with more wood than we use. A lot of it ends up rotting and then it's no use to anyone. If you could take some of the excess, it would be most appreciated."

She looked from Johnny to Emily and then seeing the eagerness in her son's eyes, she nodded.

Johnny tossed the keys to Nicky. "Here, start her up. I hate riding in a cold cab."

And before his mother could stop him, he gave a huge whoop and was out the door. Johnny watched through the window as the kid's steps slowed as he approached the truck as if it were a shrine. But he needn't have bothered looking; he recalled being thirteen and coveting big shiny black trucks. Johnny also had complete confidence in handing the keys to Nicky. There wasn't a teenager in existence that didn't know how to turn a key in the ignition.

He turned to Emily. "Are you going, too, or do you want to wait until we come back with the wood?"

"You read my thoughts," she said demurely.

In a husky voice that was rife with meaning, he asked, "Did I, now?"

"But not all of them, I hope." She grinned. "Hurry back."

"You're stepping into dangerous territory, Emily Madden."

"I can't wait."

SIX

Johnny took the long way home by way of Mc-
Donald's. Wreaths and red bows hung at the windows, with a CD somewhere playing holiday music.
The place was full of winter-wrapped kids and adults
juggling toddlers and trays of hot food. Wet tracks of
dirty snow made a trail from the door to the counter,
where he and Nicky ordered Big Macs, fries, and
shakes.

While they ate, Johnny contemplated exactly what
had been wrought in that last exchange with Emily.
Since they'd left the house to go to the Warrens', the
atmosphere had shifted. Yeah, he'd told her that his
engagement was finished, but he hadn't expected her
to do this emotional transformation from wariness to
teasing flirtation.

He bit into his burger and Nicky finished off his
first order of fries and paused before he began the
second.

"You gonna yell at me?" Nicky asked.

"For what?"

"For chuggin' down the food. Mom always yells
that I eat too fast."

Johnny leaned forward and whispered, "Your secret is safe with me."

"You Emily's boyfriend?" he asked out of the blue.

"Used to be."

"She dump you?"

Johnny stopped eating, eyeing the kid. "You don't waste words."

"Figure if you wanna know something, you gotta ask."

"Can't argue with that."

He stared at Johnny and when no answer was forthcoming, he asked, "You didn't dump her, did you?"

"Nicky, it's a bit more complicated than that," he said, sidestepping the truth, and feeling acutely uncomfortable with the fact that he had indeed dumped her.

"Yeah, but it sure would be dumb, you know, dumping Emily."

"The voice of experience, huh?"

"Nope. I just like her and she deserves a good guy."

"Agreed. Now eat."

Jesus, just what he needed. A too-savvy kid who made him look like the jerk he really was. And while Emily wasn't his girlfriend, she'd always amazed him with her generosity of spirit. No slice-and-dice nastiness from Emily when he'd walked away from her because he wanted to make big money in the big city. Emily had sensed that he needed to prove himself away from Jepson where his name was just a name and he wasn't the son of Samuel Cross. She'd simply let go as if knowing that to try and hold him would have turned their relationship into a nightmare. Because of her not turning their breakup into a sobbing battle, they'd remained friends. Nevertheless, Johnny's memory of that Christmas parting four years ago wasn't one he was proud of.

"I'll always love you, Johnny," she'd said in that soft fearless way that expected no response.

But he, of course, had to make absolutely sure she knew the score. And so he'd glared at her and said, "I don't want you to love me! I don't want you to wait for me or even think about me. Jepson is full of nice guys who will give you what you want. You'll find someone else."

He winced even now recalling the stunned look on her face. He made no excuses for himself. He'd wanted out and she'd represented all the hometown ties that entangled him. And because he wanted to make sure the break was clean, he'd hurt her and made her love for him sound as disposable as a bag of hamburger wrappers.

Now he was back home—angry and bitter and . . .

Johnny straightened. Incredibly, he had to fish deep to find much of that anger right at this moment. He wasn't angry or bitter—at least he hadn't been since Emily sneaked into the den this morning looking for her boots.

He scowled. Terrific. This was all her fault. Look how she'd screwed up his day. He'd planned to lock the den door, get drunk, lick his wounds, then sober up and crank out a revenge plan. Emily had been simply a lovely nuisance he'd intended to ignore. Instead, he was taking part in some Christmas goodwill visit that already had him thinking of new ways to help the Warrens.

Now Nicky slurped the last of his chocolate shake, then sucked some more.

"How about one for the road?" Johnny asked, picking up their papers, putting them in the trash, and then shrugging into his jacket.

His eyes lit up. "I ain't never had two shakes at one meal."

"Me neither." He winked. "Let's live dangerously."

Johnny had a couple of errands to run and when he and Nicky emerged from the last store, the late afternoon light promised darkness in a short time.

Fifteen minutes later at his house, Johnny backed the truck up to a huge wall of stacked wood. Nicky was out of the cab before Johnny had the engine shut off.

"Man, I wish the guys who worked for me were as enthusiastic," Johnny muttered as he lowered the tailgate. By the time he'd moved aside some tools and a couple of boxes, Nicky was standing there with an armful of logs.

"You're quick."

"Yeah?" He rolled the logs onto the truck. "Most of the stuff I do is for girls." He squinched up his face in disgust. "I don't mind doin' stuff for my mom, but it's not real work."

"I bet to your mom it is." Johnny stacked the wood and then jumped down to help Nicky get another load.

"Mr. Cross?"

"Hey, call me Johnny. We're pals, right?"

"Yeah?" His whole face lit up. "You really mean it?"

Johnny couldn't miss the longing in the boy's voice. "Absolutely."

They worked loading more logs, conversation

sparse but interspersed with laughter and a few jokes like it would be with two good friends.

Johnny was busy balancing the load when Nicky called out, "Hey, Johnny, there's a guy comin' over here."

Johnny glanced up and then slowly straightened. His hands clenched into fists.

In a low, even voice, he said, "Nicky, why don't you carry a load of those logs into the house? Emily will appreciate it." He dug the house keys from the front pocket of his jeans and tossed them to Nicky. "You can stack them by the fireplace."

The kid glanced at Johnny, his eyes worried, and then at the man walking toward them. "You gonna be okay?"

Johnny jumped down from the bed and ruffled Nicky's hair. "Yeah, you go on ahead."

He nodded and went to load up on logs.

Johnny walked toward the man in a gray parka, jeans, and boots. His hands were in the jacket pockets. He looked tired and pale. His name was Gabe Barry and he was Johnny's partner in C&B Construction and, until two days ago, his best friend.

"What do you want?" Johnny asked, amazed that Gabe had the guts to show his face.

"To explain."

Johnny controlled the laugh that bubbled up. "This should be good. Try not to insult either my intelligence or what I saw."

"We didn't intend for it to happen. I knows how it looks to you, buddy, but it was just circumstances that got complicated and out of hand. No one wanted this to happen."

"Let me get this straight. You were my best friend and I find you in bed with the woman I'm engaged to marry and I'm now supposed to be broad-minded and believe that no one wanted it to happen? What kind of bullshit double-talk is that? What the hell is the matter with you? You think that kind of piss-poor excuse would work if you'd caught me in bed with your woman? You'd have blown me away before I got my pants zipped."

Gabe had a hot temper and, more times than Johnny wanted to think about, he'd had to intervene when the two of them hopped the bars. Gabe usually got himself into some scrape after he'd had too many beers. Johnny could have counted his life span in minutes if he'd moved on Gabe's girlfriend.

Gabe shoved his hands through his hair and looked away, his breathing uneven. "God, what a mess. I'm sorry. I know that's not enough, but it's all I've got."

"Then you lose." He glanced up and saw Nicky coming back toward them. "You better get outta here."

"Johnny, this isn't gonna touch C&B, is it?"

He shrugged. "Things have changed. Working together after this—"

Gabe grabbed Johnny, his hands fisting around his jacket. "For godsake, it's our business. We've got jobs scheduled and if word gets out that the company's got internal problems we could be in big trouble."

Johnny shoved him away and went back to the

truck, tossing a comment over his shoulder. "You could always buy me out."

Gabe threw his hands into the air, then stalked toward Johnny, his voice trembling, desperate. "You know I don't have that kind of cash."

Johnny smiled, feeling better by the second. Maybe the best revenge was seeing the cockiness drain out of Gabe right before his eyes. "But I can afford to buy you out."

"You bastard," Gabe snarled, taking a swing at Johnny. He moved to the left and when Gabe came at him a second time, the two men ended up on the ground rolling in the snow.

From the house Nicky came running, launching himself at Gabe and screaming, "Leave him alone! Leave Johnny alone!" His fists pummeled Gabe's back.

Johnny rolled to his feet.

"Hey, who's the kid? Get him the fuck off me," Gabe yelped, and then reached around and grabbed Nicky's arm and twisted.

Johnny circled Gabe's throat and squeezed. "Let him go, Gabe," Johnny said in a cold, dead voice.

For a few seconds the three were sealed in a freeze-frame of time. A late afternoon wind blew the snow across the front of Johnny's truck and in the distance came the roar of a snowmobile.

"You're choking me," Gabe sputtered.

And Johnny pressed harder.

Finally Gabe let go of Nicky's arm and the boy rubbed it and worked it to ease out the pain. Johnny released the choke hold he had on Gabe's throat.

He helped Gabe to his feet, but his onetime friend flipped him off.

Gabe looked at him and then at Nicky, who stood with his feet apart, hands fisted, his loyalty to Johnny so deep and fierce, Johnny wanted to hug the kid. He'd always valued loyalty and where an old friend of many years had let him down, this young kid had taken a two-hour friendship and made it priceless.

"This isn't finished," Gabe muttered as he brushed the snow off his clothes.

"Say hello to Allison for me," Johnny called as Gabe walked back in the direction from which he had come. He swung around, then turned and continued until he disappeared around the corner of the house.

Johnny squeezed Nicky's shoulder. "Thanks, buddy."

About twenty minutes later, they were putting a final load of logs into the truck when Johnny casually said, "I have an idea and I wanted to run it by you first since you're the man in your family."

He glanced up, curious. "Yeah?"

"I was thinking about offering to do some work for your mom, but I'm gonna need your help."

"Work like what?"

"Like some repairs to your house."

He nodded. "Yeah, it is kinda falling apart."

"You be willing to help me?" Johnny asked, treading very carefully. He knew about pride and the last thing he wanted to do was make Nicky feel as if he weren't doing enough to make the house comfortable for his mom and sisters. It would be easy to just barrel in and do the work, but he guessed Mary would feel like a charity case. And yeah, she was poor and needy, but Johnny wasn't interested in becoming the great savior—he just wanted to help her out because he knew it was what Emily wanted to do.

"I guess so, but I ain't never done stuff like you do."

"Yeah, but you know stuff I don't know. Like you know the house and the problems and where the most important stuff needs to be done."

Nicky thought for a moment, then grinned. "Yeah, I do know some stuff, like there's a frozen pipe in the bathroom and there's a place in Mom's bedroom where I can see outside. I got it taped and stuffed with old towels." Nicky continued to list the needed repairs with details that showed Johnny that the kid had tried himself to fix them the best he could.

Johnny stuck out his hand. "Okay, we got a deal."

Nicky grabbed at the handshake. "Deal."

Then as they got ready to leave, Nicky asked, "That guy—was he a friend of yours?"

"Used to be." He pulled open the cab door and Nicky climbed in.

Looking at Johnny, he asked, "You mean like Emily used to be your girlfriend?"

"No way. With Emily it was all my fault. With Gabe, it was a mess that can't be fixed."

SEVEN

By the time they got back to Nicky's house, Johnny's mood had chilled. The evening lay ahead, an evening with Emily. Part of him wanted to seduce her and lose himself, but another part was still pissed at Allison and Gabe.

If Gabe had figured out that he'd come home, then Allison knew, too. The fact that she hadn't bothered to call or make any attempt to see him had him wondering whether she gave a donkey's ass that he'd caught her with his best friend. Maybe she was waiting to learn from Gabe what had happened or if Johnny was willing to listen to whatever tale she'd fabricated.

It was difficult to believe that a woman of her sophistication who managed the details of her life with the skill of a micromanager would remain passive and silent while her personal life was jammed in chaos. But bottom line was that for all his fury and revenge-itching thoughts of last night, he was having a helluva time stirring up those juices today. Even the confrontation with Gabe had been more sad than spectacular. So far his revenge plan had been a bust; so much for the ballyhooed fury of Johnny Cross.

Of course, he'd spent zero time today thinking about any of this, thanks to his preoccupation with Emily.

Well, that was about to change.

Now he and Nicky unloaded the wood, and Johnny made sure there was plenty stacked in the house. He also took the tarp he carried in the truck and secured it around the stacked logs to keep them dry.

Then he and Emily said their good-byes to Mary, with Emily promising to keep in touch. The girls gave them both generous hugs and Nicky stuck out his hand for Johnny to shake. Johnny resisted the urge to haul the boy into his arms. Nevertheless, a friendship had been born and Johnny welcomed it.

In the truck, Johnny adjusted his sunglasses and deliberately didn't look at Emily.

"What's the matter?" she asked, leaning forward so she could see his diverted face. "You haven't said much since you and Nicky got back."

"Yeah, well, the kid talked a lot and I'm all talked out."

"That sounds as if you don't like him."

He whipped his head around and glared before turning away. "Did I say that?"

"Then why are you acting so angry?"

"Acting angry? Acting angry? Hell, lady, I am angry! I came here angry. I was angry last night and I was still pissed this morning."

She scowled, stiffened, and folded her arms. "Fine," she snapped. "You want to shout and pout and be cranky, far be it from me to try and understand whatever your problem is."

Johnny said nothing else and by the time he turned into the drive, the silence between them had gone from hot tension to cold strain. Probably he should get his gear and split. Better to leave before he and

Emily erupted into a full-blown argument.

As he walked into the house, the scent of fresh greenery again reminded him of how separated he felt from the joy of the season. He knew part of the hostility sprang from a resistance to wanting Emily, but now even that desire seemed tainted. Sex to get even with Allison? God, he sure hoped not. He came here looking to frame a revenge plan, but no way would he use Emily for that.

Then he saw his true rationale clearly for what it was. Rejected by one woman but still wanted by another. His battered male pride—wrapping himself in Emily to salve his badly bruised ego.

Good move, pal, he concluded, stamping the snow off his boots. *You're about as honorable as a pile of dog shit.*

He flipped on the lights in the living room. Emily had gone to hang up her coat. He tossed his jacket on a chair and squatted down to start a fire in the fireplace. He set aside the screen, loaded the logs onto the grate, crumpled newspaper and kindling, then reached for the matches. Emily plugged in the tree, illuminating the ornaments and the skirt that circled the base of the tree. The fire ignited. Johnny rose and replaced the screen.

It was at that moment when Johnny grimaced at the meager amount of gifts beneath the tree. And then there was the empty stocking his mother had made for her years ago. My God, Emily and he had hauled ten times the presents into the Warrens'. He picked up a few and looked at the tags. They were for Emily from out-of-town relatives. Johnny put them back down. Why the hell hadn't they asked her to spend the holidays? She shouldn't be all alone at Christmas. Emily loved Christmas. Her feelings had never been clearer than when he'd walked in last night and seen all the decorations she'd put up in *his* house.

"Do you want some dinner? Or is that an out-of-bounds question?" She stood in the kitchen arch, a dish towel in her hand. Johnny studied her for a moment, aware suddenly that if he didn't get out of here, he was going to take her to bed. Arousal buzzed through him like someone had turned on a fleet of power tools.

The really weird part was that she wasn't doing anything to turn him on or even wearing clothes that were overtly sexy—no silk or cling or see-through. She was dressed in winter-weight tights, floppy socks, a long sweater, and any makeup she'd applied earlier had long worn off. Her hair was casually tucked behind her ears. Her demeanor was rigid and closed as if she were expecting him to take off on her just because she asked a couple of questions.

She was sending out well-aimed ice cube signals and he was turning them hot. His body felt tight and his heart pumped as if he'd run five miles and worked up a sweat. Carnal pleasure kicked and punched like a newly born encounter with an old lover.

She watched him and he shuttered his gaze but never looked away. Breaths hushed. Eyes locked. Bodies stilled. The fire crackled in the hearth as loudly as it did between them. Heat engulfed the distance separating them, pulling at them.

Johnny stared.

Emily watched.

Finally, after what seemed like a century, she glanced down and fiddled with the dish towel. Johnny exhaled, turned aside, and was amazed to find his palms sweaty and neck hot. What had she asked him? Supper. Yeah, what he wanted.

"How about if we eat out?" he asked, trying to tamp down the intoxicating need that gripped him.

"There's plenty to eat here."

Including you and me, babe. Ten minutes alone was causing them big-time sexual duress—a whole evening would be overload. He blanked his expression. "I was kind of in the mood for prime rib. And I remember that you like filet mignon. The Jepson Inn has the best."

She eyed him speculatively.

Come on, Emily, just say yes. Don't make this difficult. Come on, just a simple yes. . . .

"No."

Shit.

"But you go ahead. You have a key, so I don't have to leave the door unlocked."

Now what? Sitting alone in some bar until he either got wasted or scraped up the courage to come back here? Not a plan he relished. The seconds of silence ticked by. Of course, he could tell her the truth about himself, a spill-his-guts moment.

But he couldn't. Call it ego, call it dumb pride, but he felt a deep shame that the oh-so-savvy Johnny Cross had been betrayed by two people he trusted. He was mortified that he'd been so busy and so clueless that he'd never seen any signs of sexual tension between Gabe and Allison. He'd come home with raging thoughts of payback that ran the gamut from killing them both—good thing the old hunting rifle's trigger was missing—to figuring out a nasty way to prove that payback can indeed be a bitch.

Telling all of this to Emily? Christ, just the thought made him shudder. Just shove it aside for a bit longer. He wanted her, and damn it, he knew she wanted him.

She was almost out of view when Johnny covered the distance between them and stopped her.

Gripping her arm, he tossed the towel in the general direction of the kitchen, then backed her up to the wall and gave her a slight shake. "Look at me."

She kept her head down, shaking it back and forth.

He pressed tighter against her. "Then feel me."

She shuddered, then slowly she raised her head and lifted her gaze to meet his, but she neither pushed him away nor tried to pull away. Her fisted hands rested on his waist. "You bring back too many memories for me."

"Lately you're my only memory . . . ah, sweetheart. . . ." He lowered his mouth and kissed her, easing her mouth open, touching their tongues. "This kind of memory . . . ?" he whispered, then palmed her breast. "And this kind . . . ?" Her shattering sigh teased at the heart of a delicious satisfaction. He deepened the kiss, then lifted her hips, positioning them so that she rode his thigh. "Ah, babe, this is a special memory, isn't it . . . ?"

"You're too good at this," she murmured.

"Wanting you is easy to be good at," he whispered, kissing her ear, her neck, and then her mouth. His hands tunneled under the bottom of her sweater, drawing it up until he could flatten his fingers on the warm skin of her back. He wondered why he'd waited so long. Wanting her was more than ego-soothing, and having her had always been about more than need and sex; it was about his feelings for Emily that he'd foolishly put aside for a lousy pursuit of money and success.

They held one another, the promise of unforgettable lovemaking slipping over them.

She sighed with pleasure, and God, he hoped in acceptance. "I don't want to talk about why or if we should be doing this, Johnny." She lowered her hands to fiddle with the buttons on his shirt. "If I think about all the reasons why this is insane, I'm going to scream."

He wanted to say, *Only when you come*, but she was serious and he'd already been far too flip with her.

And so he did the next best thing.

EIGHT

He kissed her.

And after a bit of hesitation, she kissed back, and within seconds their mouths opened—eager, hungry, and hot. They stumbled their way to the couch, sinking into the cushions.

She straddled his lap, her hands busy opening shirt buttons and finding their way to his hot skin. Johnny pulled her hands down to their laps and when she looked up, he lifted the edge of her sweater and pulled it over her head. She shook her hair back and stretched, arching her back.

Her breasts filled out a red lace bra that felt like gossamer webs under his fingers.

"Merry Christmas," she said, smiling at the look of amazement in his eyes.

"You planned this?"

Her eyes sparkled with mischief. "Catching you astonished is one of my greatest pleasures."

"If I'd known you had this on, I would've moved on you a helluva lot sooner."

"A woman's secrets are ever fascinating," she said demurely.

He tugged her forward, kissed her, then nuzzled the lace at her cleavage. "Sweet . . . sweet . . . dare I hope that there are red panties to match?"

She feigned disappointment. "You peeked."

"God." He shuddered, and then he did exactly what she accused him of and wiggled her out of her tights. She sat astride him in scraps of red with the flush of the hearth fire on her skin. He simply stared at the gift before him—this special woman, a treasured gift, a value without price.

"You're so pretty, Emmie," he whispered, using a nickname he'd fashioned the very first time they were lovers. She tipped his head up, her eyes shimmering with desire and memories.

"You never forgot, did you?"

"Ah, sweetheart, forgetting is impossible." He released the catch in her bra, allowing her breasts to fall into his hands. He touched her left breast and then kissed the strawberry mark. "It's still here and still as pretty."

"I always hated it," she whispered, even as she drew his mouth back to it again and again. "I thought it was ugly until you made it beautiful."

He breathed deeply of the scent of her, grateful for her, grateful that she'd been here when he'd come home. "Nothing about any part of you is ugly. . . . Nothing."

Kisses followed kisses and she held his head as he kissed each breast again and again, then drew back and stretched out, taking her with him.

He burned with need. She blazed with want.

The rest of their clothes came off with the haste of lovers throwing away any and all restrictions. He shifted, lifting her and then curving so that she slid beneath him.

And beneath him was where Emily wanted to be.

Covered by him, absorbed into his flesh. When he entered her, her body closed around him like a silky secret finally discovered. She felt the fullness of him rush all the way to her heart. She loved this man and had for so long, so very long.

Their limbs tangled as he drew her in deeper and deeper, his hands finding places to touch that heightened her senses and burned new paths of sensation.

And then he tucked her even closer drawing her up and up and up. "Oh . . . Johnny . . . ahhhh . . ."

Hearing his name, feeling her come with such total completion, left him shuddering with undiluted satisfaction.

Johnny held her, his own climax greedy for gratification. He bore down, his breath coming hard. No more time to feast and enjoy hers. . . . His own senses were reeling, climbing fast, his fullness racing and rocking and rising. . . .

He squeezed his eyes closed, savoring the peak even more when she wrapped even tighter around him as if they were one in soul and body and passion. Neither spoke, for neither could find words to match the majesty of this wondrous mating.

A minute, two minutes, three passed as they lay in collapsed contentment.

The fire had died down and Johnny pulled the fleece throw over both of them. He must have dozed off, for when he awakened she was asleep and the fire was almost out. Carefully he pulled away from her, tucking the throw tighter, and rose to his feet. The house was chilly, and he quickly dressed before going to work on restarting the fire.

Emily slept on and he found himself glancing over at her every few minutes. She had the soft look of contentment and while the lovemaking had awakened new sexual energy between them, he desperately wanted them to have a second beginning and not just a roll in the sack.

But until he got this thing resolved with Allison, he was in limbo. He placed the screen in front of the fire, checked to make sure Emily was asleep, and then went into the kitchen to make the phone call.

A half an hour later, she awakened, disappointed to find that the warmth around her wasn't Johnny's arms. She sat up, glanced around, and not until she heard voices did she become alarmed. Company? At least they hadn't come any farther than the kitchen.

Quickly she dressed, running her hands through her hair to get rid of the tangles.

The voices grew softer as she made her way toward the kitchen, trying to control the shakiness of her body. She was nervous and uneasy and she had no idea why. Instinct? Intuition? Whatever was making her insides jumpy wasn't her imagination. She was suddenly wary, and the wonderful moments of lovemaking now seemed ill-advised and more about desire than good sense.

But damn it, good sense was what she'd always shown when it came to Johnny, and where had that gotten her? Alone and lonely.

But even at her most logical, even excusing a few moments of passion, even knowing she had no strings or rights with Johnny didn't prepare her for the scene before her.

Johnny holding Allison in his arms.

A numbness sank over her that mercifully deadened the wrenching ache of her own idiocy. She'd believed him when he'd told her the engagement was broken. Yes, she'd had misgivings, but she loved him and she'd intended to talk them all out with him. Dumb, dumb, dumb. She should have talked and asked questions before she allowed herself to be seduced by him.

She stepped back and turned toward the stairs. If she could just get to her room and close the door, she could restitch her rags of pride. This time she wasn't going to be sweet, understanding Emily.

In her room, she brushed her hair and pulled it into place with a scrunchy. She heard a car and glanced out the window and saw headlights swing out of the drive and onto the road. It wasn't Johnny's truck, so no doubt Allison was going to the Jepson Inn to wait for him. Maybe that's why he wanted to go there for dinner—in a public place, he could avoid a scene when Allison just happened to show up.

She heard him on the stairs, his footsteps coming toward her bedroom door.

She braced herself, swiping a hand across her teary eyes. She took a deep breath, kept her chin high, and waited for the knock.

"Emily?"

Instead of answering, she flung open the door. He sure didn't look guilty, and was it her imagination or did he look delighted and relieved?

"Hi, sweetheart." He hauled her into his arms and kissed her. "You smell good."

"Damn you, Johnny Cross!" She pushed her hands against his chest and shoved him away.

"Hardly the words I wanted to hear," he muttered as she stalked away to the opposite side of the room.

"Let's talk about the words I want to hear." She gave him a hard look. "You haven't told me anything about anything, and nothing about Allison."

"Allison was just here—"

"I know, I saw you kissing her," she snapped.

"Ahh." He nodded as if that explained everything.

"That sure sounds like you care a lot." Disappointment filled her.

He folded his arms. "Are you going to let me explain or are you going to jump to your own conclusions?"

"Conclusions!" She wanted to pound out her frustration on his cool-headed jaw. "I know what I saw, Johnny. And as far as explaining, you've had plenty of time to do that—like last night and all day today—and you chose not to. You were the one pouting and snapping on the way home from Mary's, not me. Now that I caught you, you want to explain." She ran out of breath, and to make it worse she actually felt light-headed. But she had no intention of sitting down and giving him any advantage.

"I couldn't explain what I didn't know," he said so easily she wondered if he'd understood anything she'd accused him of. He walked forward and again tried to take her into his arms, but she shoved him away.

"Damn it, don't touch me!" She fisted her hands

and set them on her hips. "I'm hard-pressed to fathom any reason you'd be kissing the woman you aren't engaged to, moments after you made love to me."

Johnny shut the door and again walked over to her, this time taking her by the shoulders and making her sit down in the upholstered Queen Anne chair.

"All right, I admit to being an ass since I got here."

"An admission of profound truth."

"I didn't want you involved and for damn sure I didn't want to wind up in bed with you."

"So much for your self-control." She gave him a disdainful smirk.

He raised an eyebrow and leaned closer, whispering, "And yours? Or was that a stranger who didn't hold back and came twice?"

"Only once," she snapped. Her cheeks flared red and she was grateful the only light came from a small table lamp.

"My mistake," he said easily. "Are we all finished arguing over orgasms?"

She sagged back in the chair. "You're a smart-ass, you know that?"

"I think I've been told more than a few times." Johnny went and got another chair and sat down in front of her. "I came home because I walked in on Allison and Gabe having sex in one of the model condos for a new complex we were building west of Boston."

She sat up and widened her eyes. "Oh, my God."

"It wasn't a pretty picture. I was in a rage and came home to plan out some sweet revenge." He took her hands. "Then there you were amid the Christmas decorations like some angel sent to thwart me."

"In the den . . . the rifle . . . you were going to kill them."

"Not with that weapon. The trigger was busted."

"And if it hadn't been?"

"I don't know."

She shook her head. "No, I know you. You wouldn't have even if it wasn't."

"I thought about it, Emily. I really did."

"If thinking were a crime, we'd all be guilty. The point is, you didn't go off and find a gun and then find them."

"No, I didn't do that." He rose and walked to the window, his back turned. "Gabe was here this afternoon when Nicky and I were getting the wood." He told her what had happened and how Nicky had tried to break up their fight. "Here was this kid I'd known for about three hours and he demonstrated this fierce loyalty toward me. I couldn't help but compare him to Gabe. A friend and partner for many years, and yet he shows me the worst kind of disloyalty. He sleeps with a woman I believed I loved."

Emily was pleased that Johnny had befriended Nicky, but that had nothing to do with being piqued and worried about seeing Allison in his arms. "It sure looked to me like you still love her."

He turned around, his face shadowed in the night. "That's because you don't know why she came to see me."

Emily got to her feet. She'd stepped aside the last time and let him go, but this time she was older, hopefully wiser, and definitely irritated that once again she'd managed to risk her heart so easily. "I don't think I want to hear this."

He crossed the room and stopped her before she got to the door. "Yes, you do."

"Let me go."

"Emily, I love you."

She quit struggling to free herself, a new kind of anger boiling over. "How dare you say that to me, Johnny Cross? When did that occur to you—after we had sex or while you were trying to figure out how to keep Allison in the kitchen so she didn't know—"

"Allison is in love with Gabe."

"What?"

"That's what she came to tell me."

"Why didn't Gabe tell you when he was here?" she asked, still holding some skepticism.

"I think he tried when he said there were other circumstances. At the time it all sounded like so much bullshit. I guess when he went back and told Allison I dumped him as a friend and partner, she decided to come down here and straighten it all out."

"Proving that women have more guts than men when it comes to relationships," she muttered, giving Allison credit for a bravery that Gabe lacked.

"I won't argue with that. You've always been more up front about your feelings for me than I have been with you. As for Allison, she said she realized over the Thanksgiving weekend that she'd loved Gabe." He held up his hand when she started to speak. "She knew that telling me would hurt me, and because it was Gabe, that made facing me more difficult."

"So they sleep together where you could easily

catch them? Now, that sounds wise and prudent."

He grinned. "I said the same thing to her."

"And?"

"And nothing. She had no answer beyond over-loaded hormones, and since I know what that's like when it comes to you, I didn't argue. Actually, I really didn't care anymore, so I hugged her and wished them luck and said good-bye."

Emily frowned. "How is it you were so angry and now you're not?"

"Actually, a lot of my anger slipped away the more I was around you. Perhaps it was being here with you, meeting Mary and her family, realizing that the hardest part of all of this was my battered ego. Making love to you was like being remade brand-new. I was on my way to call Allison and tell her that we were finished, not because of what she did with Gabe, but because I'd always been in love with you. I know it sounds hokey, but believe me, I came here looking for a plan to carry out my revenge and instead I found you."

Perhaps it was her heart and her need to believe him, down in some intuitive part of her she knew he told the truth. "I don't think it sounds hokey," she said softly.

"Thank God." He tipped her chin up. "Emily, I do love you. I want us to be together for Christmas and for always."

She wrapped her arms around him and held him close. "Oh, Johnny, this is the best Christmas present I've ever had."

And they kissed and held one another, slipping from their clothes and into the four-poster bed, where they found warmth and love in each other's arms.

EPILOGUE

The next morning, after a huge breakfast of waffles and sausage, Johnny made her close her eyes as he walked her into the living room.

"What's going on?" she said with a laugh, basking in all the joy and wonder of a Christmas she'd never anticipated three days ago.

"You gotta sit down and keep your eyes closed."

She did, her smile breaking into an occasional giggle.

She felt a slight pressure in her lap. "What is it?"

"Open your eyes."

She did and then gave him a puzzled look. "An answering machine?"

"Push the button."

She did and the message came on. It was from one of Essie Beene's sons. "Johnny, hey ole buddy, just gettin' back to you after talkin' to my brother. You wanta do some work at the old place, it's okay with us. Wouldn't've figured a big-city contractor would mess with such small potatoes, but hey, it's Christmas. Guess you got the spirit of the thing, huh?" Laughter followed. "Since it ain't gonna cost us nothin', do your thing. See ya."

Johnny hit the stop button and put the machine aside. Emily threw herself in his arms. "This is wonderful and Mary will be so grateful. When did you do all this?"

"Last night. When I couldn't get Allison, I called the Beene boys. I told them I was moving back to Jepson and my bride-to-be was friends with Mary Warren and would the boys mind if I did some work at her place? Gratis, of course. He called back last night while we were, uh, busy."

Emily vaguely recalled hearing the phone ring around midnight. "And it's all true? You're moving back? Forever?"

"And ever and ever."

Then her eyes misted. "Oh, Johnny, this is just so unbelievable and so wonderful."

He hauled her to her feet. "Come on, we have a lot to do."

She laughed as he urged her up the stairs. "Wait a minute. You also said something about a bride-to-be?"

"I said that?" he asked, his expression innocent.

She gave him a friendly punch. "You know you did."

"Oh, yeah, that's why we have to go shopping."

She pouted. "I thought we were going back to bed."

"Bed first, then shopping."

"But does it have to be today? It's Christmas Eve."

"I know, and I sure hope they didn't sell it," he said mysteriously. "I saw it yesterday when Nicky and I ran some errands before we got the wood."

"Sell what? What are you talking about?"

"The diamond ring I saw at Swan Jewelers. It had emeralds around the diamond that reminded me of your eyes. Anyway, I thought it would make a great engagement ring, so when I get down on my knees and beg you to marry me, I've got something to offer you besides me."

She halted at the door of the bedroom. Tears streamed down her cheeks and she made no effort to stop them. "An engagement ring? I think I'm in some kind of fantasy. But Johnny, as wonderful as a ring would be, it's not as wonderful as having you."

He tipped her chin up and kissed away the tears, his voice as serious as she'd ever heard him. "Having you become my wife would be the best gift I could ever have."

"Oh, Johnny, I love you. I've loved you forever."

And with those words, he lifted her into his arms and carried her into the bedroom.

"Merry Christmas, sweetheart."

"And to you, my love."

And along with the heart-stopping happiness that enveloped them both came the joy and peace that promised many more Christmases to come.

HEROES and
Heartbreakers.com

Contemporary · Paranormal · Historical

WE SCOUR THE ROMANCE WORLD TO BRING YOU THE BEST.

♥ Original stories from new writers and authors you already love
♥ Exclusive excerpts from upcoming releases
♥ Non-stop discussions that run the gamut from Acheron to Zeke
♥ New covers as they're revealed
♥ Giveaways including advance copies and other ridiculously awesome stuff

Discover. Share. Obsess.

JOIN US AT
WWW.HEROESANDHEARTBREAKERS.COM/OBSESS